Connie J. Jasperson

Julian Lackland

Copyright © 2020 Connie J. Jasperson

First Edition

ISBN-13: 9781680630695
ISBN-10: 1680630695
Graphics & Maps © Connie J. Jasperson
Cover Image: Stained glass at monastery© Emi Cristea | Dreamstime.com

Portions of "Julian Lackland" first appeared in the book "The Last Good Knight" by Connie J. Jasperson

Published by
Myrddin Publishing Group
Contact us at - www.myrddinpublishing.com

Contact us at: www.myrddinpublishinggroup.com

Julian Lackland

Portions of this book first appeared in novel form as *The Last Good Knight*. Following a dispute with my first publisher it was unpublished and languished for the next eight years. It has been rewritten with the addition of scenes that were originally mentioned only as backstory. Irene Roth Luvaul, Johanna Flynn, and Sherrie Degraw, your diligence and keen eyes were invaluable in this process, were those of Alison DeLuca and Carlie M. A. Cullen.

Special thanks to Lee French, Ellen King Rice, Melissa Carpenter, and the Tuesday Morning Rebel Writers for your unconditional support and encouragement when I felt I couldn't straighten out what began as an unholy mess. Thanks to you all, I had the courage to let this novel become what I always believed it could be.

Connie Jasperson, September 2020

Table of Contents:

JULIAN LACKLAND
The Last Good Knight
By
Connie J. Jasperson

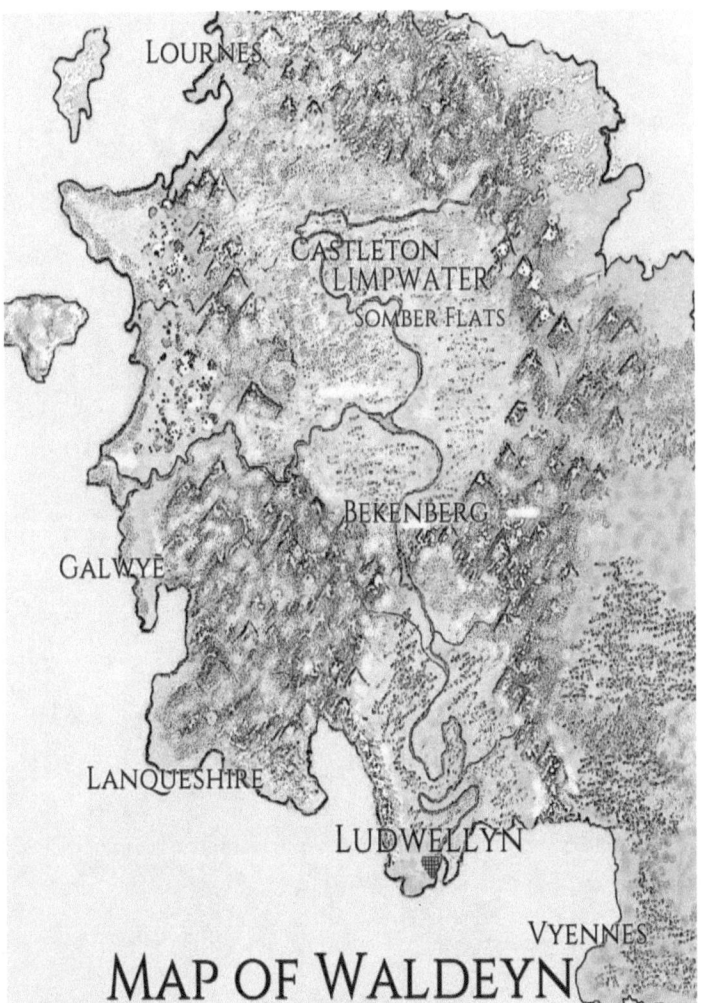

LOURNES

CASTLETON
LIMPWATER
SOMBER FLATS

BEKENBERG

GALWYE

LANQUESHIRE

LUDWELLYN

VYENNES

MAP OF WALDEYN

PART ONE
The Young Knight-at-Large

AT EIGHTEEN YEARS of age, Julian left the court of his royal cousin, fleeing the unasked-for advances of King Henri's unlamented first wife, joining the mercenary company known as the Rowdies.

I met him not long after. He was a peculiar mix, wise in the ways of politics and war, brave beyond belief, a warrior like no other, and yet innocent about the most ordinary things. He was slightly mad even then, but mystery swirled around him. Instantly, I knew my path, knew my future lay wherever he was. If I could find him, I would never lack for new stories, tales of daring and bravery. Accordingly, I made my way north to Billy's Revenge.

Excerpt from *The Life of Julian Lackland De Portiers, Waldeyn's Last Good Knight*,

by Huw Owyn, Master Bard of Waldeyn

Connie J. Jasperson

CHAPTER 1

JULIAN "LACKLAND" DE PORTIERS rode out of Castleton Keep, his mood improving with every step taken by his fine, white stallion. Farroll was one of several princely parting gifts from his cousin, King Henri. Although he had only owned the horse for two days, Lackland thought he would be a fine companion for the next few years. Tied to Farroll's saddle was a pack pony laden with all the eighteen-year-old knight owned, items of value only to him.

Once outside the castle grounds, Farroll strutted as if he knew every eye was upon him. The immense warhorse paraded past the tall peak-roofed houses and shops crammed against the massive stone walls. Unaware of his horse's antics, Lackland smiled and waved to the many vendors and people he knew as he rode through the narrow streets teeming with people. Though the city had been his home since he was a boy of twelve, he wouldn't miss it.

At last, they rode through the less-traveled southern gate. The change in scenery when they emerged outside the city walls always surprised him, even though he expected it. He thought it mysterious, the way the forest closed in on either side.

Unfortunately, the cobbled lane became a packed-dirt road, which soon became a narrow, rutted track.

Bad weather plagued the month of March. The gray clouds lowered, and rain fell, lightly at first. By noon, it was relentless. Occasionally, deep mud and driving rain made the winding road slick and dangerous for the horses, forcing Julian to travel slower than he wanted. As the daylight faded, he was still two hours from his destination.

He stopped at the clearing just before Psalter Pass, where he dismounted. Sitting on a fallen log near where the horses nibbled grass, Julian finished the last of his bread and cheese and watched the sunset, turning the clouds in the western sky an angry, bruised color. "I have a decision to make," he said, thinking aloud as he often did. "Should I make camp here and continue on in the morning or risk traveling the pass in the dark? The stable at the Rowdies' Bolthole would be nice and dry. I'm sure Farroll would like that."

The horse nodded, looking meaningfully into Julian's eyes.

Nonplussed, Julian said, "What? Camp here?"

Farroll shook his head violently.

"You want us to continue on to the Bolthole in the dark?" Unsure if he imagined the horse's reaction, Julian's voice sounded strangled.

The horse nodded.

Mystified, Julian said, "But we have a good two hours' ride ahead of us in the dark and rain. Don't you enjoy camping? We could meet a wood-wraith along here in the dark, or a firedrake. That would be bad."

Farroll snorted and shook his head violently.

"You... you're a most unusual horse. You're sure you don't want to camp?"

He snorted again and pawed the ground once.

"I see. Do you talk to everyone?"

The horse made no reply, ignoring him as if he hadn't heard the question. Or as if Julian had only imagined he could answer.

Feeling lightheaded about the whole thing, Julian decided to just go along with it. He rose, taking the reins of his pack pony, tying them once again to Farroll's saddle. After fishing around in his saddlebags, he produced a small lantern which he tied to the end of a fresh-cut alder pole. He lit the lamp and mounted, settling the pole in the lance-rest of his stirrup, holding it upright as if it were a flag.

Always an optimist, Julian put a cheerful spin on things. "This will help us find our way and may ward off the less courageous beasts. Or else it will attract them. Either way, off we go."

They entered the most dangerous stretch of the journey, the Psalter Pass, with Julian keeping up his spirits by singing a few of the jollier ballads he knew. As they came through the narrow stretch, he was well into the third verse of *Mary MacReedy's Knickers*. He'd just gotten to the part about the squirrels when Farroll suddenly stopped.

A group of highwaymen blocked the road ahead with their swords drawn, alerted to a victim by both the light of the lantern and Julian's singing. Farroll had stopped well short of where the four men now stood in the road. They eyed the immense warhorse warily, keeping as much distance as they could between themselves and his hooves.

"We'll just take your fine lantern," said a burly man with a patch over one eye. "We'd not want it starting any forest fires now, would we?"

Julian made no reply.

"Well? Throw us your purse, nice and slow," said a gaunt, skeletal-looking man, looking nervously at his friends.

Julian sat in his saddle, holding fast to his lantern pole.

Angry at Julian's lack of response, the third man said, "Well? What're you waiting for? Throw down your purse."

In answer, Julian drew his sword and dismounted, stabbing the lantern pole into the deep mud at the side of the road to light the scene better. He advanced on the highwaymen, who appeared disconcerted at his bold response. "Gentlemen... you should flee," he said. "I outnumber you, so it's not really a fair fight."

"Are you daft?" One-Eye rushed him, swinging wildly. "C'mon boys."

Julian neatly lopped off his head, which fell to the mud with a splat, followed by the man's body. A cold smile played on Julian's pleasant face. "I warned him, but he wasn't taking 'no' for an answer. You can flee now. I don't want to harm you."

In answer, two of the three remaining swordsmen rushed him, shouting, and slashing wildly. In no time, the thin man had doubled over, screaming, trying to keep his guts inside. Another man's head lay fallen into the mud.

Julian pitied the now-frantic attacker who clutched his belly. "You just had to run yourself onto my sword. Once your insides are on your outsides, you're done for." Julian's sword flashed in the lantern light as he decapitated the gutted highwayman. "That's the only remedy for such misery."

From some distance behind Julian came a strange, thunking sound, and a man cried out in pain. He turned to see the fourth thief doubled over beside the pack pony. Farroll whinnied and bucked again, and this time, his flashing hooves sent the man flying past a somewhat surprised Julian. The unfortunate thief landed headfirst in the bushes. He lay in the shrubbery with his head twisted at a dreadful angle, unmoving except for his mouth, which stretched and gaped like a fish out of water.

Julian asked, "Are you injured?" He held the lamp up, looking closely, seeing the thief had broken his neck. After a series of vain, strangled attempts to breathe, he too was dead.

In the absence of battle noises, the hissing of rain on the foliage was loud in Julian's ears. A trickle of water ran down his spine. Hearing horses splashing through the mud, he turned and saw Farroll walking toward him, the pack pony's reins in his mouth. Julian took them. "So, this poor fellow was trying to sneak off with the pony and our things? Good work. But now I must dispose of these fellows, or they'll attract the bigger beasts, and they'd soon be preying on unwary travelers." A short while later, they were back on the road, plodding through the mud, the lamp once again lighting their way.

It was late when Julian arrived in the stable yard at the Bolthole, the home of the Rowdies. The young ostler who usually handled the horses wasn't there. The stable was nearly empty, with only a few horses in the stalls. Fortunately, the horse he recognized as belonging to Billy MacNess was there. Julian groomed both his horses before he went around to the front with an armload of his belongings.

He could see the lamps were lit, so someone was up and about. He made two trips, climbing the steps with his possessions, stacking them by the entrance. Tucking his helm under his arm, he knocked.

The door opened, and an immense man filled it. Sandy-haired, blue-eyed, and appearing far younger than his age of twenty-two, Billy MacNess was easily the tallest, largest man in Waldeyn.

"My apologies for dripping on your clean floor," said Lackland. "The weather's been wretched. I left the Keep this morning, and it's taken me all day to get here." He looked around. "Did you get a new housekeeper? This place looks as cozy as my grandmother's rooms at House Portiers."

"Just me. With this injury to my sword hand, I've had to leave the road. I'm a proper housewife these days." Billy laughed. "I'm sorry, Lackland. I have no Rowdies available to send the king for at least two weeks. They're all gone on long jobs, some to Galwye and the rest to Wister," he said. "But come on in and get dried out. I'll find you a bunk for tonight."

"Thank you," replied the damp knight. "I'm not here on King Henri's business—I'm here on my own."

"Is your horse in the stable? I've had to send my ostler out on the road to make a full crew, so I'm doing my own scheduling and taking care of the place myself. Willy just turned sixteen and can legally sign a contract, so he's a full Rowdy now."

Lackland peeled off his gloves, laying them out to dry. "Yes, my horses are both settled. I thought the place looked empty. My new horse, Farroll, was happy enough to lodge next to your old fellow. Apparently, he's a delicate flower which surprises me, as he looks quite studly. He absolutely insisted he didn't want to camp even though it was nearly dark, so we came straight on here."

Billy stared at him. "Your horse said that?"

"Yes, firmly." Lackland didn't notice his host's confusion. "Actually, I've left the court. I was wondering…do you need another good sword-swinger? It's different from the fighting I'm used to, but I can be trained."

Billy's eyebrows rose in surprise. "Well, yes. I can use your help. And don't be ridiculous. You're better trained than any man in Waldeyn. But why? Other than the king, you're the only one there with any brains. Who's running the country?"

Lackland sat on a bench and divested himself of his armor, talking all the while. "Henri finally exiled his royal mother back to her family in Vyennes and seized the reins, much to some people's dismay. I don't want to go into it too closely, but his wife seeks to drive a wedge between him and me. I had to throw Queen Morganna out of my rooms in the middle of the night, and in the process, she discovered evidence of my, ah, *close* relationship with Lady Mags De Leon. The queen didn't take the rejection well. Besides, I'm tired of being a glorified messenger for a bunch of addlepated dimwits who couldn't think their way out of a room with all the doors nailed open."

Billy laughed and agreed with him.

Lackland shrugged and continued his tale of love found and lost, finally winding down to the end. "So, with this disgrace hanging over Lady Mags's head, there's no reason for me to remain at court. Besides, I'd much rather do some good in the world if I can. This way, a few more merchants will be safe, and King Henri can freely consult with me between jobs without putting some pudding-faced duke's nose out of joint. We worked this out before I left."

Lackland was exactly the man Billy wanted in his Rowdies. "I always thought you were too good for court. But it figures you would fall hopelessly in love with an earl's daughter." Billy chuckled at Lackland's misfortune, his boyish face openly displaying his glee.

"My brother named me Lackland, and the bullies at court made it stick. It means I have no land, no position, and no chance to marry Mags. I embraced it long ago, and now it's a part of me." Julian placed no stress on his words, but resentment flashed through his eyes, immediately hidden. His features lit up with a wicked grin. "But it also means I have no reason to toady to anyone, so I've come to you for a chance at a real job."

Billy laughed, holding up his maimed hand. "And I must embrace the fact I am now Billy Ninefingers. This injury to my sword hand is why I'm off the road, and young Willie Besom is a Rowdy sooner than I'd planned. But I have a plan I hope will enable me to remain captain of the Rowdies. In the meantime, I've got no one to fulfill the local jobs that might come in, so you've joined us at the perfect time. I'll send you out on the next one that comes along. Put your things upstairs in the north end bunk room. Two bunks are free in that room, and I just cleaned up there, so it's ready for you. Pick one with no bedding. I'll be up with sheets and a blanket in a few minutes."

They passed the evening companionably. Lackland listened with interest as Billy explained how Bastard John, captain of the Wolves in Somber Flats, had maimed him while in a drunken rage. "But, I still have nine fingers and all my wits." Unrolling a long tube of paper, Billy showed Julian his plans for building a fine inn there in the wilderness, as grand as any in Castleton. "It'll have a proper bathhouse, one with running water like the Queen's Garter in Castleton, only much bigger. My bathhouse will have four tubs on each side and plenty of flushing toilets for both the ladies and the gentlemen. No reeking privy for my Rowdies—we'll be set up better than any mercenaries anywhere. Even better, I'll make a tidy income from those of the traveling public who, like your horse, prefer not to camp."

Laughing, Julian said, "Building an inn here is a great idea. It's the perfect place, being exactly halfway between Castleton and Somber Flats. You've no idea how much the ladies of the court hate to camp along the road when they must go south for any reason, and with this being a one day's ride for them, you'll have plenty of court business. And, now I think of it, this would be a perfect place for a town. You can design it properly from the outset." His blue eyes twinkled as he added, "I too have a fondness for the modern plumbing that makes life bearable at Castleton Keep. You'll have your pick of mercenaries begging to be Rowdies with that to sweeten the deal."

An hour passed, and the two men went to their respective beds.

Julian had had many lovers, being a man who easily fell in love with a person regardless of their gender. But he'd been smitten with Mags in a way that no other lover had ever matched. Losing her weighed heavily on his heart. Her burnished mahogany hair and the saucy swing of her hips were paired with a wit sharper than any sword. No woman would ever match her fiery beauty and tempestuous nature.

No man could outmatch her in a swordfight, either, something that few would admit to. He consoled himself, thinking the Duke of Silenia might have a dragon by the tail on his wedding night.

Just before dawn, Lackland suddenly woke, having realized how he could win the battle for his darling Mags.

Whatever else Lackland was, he was a wily tactician. His instructors in the military arts would have been the first to say that no one was better at making the best of a bad situation and turning what should have been a miserable defeat into a last-minute victory. Julian understood his enemy's weaknesses and ruthlessly exploited them.

It occurred to him that the Earl of Bunder's weakness was his daughter's unladylike fear of wedlock and her deep desire to be a knight. He also knew full well the poor earl was pretending not to notice just how strong that desire was.

Rising immediately, Lackland went downstairs and sat before the fire at one of the large tables, writing the letter that was his one chance to win his lady back.

My Dearest Mags,

The only thing that would make my life complete would be to have you in it once again, but I have accepted it is not to be. I'm sure you'll be just as happy married to your cold, foreign duke as you would have been with me, despite his serious lack of a chin. Perhaps your many children will be more fortunate in their appearance than their noble father and take after the De Leon side of the family in both looks and adventurous nature.

I've left the court and become a mercenary knight. Should you wish to send me a wedding invitation, you can find me lodging with the Rowdies on the big bend of the River Limpwater. Remember Slippery Jack Fitzmarion? He is here, as are Lady Barbara Gentry and Lady Susan De Neves. You may remember Lady Elinor St. Clair—she's here too. Apparently, they chose not to marry the lads their fathers had selected for them. Captain Billy tells me he couldn't get anything done without his Lady Rowdies, as they are his best fighters. He pays them handsomely, the same as the men.

But enough of my small talk. I'm sure you have fittings for your wedding gown and monogrammed nappies to embroider, so I'll just wish you the very best in your new life.

Sincerely yours,

Julian Lackland

At breakfast, he told Billy what he'd done.

Billy said he expected a merchant from Castleton that day to deliver materials for his as-yet-unnamed inn. "He'll take your letter back with him and leave it with the royal messengers, so that'll speed things up for you. If your lady's willing, I have a place for her here. I need more Rowdies. I can't keep up with the demand for our services as it is."

"She'll take the bait." Julian knew with certainty Mags would join them. "She won't pass up this opportunity to swing her sword."

"Lackland, you are aware lady mercenaries rarely give up the sword to marry anyone, right?" The fleeting loneliness in Billy's expression gave evidence of his own struggle to convince the love of his life to marry him. "Unless the Earl of Bunder has his daughter chained in the cellar, she'll come to the Rowdies, and she *will* swing her sword, judging by what you've told me about her. But she'll never marry you, and she won't be faithful, so don't expect it. Mercs make terrible spouses."

"I'll be glad to have her any way I can, and if a loose arrangement is all I can have, fine. I'll do my best to be content," replied Julian. "I love her, and this way, I'll still be with her." He shrugged wryly. "I'm not a jealous man, and I'm not always as faithful when I'm away from her as I should be, either. We just try to live the best way we can."

"And you don't mind out-foxing the wily Earl of Bunder, either." Billy laughed at Lackland's slight blush. "But it's one thing to *know* she won't marry you and another thing to *live* it," replied Billy, with the voice of experience. "It's not an easy life being a mercenary, but the merchants and travelers will be grateful to you for choosing it."

"I know. But life's too short to waste it by worrying about what you don't have." Lackland felt he'd made the best decision he could under the circumstances. "And you're right, I don't mind out-foxing Edward De Leon. He's a good old thing, and my quarrel with him isn't personal. But he doesn't understand his daughter or how much she loathes the idea of marriage. Even if my letter misses her and Mags marries the duke, she will not go quietly to the cold wilds of Fornost, no matter what her father believes, and the duke's life will have taken a turn for the worse. I guarantee it."

Two weeks later, a gentle knock at the door announced the arrival of Lady Mags.

Gertie Smith, Billy's stepmother, was at the Bolthole, being between jobs. "Mags! When we discovered Lackland was here, we wondered when you would follow. Babs is a merc now too. So is Bess, but they're off on a job. Lackland's crew should be home this evening."

Billy was glad to have her, but her father's reaction worried him. "Your father won't send an army after you, will he?"

"He's hopping mad, of course. But he has no one to send who isn't terrified of me and my sword." She looked around, smiling, seeing several people she had known at court. "He'll cool down in a week or two. I just don't see myself as a duchess. I'd prefer to do some good in the world. Do you need me to sign anything?"

Gertie led Mags upstairs to the ladies' bunkroom and left her to unpack. Mags hung her dresses on the hooks at the end of her bunk and stowed her possessions in the locker at the foot. Looking out the window, she congratulated herself. The Rowdies were the perfect solution.

She laughed, thinking that she was damaged goods now. Even the ugly Duke of Silenia wouldn't want her disgracing his family's name. She could have Julian on her terms. She loved him but had no intention of marrying, ever. Most importantly, she fit right in with a group of women she could call sisters, some of whom she had known all her life.

When he arrived home, Lackland was ecstatic but behaved with dignity. After supper, he casually invited her to view the river with him, the hopeful expression giving away his wish.

Mags accepted, an answering spark in her gaze. "I'd love to examine the brush with you. Sneaking around with you was the best part of being at court. Shall we bring a blanket in case it rains?" Gertie had told her that since there was no privacy in the Bolthole, trysting lovers "went to view the river."

Toward midnight, they returned, going to their separate beds.

After getting into his bed without disturbing the other sleepers in the bunk room, Julian couldn't relax. Wide awake, he lay looking out the window at the starry sky.

Seeing the smile on Mags's lips made his heart sing. Hope filled him, and joy. She loved him, and now nothing stood in their way.

The next day he went out to the stable to chat with Farroll, as he often did. Brushing the big horse's mane to a glossy sheen, he confided, "We're young.

We've plenty of time. I've won this battle. Surely she'll marry me once she grows tired of life on the road."

Farroll looked at Julian sympathetically but clearly, the horse doubted that would ever happen.

CHAPTER 2

MAY HAD ARRIVED. Construction on Billy's new inn was well under way, and the Rowdies were busier than ever. They liked and accepted Lackland despite his admittedly odd ways. He and Mags were mostly together, but as Billy had warned him, she had no intention of settling down.

Percival St. John, a younger son with no inheritance to look forward to, had also left the court and was considering joining the Rowdies. Julian and Percy had once been lovers and remained good friends. Julian's heart remained set on Mags.

Billy Ninefingers received a request from King Henri. Despite his misgivings, he obeyed, sending Lackland to the South to deliver a message to a southern duchess. The fact the knight was to go alone bothered Billy, but if anyone could travel alone in the wilder parts of the country, it was Lackland.

A separate note for Julian gave him a task only he and his longbow could accomplish, as a special side trip. The second task was not to his liking, as he disliked resorting to assassination. However, archery was a passion of his. He'd developed a bow few men were strong enough to draw, one that shot much further and with greater accuracy than normal longbows. His skill with that weapon meant he was the only person for the job.

The next morning, Lackland and Farroll took the road south, catching up to a convoy heading to Bekenberg. On arriving there, he ran into Lord St. John. The governor of the Eynier Valley, he was also Percy's father and was going north for the spring parliament.

Lackland explained his mission, and after hearing what Lord St. John had to say, he then spoke with another old friend of his from court. A younger son, the same as Lackland, Sir Bry Dale had no inheritance to look forward to and was now a mercenary of the Ravens, working out of Bekenberg. With St. John's agreement, Lackland made a proposal to Dale, received the answer he wanted, and departed immediately. He travelled south to Clythe, a village that stood at the entrance to the Eynier Valley. The two-hundred-league-long valley comprised the southern half of the country of Waldeyn, but it was an unknown place to Lackland.

The valley was insular and rarely shared its secrets.

Lackland rode into the stable-yard at the Green Man, the inn that stood well outside the walls of Clythe. He stabled Farroll, noting he was the only mount there. There was no ostler, so guests had to see to their own mounts. Few commoners owned horses in that strange, long valley.

Once he had done that, Lackland carried his saddlebags into the common room. He looked for the innkeeper, a man known as the Bear, and secretly, as a friend to those from the North. Julian had been to the Green Man several times on business for the crown but had never been further south. He hoped the Bear could give him an idea of what to expect on his travels.

"Lackland!" The big man behind the bar rumbled a welcome. "What are you doing down here in the civilized world? Who's taming the wilderness? If you've come to meet with Lord St. John, he left for the North last week and won't be back until next month. Things have gone to hell down here, truth be told."

"I ran into St. John in Bekenberg, and we talked. This time, I need to travel all the way south to Ludwellyn, with a stop in Imrysdock," replied Lackland. "Henri's sending me to aid the Grand Duke Weyllyn with an internal matter."

"So, you've some idea of what's going on. Younger Murfee was supposed to have a ship coming in, but with the fire in Ludwellyn, shipping's ground to a halt."

Lackland nodded. "A fire overtakes much of the port city of Ludwellyn, and the heir to the Weyllyn duchy disappears in the same week. These might be coincidental or might not. Henri wants me to find the heir. St. John felt the man may have left voluntarily but could give me no reason for such a thing."

The Bear's eyes widened. "I haven't heard of a caravan heading south, so you must wait."

Lackland demurred. "I don't have time. I'll head south tomorrow, so if you've got a map, I'd be grateful to see it. I've never been beyond your fine inn."

"You'll never make it without an escort of local lads. You'll be mistaken for a lone Crow and be run out of every village, possibly even murdered in your sleep. Crows are naught but trouble these days."

"Lone crow?"

"A merc for Clan Grefyn. The war between Grefyn and Weyllyn is a spark short of a blaze right now. The whole valley is about to go up in flames. It's not safe for strangers to go alone these days."

"I must get to Imrysdock to make sure Clan Weyllyn does as Henri wishes. So… I'll be off tomorrow," Lackland replied. "Don't worry. I can take care of myself."

The Bear considered the knight's golden hair, cut short in the military style but with the beginnings of a mercenary's tail growing just beneath his left ear. "I see some things have changed for you since you were here last. Your hair tells me you've left the court. But that light hair and your accent declare you to the world as a northern mercenary. The Crows are hiring thugs from as far north as Lournes and also from Lanqueshire in the west. You'll be mistaken for a Lournesque highwayman and find no friends between here and Imrysdock, even though it's Dragon country."

"I'm not from Lournes—good god! My accent is nothing like theirs."

Lackland's shock drew a smile from his host. "It won't matter. You northerners all sound the same to us. Even if you survive the journey to Imrysdock, you'll be murdered long before you make it to Ludwellyn. You'll be passing through the Grefyn's lands to get there, you know. They despise the king, and it's not mere dislike. It's rabid-mad hatred. They'll mob you and kill you.

The Crows of Grefyn love a good lynching before breakfast to start their day off well. Hanging a lone Dragon would give them reason to smile."

"I see." Lackland stood thinking. "Well... I must chance it. Henri wants me to get to Imrysdock as quickly as I can. I'll figure it out as I go, I guess. If I lie low, I may avoid notice. In the meantime, I'll need a bed for tonight."

The Bear saw it would do no good to continue trying to dissuade him. Shaking his shaggy head, the innkeeper turned to get his guest settled and fed.

The next morning, he attempted one last time to change Lackland's mind. "Put the armor in your saddlebags. You look like a lone Crow, dressed like that. Trust me, you really don't want that. If you won't wait for a caravan, at least hide the armor and wear a hat."

"I'd be naked, riding in a strange country unarmored! And I've no time to wait for an escort. Henri gave me a second task that must be done before the social season ends in Ludwellyn," said Lackland, as he prepared to depart in the early light of the dawn. "I'll return, never fear. This is a civilized land. Surely some folks will help a knight along the way."

"Yes, they will," replied the Bear, with a grim attempt at a smile. "They'll laugh and joke like good friends do, as they help you to an early grave."

The journey proved more difficult than Lackland had thought it would be. Paranoia infected the countryside. No tradesman would sell him so much as a sliver of cheese. Despite his struggles, once he arrived in Imrysdock, the young duchess met him with relief.

Lackland sat in the private drawing room of the lovely Duchess Madewyn, granddaughter of the Grand Duke Daffyd Weyllyn, the most powerful man in the Long Valley. Now, with her sickly grandfather as their chaperone, they discussed the disappearance of her brother, Dayved, the heir.

That is, Lackland and the duchess talked, and the old man remained silent. If he heard their conversation, he gave little sign.

The Weyllyn Duchy was critical to Henri's rule. They were of the same house, House Dragoran, and the two people whose hospitality Lackland now enjoyed, were nearer to the throne of Waldeyn than anyone, save any children Henri should beget. Dayved's disappearance had caused a crisis, as they had trained him from birth to succeed both his grandfather and King Henri if no heirs were born of the king's body.

The duchess explained that her brother had abdicated for private reasons. Madewyn spoke softly, her lilting Eynier accent sounding musical to Lackland's northern ears. "Dayved left me a note, but I can't tell you his reason for leaving. It was a private matter, and I won't break his confidence. I swear on my hope of heaven my brother left of his own will, just after the terrible quarrel he and Grandfather had. He abdicated and walked away from this house with nothing, vowing he would never return no matter what happened. I know my brother, and it was no idle threat. He's gone and won't return."

Julian thought he had a plan that would resolve the situation if only the duchess and the grand duke would agree to it. "And it was this quarrel that broke the old man's health?" Lackland handed the note back to Madewyn. "You're right that he's unable to rule as he is now."

"He's been ill for a long while, but we've kept it quiet, or Anvel Grefyn would have seized it as an opportunity to bring us down. The trouble is, Grandfather has been growing ever more unpredictable with this infirmity, and some of his decisions have weakened us. He went mad when he found out... but never mind." She shook her head, tears in her eyes, and rose, putting her arms around the old man's neck. "Grandfather would never have done such a terrible thing if he weren't in the grip of this illness. He has no control over his body and goes mad with the frustration. He is a good man and didn't mean to quarrel so harshly with Dayved." Madewyn said it as if she were trying to convince the grand duke. "He's not old; he could live another twenty years but for this disease. The healing sisters say he may live that long anyway, even though he tries to abandon his body every day." Kissing her grandfather's cheek, she crossed back to the settee and sat opposite Julian once more.

Lackland wanted to offer comfort, but nothing he could say would change the facts. "Your grandfather will find a reason to live or not, but only on his terms. He was a strong leader, and all know him as a good man. *You* are the heir now. You must seize the reins and guide your clan in the absence of your brother. Henri will support you with gold and armsmen if it comes to that, and I'll ensure you have the support of all the Weyllyn lords here. They know me. None will go against me in this matter if they intend to keep what is already theirs."

Madewyn stood nonplussed. "What do you mean? Grandfather was a powerful ruler, and men flocked to him. They won't support me."

"I have a solution, but time is short for me." Julian felt the weight of his other pressing task. "I must leave in a few days as I have another task I must accomplish before the end of the month. We must assemble as many of your earls as can get here in three days. Also, you must make some key appointments to cement their loyalty to you."

Madewyn sent a servant for both the scribe and the herald. "I'll want your fastest messengers for this," Julian told the herald when they arrived. "Your task is to impress upon these earls to drop whatever they are doing and come to this house immediately. The grand duke requires it!"

With the messages sent, Lackland and Madewyn resumed their discussion.

"Our lords will never follow a woman. How will I keep them from going over to the Grefyn? Noblewomen are property here, just as they are in the north. Southern men don't follow property. They own it, display it, and then hide it from the sight of others." Madewyn's dark eyes flashed, and her cheeks flushed. "With Dayved gone, I've been giving orders in Grandfather's name and keeping him secluded, but soon they'll realize he's too ill to lead, and Clan Weyllyn will be no more. This branch of House Dragoran will have a new master. I can only pray it isn't Amstyce Lyndys." She shuddered. "He's the heir to Grefyn, and he would love nothing more than to wed me. He would own me, and the valley. You don't know what that means."

Lackland's eyes narrowed. "I do, actually. As a youth, I trained with him in military tactics one summer when his family guested with Henri's mother. While he's a boor, he's not completely stupid. Amstyce's first move would be to seize the port, and then he would block the trade road at Clythe, cutting the Long Valley off from King Henri. I believe his noble uncle, Anvel Grefyn, would crown himself King of Eyn even now if he dared attempt such a thing."

"He would indeed." Madewyn's anger flared. "The Grefyn has ambitions some would deem treasonous."

"Henri is aware that Grefyn consorts with Lanqueshire. That is why *you* must be bold. Seize power and force your men to follow you. Give them no choice by presenting it to them as done and irreversible. You can do this, and I know the right man to assist you. I know him from my early days at court, Bry Dayle. His father was the younger son of one of your nobles here."

"I know the Dayles, but not well."

"If I were you, I'd cede Bry Dayle the lands near Clythe and make him an earl. Not only would you have a better commander for your forces than you could ever wish for, but you would also have placed him at the gate to the valley. He would keep the pass open with force if needed. As an earl of tenanted lands, he would have the men-at-arms needed to support you, and he's as fine a strategist as I am. He's been working as a mercenary for the Ravens in Bekenberg. I've spoken to him."

Madewyn paced, thinking. "But even if we could get a message to him, could he be here in time?"

"He'll be here tomorrow or the next day, regardless of your decision regarding giving him a title, because he is the only man available with the abilities you need, and he loves this land with all his heart. He doesn't want to see the Eynier Valley return to the feudal days when the Lanques were your masters. Your aristocracy will accept him as he is of noble birth and has the added benefit of being a loyal man of this valley."

Madewyn was silent as she looked at her grandfather, trembling with palsy, seated in his invalid chair near the window. Her features displayed love for the old man as well as sorrow.

Daffyd Weyllyn opened his eyes and looked directly at her, lucid for a moment. His voice was weak, and his palsy increased in its intensity as he struggled to speak. "Take the man's advice. You'll never have a better opportunity. You have the ability and the will to lead Weyllyn. You need only draft a man with the skill to command and the understanding of how to wage a war. That will show the nobles you know what you're doing. I've already signed the papers naming you regent." With that said, Daffyd Weyllyn resumed staring out the window. The severe tremors of his head and hands abated, as he once again lapsed into his thoughts.

Madewyn turned to Lackland, filled with uncertainty. "What makes you think this mercenary will follow me? He owes me nothing. I was educated alongside my brother which means I know how to manage our concerns. But I don't know if I have the audacity." Suddenly she laughed, looking like a mischievous girl. "I believe I have the ambition, though, which my brother never had. Dayved and I often wished our roles were reversed."

"Bry Dayle will follow you," Lackland replied. "He's a good man and a true knight. But, like me, he has no land and no hope of gaining any. This plan resolves that and puts the best man for the task in the position to be most useful."

Once again, the halting voice of the old man sounded, though he remained looking out the window. "Give a man an opportunity like that, girl, and he'll follow you through the gates of hell."

Three days later, a hurried assembly of the nobles met at Imrysdock. As Lackland had hoped, the duchess impressed them with her force of personality. With two such respected soldiers as Lackland and Bry Dayle supporting her and speaking on her behalf, the nobles unanimously approved Madewyn's regency. The men who stylized themselves as the Dragons of Clan Weyllyn had been disorganized in their efforts to halt the depredations of Clan Grefyn. All the earls, including newly made Earl Bry Dayle, signed oaths of fealty to Madewyn Dragoran and to Clan Weyllyn. The swearing of fealty formally allied them with Henri Dragoran, King of Waldeyn, and that was what Lackland had come to Imrysdock to ensure.

Lackland immediately prepared to depart for Ludwellyn, intending to follow a map given to him by the duchess. In the stable, Bry Dayle tried to convince him to take some men. "You can't rely on your luck here, wonderful though it is. You'll be one man against a mob."

Lackland balked. "My task is one a lone man must accomplish. I'll return in a matter of days and ride north with you to Clythe. Don't wait for me, though. I must take the little-used ways now and go unnoticed."

"You're an idiot, you know. You're the last man on earth who'll ever go unnoticed. I don't know how you made it this far unmolested." Bry smiled, but he was serious. "You don't understand what you're riding into."

Though the young earl tried, he couldn't dissuade the knight. Lackland left Imrysdock, taking a lane he'd seen marked on the map, riding down a weedy, rutted road toward a village called Maldon.

CHAPTER 3

A SCRAPING SOUND impinged on Julian's nightmares, stirring him to consciousness. He gradually woke to a raging headache, seated in an awkward position, unable to stretch his legs. As his vision cleared, he realized he was in a cage, swinging from a tree, swaying in the wind. The movement of the cage caused the chain to make a mournful, creaking sound as it rubbed on the immense branch that held it. Townsfolk strolled by, pointing and mocking.

Julian's confusion slowly cleared. *Maldon...I remember seeing the sign on the gate. I handed Farroll to the stable master and talked to the innkeeper, but then what? I can't remember.... What do they want? Why have they done this?*

Lackland hung in the gibbet-cage under the burning sun with no water or food. The shade of the tree fell everywhere but on him, and now he was unpleasantly hot in his mail. In fact, he was more than uncomfortable.

He was in misery.

Occasionally the townspeople surrounded his prison, taunting him and ignoring his appeals for release. They refused his pleas for water, insulting and reviling him for begging.

An old man threw rocks at him, opening wounds over his eye. Two enterprising layabouts lobbed dog shit at him, and the villagers wagered on who could land the most accurate toss.

At first, Lackland was sure that once the people had their fill of entertainment, they would relent and let him go. Strangely, when the sun went down that first evening, the village became silent, the streets empty and abandoned.

The second day passed the same way. By the evening, Julian had no past and no future, only suffering. His waking moments were a wilderness of thirst and pain, and he believed he had died and gone to hell.

As night fell, alone and abandoned in the cage, all he had for company was the mournful sound of the gibbet creaking in the wind and his own pitiful moans in the dark.

On the third morning, with the first rays of the sun, the villagers were back, and the torments began anew.

By then, the agony of thirst was all Julian knew; nothing else mattered. Being denied water was the most terrible torture to endure, worse than the pains of his limbs, worse than the hunger, worse than the stench of living in his own filth.

Of all the cruel villagers, the most dreadful was the ghastly woman with the garish, painted face. She leered at his misery, mocking, and taunting him as she stood just out of reach of his cage. Her cheap red dress was cut so low her breasts were nearly falling out, and her skirt was tied on one side above her knees, showing off her stockinged legs. Slowly, the woman sipped from a goblet, deliberately allowing drops of water to spill from her mouth to her white breasts. Leisurely, they rolled down the cleft, drops Lackland yearned to lick from her although she was a common street whore, not because she excited him, but because it was water.

He sobbed at the waste of it and would have done anything to feel the drops on his parched tongue, begging her to relent. Seeing the cool liquid so tantalizingly near and yet denied to him sent Julian into a mad frenzy, exhausting what little strength he had. Glassy-eyed, he lay crumpled in his cage unheeding, despite the devils who poked and jabbed him. The villagers took joy in his suffering, many of them dancing and laughing, mocking his cries for mercy.

At last, darkness fell, and once again, Lackland hung abandoned in the cage, too weak to sob, too despondent to pray. Cloaked in hopelessness, he waited for sunrise and for the misery to begin anew.

A young man had taken the little-used back roads for his own reasons and stumbled into the abandoned village in the dead of night. Mystified at finding the hamlet empty, the man calling himself Jak the Tinker followed the weed-infested street to the town square where he found Lackland hanging in the tree, his sword belt lying on the ground below the cage.

Although circumstances had forced Jak to commit a murder, he was not a cruel man. After some thought, he climbed the tree, shinnying out on the branch until he could reach the cage. Seeing the lock, he used his sword to free Lackland. "Wait until I get below and can catch you. Your legs won't work for a while." He climbed down and caught the knight as he fell out of the cage, unable to feel his feet or legs. Jak supported him while Julian endured the pain of blood rushing back to his long-dead limbs.

The stranger half-carried him to the well and dipped out water to slake his thirst.

No drink had ever tasted so good, so sweet in Julian's life, and he moaned with pleasure. The man stayed with him until his head stopped swimming and he could stand. Once he had quenched his thirst, Lackland poured the cold water over his head, reviving himself somewhat, although nothing eased the pain in his feet. They exchanged names, and Lackland thanked his rescuer, barely able to speak through his cracked lips.

"Well, now I can walk a little. I must rescue Farroll." Lackland clenched his teeth against the pain in his legs and feet. "Where are all the people? They have my horse somewhere, and I want him back." He leaned against the stones surrounding the well and then slid down again to sit, as his legs gave out. "My feet are swelling now, I think. But never mind, I'll get used to it. Where are the people who were here tormenting me just this afternoon?"

"This afternoon? Really?" Jak appeared puzzled. "It looks as if it's been abandoned for years. What does this remind me of...? Oh no; it can't be. What sort of idiot am I that I'd forget such a thing? If I'd remembered the tale of Maldon, I should never have taken this road." The whites of his eyes showed his sudden terror.

"What is it? You look ill." Lackland pulled himself together as well as he was able. "If you hadn't come here, I'd surely have died since none of the villagers would release me. Cheer up! We'll soon be on the road once I find my equine companion."

"This is the village of Maldon. It's haunted! How could I have forgotten?" Jak groaned. "I'm an idiot!"

"Well, it seems a bit bleak and rundown, but really...." Lackland couldn't hide his incredulity. "Haunted? Like spirits and ghosts? Haints?"

Jak told the story, finishing with, "So, there are no villagers here because they're in hell for all eternity, doing the work of Old Grim. They've been gone for nigh on fifty years." The cadence of the tale and the timbre of Jak's voice fired Lackland's imagination, better than any master storyteller he'd ever heard.

"You tell that as well as a bard."

"Oh...er...thank you, but it's just an old story anyone would know." Jak fell silent and then said, "I can't believe I forgot it. We need to leave. *Now.*" He groped around, gathering his possessions.

"Well, fifty years is a long time. You can be forgiven for not remembering. But it can't possibly be this village." Lackland was unwilling to believe ghosts had deceived him. Nevertheless, the place had become deserted after dark each evening.

Finally, Julian admitted it was strange given the enjoyment the people took in his misery. "I came to this place three days ago, and the innkeeper took my money in exchange for a room. Of course, then he knocked me out and put me in a cage, but he was real. They've been poking and prodding me daily ever since."

"Yes, he was real, and your tormenters are too," agreed Jak. "It was a sunny day, am I right?"

"Yes! It poured cats and rats until the moment I passed through the gate and stepped into the village." Lackland gazed up, seeing the stars shining overhead in the cloudless night sky. "In fact, the sun shines all day long in this town, burning with the heat of hell. I thought it was strange, but many things are strange in this valley."

"It's the bargain." Jak clenched his teeth together to keep them from chattering. "The bargain they made with Old Grim in exchange for eternal life. In the light of day, they're allowed to take any innocents who walk into their trap, but they must spend their nights in Hell. We have to get out of here, or we'll be done for!"

"I'm not leaving without Farroll," replied Lackland firmly. "My horse trusts me with his life, and I must honor that commitment."

Reluctantly, Jak agreed, and the two men made their way to the overgrown and weedy yard behind the abandoned inn. After a great deal of trouble, they found Farroll in the tumbledown stable and in as bad a state as Lackland.

With Lackland helping as much as he could, Jak saddled Farroll while Julian warned the horse not to drink too much. Once watered, the unhappy horse desperately munched on the grass while Jak got him laden with Lackland's many heavy saddlebags and weaponry.

"I have no strength in my legs, and I doubt you could lift me into the saddle. I'll have to walk as best I can." Lackland's feet ached, getting worse with every moment, but he tried to hide it as best he could.

Nodding, Jak jumped nervously as the predawn sounds of birds stirring alerted him to their danger. "We must leave now!" Jak picked up his kit and looped his arm around Julian's back, half carrying him. He grabbed the startled horse's bridle and tugged. "Come, Farroll! They'll have you back in the hellhole we just left unless you help me get your master out of here!"

With Farroll supporting his other side, Lackland staggered as swiftly as he was able.

The occasional call of the birds spurred them on as nothing else could have. They stumbled to the open gate just as the first ray of sun pierced the dawn. With the light, the gates shuddered and slowly swung closed, creaking and groaning. Struggling desperately, Jak pulled Julian and his horse through the opening just in time. With a loud thunk, the gate swung closed behind them, catching the horse's silken tail.

Farroll kicked and bucked, but his hooves passed through the wood as if through fog, although his tail was trapped. Skeletal hands appeared, pulling the great beast backward by the tail. He whinnied, his eyes wild.

Lackland hung on to his bridle, struggling to keep him standing still. Jak raced back, dodging the stamping hooves. He cut the tail free with a flick of his knives and slapped Farroll's rump. The horse shot frontward, knocking Lackland down.

"Gah! They nearly had us!" Panicking, Jak pulled Lackland to his feet. He grabbed Farroll's harness. Soon he was pulling the two down the rutted, overgrown road, urging them on until they were out of sight of the gates. Some distance down the road along the river, well away from the haunted village, they found a place to rest and made camp.

The young tinker spent the next three days nursing Julian back to health. During the time they were together, Lackland came to know the man. Instinct said he could trust Jak, even though he could tell the man was lying about his name and was obviously on the run. A Grefyn earl had been murdered, and while he admitted he knew the countess, Jak was eager to avoid discussing it, which made Lackland suspicious.

Realizing he had to have help, Julian explained his mission. "I hope you are no friend of Anvel Grefyn. I intend to stop him from consorting with Lanqueshire. To kill a snake, you must cut off its head."

Jak stared. "You have my sincerest blessings, but I heartily doubt you'll achieve such a wondrous thing. He is extremely paranoid and better guarded than most men do their gold. His guards are mostly ruffians of the Lanque persuasion, as he doesn't trust his own heirs."

After much discussion, Jak devised a plan. He knew a woman who had grown up in the villa where his quarry lodged and devised a cover story for Lackland. "The dowager countess will help you. She's the only hope you have of getting out of there alive."

"I see. Would this acquaintance be the same young dowager countess we were discussing yesterday?" Lackland grinned at Jak's obvious discomfort. "A fine-looking, scholarly lad like you and the bored young bride of an old man…. It's a volatile combination in any strata of society!"

"I'm sure I don't know what you're referring to." Guilty dismay spread across his dark, handsome features. "In any regard, I feel sure the lady in question will assist you." He made a shrewd guess of his own. "Your unusual blond hair and romantic demeanor might well appeal to her adventurous nature, nearly as well as they did to a prominent duchess!"

"I'm sure I don't know what you mean." Lackland's smile gave away his enjoyment of the mocking exchange. "Although Madewyn is a wonderfully warm and generous hostess."

CHAPTER 4

TWO HARROWING WEEKS after he left Imrysdock, a much chagrinned Lackland rode toward the country estate known as House Dwyn. It was a house known to be aligned with the Crows of Clan Grefyn. He talked to Farroll, as always. "Remember, if you must gossip with the other horses, I'm a Lournesque mercenary. I'm sure Jak's right about this. Thanks to his advice, this part of the journey has been much easier."

Farroll apparently agreed although he said nothing.

"Jak is more than merely a tinker although he has the looks. But what? He's lying about his name, but he isn't the missing heir. Although at first, I thought he could be. Still, he's too familiar with the current politics and the nobility in this valley to be a simple scholar on his way to Vyennes, no matter what he says. He's a mystery; those knives of his aren't ordinary blades. They're the weapons of an assassin, and he's quite adept with them. Jak thinks like a spy, the way Slippery Jack does. But who is he working for? Is he on Henri's side, or is he with Grefyn? I'll find out soon enough, for good or ill."

Entering the stable yard, Lackland dismounted and handed Farroll over to an elderly man wearing a black armband signifying a house in mourning. As Jak had advised him, he introduced himself using the full formal Lournesque translation of his name, Julian De Portiers. "I am Giulian, youngest son of Baron Malcolm, Defender of the Gates." In the old days, a portier was a gatekeeper or door man. Thankful for his long friendship with Slippery Jack, the clipped, old-fashioned, overly proper speech of Lournes came easily. "I've come from Val Halle to assist House Dwyn in recruiting and training men-at-arms, as has been requested."

Lackland bowed formally. The Lournesque bowed at every opportunity, although Jack had toned it down a bit. "My sword and honor are at your lord's service. This letter contains my orders." Julian handed the man the first of the two sealed missives Jak had written for him to give the countess. If Jak was wrong and the earl was not dead, Lackland would still claim to be an agent of the king of Lournes and then find an opportune moment to kill the earl himself. "I bear a private message from Prince Maldred of Lournes for your master, or your mistress if your lord is not at home," said Lackland.

"I'm sorry, sir. Earl Rann Dwyn was murdered twelve nights ago, so we're in some disarray. We weren't warned of your imminent arrival, so we're not prepared. Please don't be offended if I have you wait here while I inform the countess of your arrival."

The man bowed and left Lackland seated on a bench in a well-ordered kitchen-garden, with only himself for conversation. "Well, then. Jak was telling the truth when he said the earl was dead. The earl... murdered twelve nights ago, but Jak knew he was dead when we met only two days afterward. That confirms it. Jak must be an assassin and an expensive one at that. Hopefully, his employer is on Henri's side. If he murdered the earl, he's finished his contract, so he's free. He said he was unwelcome here in the South now. Perhaps he'll go north to Billy Ninefingers. He seemed interested when I suggested it."

Soon a young page appeared and greeted Lackland. Someone had dressed the lad in livery with a black armband, clothing that had been neatly cut down to fit him. "I'm Ned, sir. Madam wishes you to guest with us tonight," said the boy, imitating the manner of the older man who'd taken Farroll. "If you would like to wash away the dust of the road, I'll take you to your rooms, where a bath is being prepared even now. Countess Ilene will meet you and speak with you in the small drawing room before dinner. I will come to get you at five thirty and guide you to the drawing room if that is agreeable to you. We'll serve dinner at six thirty." The boy spoke carefully, as if attempting to correct a low-class accent.

"It is most agreeable," replied Lackland, smiling at the serious lad. "I've been on the road a long while and would appreciate a bath." As he followed young Ned through the corridors of the rambling manor,

Lackland prayed he hadn't made a mistake in trusting the handsome tinker, but he was committed now. *At least if I die here, it won't be of thirst*, he thought, shuddering.

Lackland sat in a small, pleasant sitting room watching Ilene, the Dowager Countess Dwyn, as she read the second letter from Jak. A beautiful dark-haired woman, Ilene was very young. She wore the traditional black of recent widowhood, but something about the way she wore it was anything but traditional.

She was stylish, glamorous, as if the black she wore was a badge of honor. She was a young woman full of ambition and energy. Ilene reminded Julian of a flower just bloomed, filled with joy, and poised on the edge of her new life. It was as if she intended to live her life to the fullest, as if every moment were precious to her.

At last, she looked up from the letter, her dark eyes sparkling. "So, you are the infamous Julian Lackland, eater of babies and slayer of gods. I never thought to see you of all men in my drawing room," Ilene laughed. "My late husband must be turning in his grave!"

"I am all that? I sound terrifying! But in truth, I don't know what to expect here, Countess," replied Lackland with a twinkle in his eye. "Jak the Tinker told me you might consent to help me, but as far as I know, your house is aligned with your noble uncle, and against King Henri."

"Call me Ilene, as we are friends and equals. House Dwyn has turned to Weyllyn," replied Ilene with a mischievous grin. "I've sworn fealty to Duchess

Madewyn, the Regent of Weyllyn. I received a letter welcoming us into the fold several days ago." Her fine brows drew together. "Immediately after my husband's funeral, I gave my armsmen a choice to stay or go. Of the hundred and twenty, only thirty-two departed. They were of the Lanque persuasion and are most likely owned by my uncle, Anvel Grefyn. The others swore to serve me and this house and to serve Weyllyn and King Henri.

"The only difficulty I have now is dealing with the rotten apples of my late husband's personal guard who insist on hanging about in the nearby town. I paid those men off and sent them on their way. But they keep returning here trying to bully my faithful men and convince me to return to my uncle's hearth, each time with greater force. My loyal armsmen have so far prevailed, but I fear trouble looms. My uncle can't accept that he's lost control of me, and I know he'll send my brother, Amstyce, to bring me back to Grefyn by force."

"You may have to kill your brother." Lackland's regret was clear on his chiseled features. "If the men who defected are of Lanqueshire, they're committed to fomenting rebellion against the crown. They're not merely hired armsmen. They'll return with your brother, knowing all your weaknesses."

"I would regret killing Amstyce, though I doubt he would regret killing me. Will you remain here at Dwyn in your guise as Giulian and assist me in gathering armsmen on my lands? Would you help me find the right men to be my captains? The captains my late husband employed didn't remain with me, nor would I have wanted them to. In return, I'll gladly help you achieve your goal in Ludwellyn." Ilene stood and crossed to a tall window. Her brow furrowed as she thought on the ramifications of Lackland's plan.

Julian joined her. "I must do my task before the Grefyn departs Ludwellyn for the summer." He thought for a moment. "I'll never get near him once he leaves the city. But yes. I'll help you."

She turned back to Lackland. "If you're successful, you'll send Clan Grefyn into a feeding frenzy. That chaos will keep Amstyce out of my hair while I consolidate my position here."

"What do you mean?"

"Amstyce is my uncle's heir, but that doesn't mean he wouldn't have to fight an inter-clan war to gain the coronet. If he and the other houses are occupied with that, they won't worry about an 'untutored girl with delusions of grandeur.' My brother won't even think about me until he's been acknowledged by every other house that looks to Grefyn. By then, it will be too late."

The complexity of Southern politics astounded Julian. "Who would stand in your brother's way?"

She snorted. "He'll first have to deal with House Doleyn and House Denvyr. But Doleyn will be the true thorn in his side. If Doleyn and Denvyr were to put aside their differences and work together, they could topple him. But they won't because they're too shortsighted. Greed will always be the downfall of Grefyn."

"You say you're young and untutored, but I say you're sharp and perceptive. You're exactly what Madewyn needs among her nobles." Lackland felt some of his burdens lift. "I will see your house strong and well-able to defend your land before I depart for the rest of my journey. I have a plan that will cost you nothing and will give Henri a presence here, which will deter your brother."

She looked at him questioningly.

"When I get to Ludwellyn, I'll ask the governor's liaison to billet a squad of crown soldiers here at this house, to assist you in recruiting and training your men. I have the authority to order it myself, but I don't want my presence in the valley known."

Joy graced Ilene's features. "An excellent suggestion for several reasons. I've only just discovered my late husband has nearly run this family's shipping business into the ground, which means I must go to Ludwellyn. Madewyn has asked me to be her guest while I am there, so our lodging is sorted. I must assume Amstyce will attempt to withhold the inheritance my mother left me, delaying it for as long as he is able. This means I must right the finances of this house using whatever means I can." Mischief sparkled in her dark eyes.

"Not an easy task." Lackland's raised eyebrow showed his concern.

"It will be less of a problem now, thanks to you. You've resolved paying the extra soldiers' stipends for me. I was raised in House Lyndys and I will tell you this—no one can count gold better than a Lyndys. We cut our teeth on business and financial dealings. I'll sell off the dreadful art in this mausoleum to finance both the outfitting of my armsmen and the rebuilding of my ships."

Lackland interviewed and tested her men-at-arms. He found she had many good loyal men qualified to lead the various squads. They voiced relief on hearing a contingent of crown soldiers would soon be there to bolster their ranks.

With Ilene's help, he devised a disguise for himself once they arrived in Ludwellyn. Soon, he had a plan, devised from her intimate knowledge of his quarry's daily habits. He saw the one weakness he could exploit if all went as he hoped.

Ilene left her steward in charge, saying she had to attend to her shipping business. As no woman of her station would travel without guards, Lackland rode beside Ilene's carriage, traveling as captain of her personal guards.

Madewyn was in Ludwellyn, tending to her own business interests. She welcomed Ilene, winking at Lackland's disguise. She felt that leading their houses made them sisters of a sort, and the two women bonded instantly.

The Weyllyn Villa stood at the opposite end of the long, winding boulevard from the Grefyn Villa. Highborn Street ran along the high bluffs, with the grand winter homes of every great family from both clans between the two powerful houses. All the highest of society spent the winter along that street.

The last balls of the season were scheduled for the following weekend, so time was short. Lackland began plotting how to accomplish his task.

The first thing he did on Monday was to visit the exchequer, meeting in private with a certain man. He arranged for a squad of crown soldiers to return with Ilene to House Dwyn when she departed the city. Then, he dressed in the garb of a local noble, wearing a plumed hat of a common style to hide his hair. The ubiquitous gray cloak worn by the nobility covered him against the chill morning fog rolling in off the harbor.

As the day warmed, it grew humid. People came out to sit in cool gardens, dining or passing the time in conversation. Strolling idly, he walked the length of Highborn Street, listening to the gossip of the servants and their masters as he passed each villa. He noted the landscape and the style of the architecture of the great houses. He did this off and on all day Tuesday also, spying and thinking until he knew exactly what he would do.

At ten o'clock on Wednesday night, Lackland sat high in a tree on the bluff behind House Grefyn, just outside the wall surrounding the palace. Guards strolled in the gardens, following a regular pattern. He had a perfect view inside a certain third-floor window, but the timing had to be perfect. According to Ilene, the old man had a fetish for breathing the night air before bed, frequently carrying on at dinner about the health benefits of fresh air to the utter boredom of his heirs.

Minutes slowly passed, and Julian wondered if he had mistimed things. He was just about to climb down when the window was thrust open, and an older man stood framed in the opening. Julian held his arrow nocked, with his great bow drawn, waiting for the guards to pass out of view, hoping the old man would remain there long enough.

At last, the guards paced out of sight, and Julian let fly the bolt.

An immense shaft appeared, perfectly lodged in his target's heart. Clutching his chest, the man staggered, unable even to cry out. The old man's body fell against the window frame, sliding to the floor, and vanished from Lackland's sight. Unaware of what had occurred, the guards still paced the garden below, walking their regular circuit.

Julian slipped back to the Weyllyn villa, unseen in the dark streets.

The next morning Countess Ilene was enjoying a pleasant breakfast in the dining room with Madewyn and several other guests when a crown messenger brought the news that the Grefyn was dead. "An arrow the size of a tree-branch run him clean through, your ladyship. Shot at his window, he was. House Lyndys has taken possession of the Grefyn Palace, and they've executed the guards who failed to protect the old Grefyn. The port is under martial law until House Grefyn gets themselves sorted. In the meantime, it's not safe for anyone here on the Highborn Street. The governor's liaison wishes everyone to return to their country houses until things are more settled."

"Of course. I'll collect my guards and depart for House Dwyn immediately," Ilene replied solemnly.

As soon as the two of them were alone, Ilene threw her arms around Lackland's neck and laughed. "Thank you, my knight in shining armor! You're the most amazing of men, to have accomplished so much in so short a time! But now I feel sad for the women and children of Houses Doleyn and Denvyr, and indeed of any house that attempts to take the coronet from my brother. They're about to lose everything. They'll be reduced to less than chattel."

Three months had passed. Lackland rode into the stable yard behind the newly finished inn, appropriately named Billy's Revenge. He had beheaded the snake, but the experiences of his journey had tamed his youthful arrogance. It was a quieter, more thoughtful man who handed Farroll off to Cob John, Billy's ostler, in the stable.

"Lady Mags is out with Annie Fitz, but she'll be home tomorrow," said John, as Lackland dismounted. "You're all moved into the new place now. I think you'll like the room Mags selected for you. She fixed it up with your things, so it looks quite homey."

Somehow, Julian wasn't surprised she'd opted for separate quarters. Disappointed, but not surprised.

Thanking John, he walked to the front and stood on the porch looking around, stunned at the way the town was rising before his eyes.

A shadow loomed, and Billy stood next to him. "It's hard to believe, isn't it? But you were right. A town *is* growing here on the Limpwater River." Billy's hand rested on Lackland's shoulder. "Thanks to your foresight, we've had the chance to plan it right, so it'll grow properly."

Lackland counted four shops in various stages of completion across the muddy square from Billy's Revenge. Cottages were going up along two side streets, and a man he recognized as the Patriarch of the Church wandered around, masquerading as a portly friar, directing the various building projects. "What are you calling this town?"

"Limpwater, after the river. It makes sense, since we're right here on the big bend," replied Billy, shrugging. "I hope to have the streets cobbled before

November when the rains set in. So, what the hell kept you away for so long? I feared you were dead, but St. Coeur from the Ravens passed through here two weeks ago and said he'd heard you were on your way back."

"Well, show me to my new home then. I'll tell you all about this trip, as much as I can anyway, over a nice mug of cider," said Lackland. "I'm not inclined to go thirsty anymore!"

Unfortunately, when Julian got to the part about the haunted village, no one believed him.

Billy laughed and asked him what sort of mushrooms he'd been dining on.

"Ask Farroll if you don't believe me." Lackland went hot with indignation. "Everyone knows horses don't lie!"

The room erupted with laughter, leaving him at a loss, wondering what he'd said.

"Oh, we don't doubt evil villagers held you captive and tormented you. I've heard stories of the South that would curl your hair! We don't even doubt a handsome tinker lad rescued you, although it sounds a bit convenient." George Finch laughed at Lackland's obvious annoyance. "It's the ghosts and haints we're disbelieving. But it makes a wonderful tale. I've never heard such an astonishing story!"

"Well, doubt me all you wish." Lackland saw it was useless to protest. "But if you ever chance to go south, don't pass through Maldon, whatever you do."

September had arrived. Lackland and Lady Mags entered the common room at Billy's Revenge, having just returned from guarding a pottery shipment to Castleton. The room was full, and several Ravens from

Bekenberg were there. An entertainer sat in the corner, softly playing pipes in the style Lackland had only seen in the South. He was sure he'd seen the man before. It took him a moment, but at last, he recognized him. Gone was the mass of waist-length curls, and in their place was a mercenary's haircut, but he was most definitely Jak the Tinker. Best of all, he wore a Rowdy's armband.

"Jak! Jak, the tinker's son! You've cut your hair—I knew I would see you again." Lackland was wild with joy. "Billy, Mags—everyone—this is the very tinker-lad who rescued me from the cage in the haunted village and saved Farroll from a miserable death." He embraced the bard again. "And what are you calling yourself now, Jak? Will we know your real name? I knew you were no scholar."

"I'm called Huw Owyn, pronounced Hugh in your Northern language. And yes, it's my true name. Sadly, I am most definitely a scholar, as are all tinkers." He laughed as he sat at Lackland's table. "You must be the lovely Lady Mags, about whom my exuberant friend here waxed so poetic while Farroll and I were nursing him back to health after his ordeal in the South."

"I'm pleased to meet you at last. None of these louts believed my poor Lackland when he told them about the ghosts," she laughed. "He's a bit imaginative, but even Julian couldn't hallucinate a haunted town and a gibbet-cage."

Matt St. Coeur, the leader of the Ravens, sat down with them. "Huw—you never told me *you* are the famous tinker who rescued the Great Knight. Everyone's heard Lackland's story, but now we'll hear what really happened. Huw the Bard will tell us the truth!"

"And so, I will. I've made it into a ballad," replied Huw, his dark blue eyes sparkling with mischief. "I hoped I would have the chance to play it here first since it's Lackland's story."

That was the first time the world heard the tale of *How Jak Rescued the Great Knight*.

CHAPTER 5

YULE HAD COME and gone. Billy Ninefingers felt satisfied with the way the roughest year of his life had turned out. His inn was earning money, and Bess had married him before the birth of their son.

It was a difficult year, no doubt.

But he'd survived it.

And thanks to the efforts of his Rowdies, Lackland, in particular, Billy's Revenge was the first inn south of Castleton to have right to display the King's Seal on the corner of his sign.

It had been a decent afternoon considering it was January, but now it poured rain, and few people were out. Billy was almost dozing when the door flew open, startling him awake.

Ben Baker hurried in as fast as he could on his two canes, white-faced and in a state. "It's Beau! The boys were all fishing—he's in trouble. The lads he was with are frantic, but they swear it was a waterdemon. From what they're describing, it must have been. But with my bad leg, I'm stuck. Please, help me find my son!" Ben's leg had never properly healed from a bad break.

Billy immediately sent the only two Rowdies he had available, Lackland and Slippery Jack, out to look for the missing boy. He warned, "Waterdemons are sneaky, and darkness is their time to hunt. The boy might still be alive because these things are like spiders. They take their prey when they have the opportunity and put them to sleep. Then they store them, like in a larder, to eat later. It's getting dark now, so it should leave its den to go fishing. Be careful and see if you can sneak Beau out without getting involved in a fight you will lose." He told them where the boy was last seen and sent them off.

Slippery Jack's real name was Johan Fitzmarion, and he'd been born an illegitimate son of the late Duke of Marionberg. His mother was Lournesque, and despite his having grown up in Marionberg, his accent betrayed his roots. Like Lackland, he'd had the benefit of a court education, but his talent as a spy and a scout was without peer. The two had trained under the same arms master and were old friends

When he saddled up, Julian noticed his horse was in an equine snit, but ignored it, as always. He'd concluded that for all his fine lineage, Farroll was a whiner. He stood his ground in a fight, though, and was a loyal friend. Julian had grown fond of him.

"I think your horse is sulking," Jack said, as they left the stable yard.

"I suppose he is. He has delusions of grandeur," Julian replied. "His dying ambition is to be put out to stud for the rest of his days, the randy old beast."

"I have the same ambition." Jack sighed. "I have little hope for it, though."

"No, I suspect not." Lackland chuckled. "Merry Kat might disapprove—she seems more than a little fond of you."

Jack blushed, sheepish glee sparkling in his eyes, and changed the subject. "How did young Beau get caught by a waterdemon? He's smarter than most of the boys his age. Huw seems to think he'd make a fine bard."

"I don't know. The children in this town are pretty well behaved, and he seems like a good lad, but you know how boys that age are. They're too adventurous for their own safety. At least I was."

"He's twelve—he'll be a man in three years if he lives through this. He's determined to ride with the Rowdies as soon as Billy allows it." Jack shook his head. "What if we must fight this waterdemon? We have no majik amulets. I don't, anyway. Stella One-Eye has a nasty little lightning-spelled amulet that these beasts just hate. Too bad she's out on a job."

Lackland patted the longbow strapped to the saddlebag behind him. "I have no majik amulets either, but I'm thinking arrows. If we can lob a few arrows at the beast, maybe we can get his attention."

"I doubt it," replied Jack. "I've heard you can't kill them with a sword, so I don't know how you could with an arrow. But I've only seen the one, and Stella zapped the bugger straight to hell, which worked miraculously."

"I've never fought one, so that's good information. Maybe we won't have to fight it." Lackland fell silent, considering the problem.

Jack agreed. "Normally, I enjoy sneaking around in the dark, but waterdemons aren't my sort of job."

"I don't relish fighting in the dark," said Lackland. "But I like seeing something new, fighting something I've never seen. It keeps life interesting." He fell silent, listening to the wind and hissing rain.

"You're mad, did you know? Anyway, I couldn't let you get killed all by yourself. Someone has to bring the bad news back to Lady Mags." Jack fell silent too.

The occasional soft clinking of harnesses and the sounds of their horses walking through the mud accompanied the hissing sounds of falling rain. They held the lantern up as they rode, trying to find some sign of the waterdemon's passing. However, the dark and the wet hid any signs well.

They quickly arrived at the place where the other boys said the beast had grabbed Beau. A strange smell filled the air, which the horses didn't like. Jack said, "If that doesn't stink, nothing does. It smells like we've found our quarry's nest."

A small trail led off toward the river. Even in the dark, it was easy to see something heavy had been dragged down it. Dismounting, Lackland and Jack tied the horses to a bush. Jack said, "I'll make a quick trip down to see what's there. There should be a hole in the bank if it's a waterdemon's den." He slipped off into the dark while Julian held the horses' reins.

In what seemed no time at all, he returned.

"It's a den all right," Jack whispered. "I can't tell if the boy is in there. I couldn't see much of anything. Maybe it's out hunting. Either way, we must chance the lantern light."

"Is there a place for me to fire off a bolt or two?" Lackland turned, reaching for his longbow. Pulling his bowstring out of a dry pocket, he strung it.

"There is, near the river. I've never seen a bow that long. I don't think I could draw it, much less string it," Jack commented, watching him.

"Sometimes it's too long. I need a certain amount of free space for drawing it unheard in the forest." Lackland finished and looked around. "You're right. It's uncommonly dark here."

Jack glanced around, nervous. "We need light, but it'll alert the creature. That will be a problem."

"I agree, but we'll never find the boy without it."

Soon the two men crouched before the dark hole in the bank. Jack said, "Perhaps you should get the boy. There's probably not room for more than one of us in there, and the boy is heavy. You're much stronger than me. I'll hold the lantern and hope the beast doesn't catch his fish and return anytime soon." Jack broke off as from somewhere at the back of the den, a glimmer moved, reflecting the light of the lantern. Suddenly, the horrifying figure of the waterdemon filled the entrance to the den. "Oh, god. He's still here."

Once out of the den, the demon glowed in the weak light of the lantern. Its chest was barrel-shaped, and the limbs were manlike. Its huge, grotesque head was disturbingly alien. Tiny, mean-looking silver eyes glared out of its ghastly face.

Sniffing the air, it roared its defiance, shaking its head and snarling.

"I'm not comfortable facing him this way." Jack looked at Lackland, who paid him no mind. "Julian? I'm a spy, not an idiot. Oh, hell. You never listen."

Lackland already had a huge arrow nocked, and quickly drawing it back, he shot the demon squarely in the chest. The beast yanked the arrow out and came racing toward him. Quickly, Lackland fired off another bolt, which lodged in the demon's head. The creature yanked that one out too, swinging it at Jack as if it were a club.

"Now, we're done for!" Desperately Jack swung and chopped with his sword. "I could use your help here." He lopped off a gooey hand, and the demon immediately grew another. "Lackland—help, please!"

"Just keep him busy. I know what we need!" Cutting off part of his new shirt, Lackland wrapped it around the head of an arrow and touched it to the lantern, setting it alight. Nocking the bolt and drawing it back, he held it, wanting to aim for the beast's back, which was not facing him.

"Shoot the arrow! Shoot the arrow!" Jack lopped off the newly grown hand again, nimbly dodging and ducking as the waterdemon flailed blue-bloody stumps at him, spattering him with jelly-like gore.

"Not yet! I must shoot him in the back, or he'll yank it out. Get him turned, so his back is to me. Hurry!" Lackland prayed his flaming arrow would last long enough to cause grief for the demon.

After a spate of cursing, hacking, and slashing, Jack got the waterdemon's back toward Lackland, who shot the arrow.

The demon shrieked, trying vainly to reach it. Jack scuttled out of its way. The creature started toward the river, the inside of his body aglow with the burning arrow. For a moment, they just stared at the beast, all alight inside. Suddenly realizing their peril, Jack shouted, "Don't let it in the river for the love of God, Julian! It'll heal itself, and we'll be dead men!"

Lackland drew his sword and quickly sliced through the back of the demon's left leg, causing it to pause. Jack pressed forward, hacking at the creature's torso and arms, confusing the writhing beast.

Using the last bit of his shirt, Lackland shot another flaming arrow, this time into the back of the creature's head. It stumbled to its knees, trying vainly to reach either arrow, but Jack kept lopping off its arms. Lackland immediately drew his sword again and set to hacking at the brute. A thin, high screech shredded their ears, as the beast tried to claw at its chest with first one bloody stump and then the other.

After what seemed like hours, the demon finally toppled to the earth. First, it shuddered, and then, at last, it stopped glowing.

Exhausted, Lackland stared down at the reeking corpse. "We should burn this carcass, so it can't come back to life by some miracle."

Jack agreed. While he did that, Lackland took the lantern and entered the dark lair, looking for the boy. With relief, he could feel Beau was breathing. He carried him out of the den, covering him with his cloak.

Jack was just finishing burning the creature's remains. He shook his head. "I never saw anything burn so fast in my life."

Lackland nodded. "Let's go then. I'm worried about the boy. I hope he doesn't die."

Jack lit the way with the lantern while Julian carried the unconscious child back to where they had tied the horses. He took Beau while Julian mounted

Farroll, then attempted to hand the boy up to him. "Gah! He's heavy. I think I just sprung myself." He struggled to lift the unconscious boy. "Good lord. What is Ben feeding him? He's only twelve, but he's as big as me."

"He's definitely big for his age. If he keeps growing like he is, he'll be almost as tall as Billy," Julian agreed. Reaching down, he pulled Beau up. Once Lackland had the boy securely settled, the shivering knight wrapped his cloak around them both.

Still grumbling, Jack mounted up, and they rode through the miserable darkness back to Limpwater. At last, the two gore-covered heroes delivered the boy to his worried parents. Jack went to get the healing priestess while Lackland waited. "I want to be sure he'll live, but I'll wait out here, so I don't dirty your floor." Lackland remained on the step. "It was a mess in that den."

Sister Naille hurried back with Jack, and after she checked Beau over, she told them he would recover with no lasting effects and would have no memory of the incident. Turning their tired selves toward the warmth and welcome of Billy's Revenge, Lackland and Slippery Jack silently walked their horses through the mud.

Cob John met them at the stable. "I'll take your mounts here, lads. I don't want you upsetting the rest of the horses with that stench." He took the reins of both, waving Julian and Jack off to the bathhouse. "You reek worse than George's boots. Hose yourselves off good before you dirty up the tubs. Then burn your clothes." He looked at the unhappy horses. "Don't you ponies worry," he told Farroll and Bruiser. "I've got a nice hot bath of sorts for you too."

Once they were finally sitting in well-deserved tubs of lovely, clean, steaming water, Jack looked at Lackland. "Where did you come up with the idea to use fire against him? It saved us."

"It wasn't an elegant solution, but it was all I could think of. When he yanked the arrow out of his head and beat you with it, I knew we were done for unless I could find a bit of majik we could use." Julian shivered, despite the warmth of the tub. "But I didn't reckon on how chilly a coat of mail gets on a cold and rainy night in Limpwater when your shirt is gone. I nearly froze my arse coming home."

The two men reentered the common room where Billy greeted them with warm bowls of stew and mugs of ale. "I knew you'd find the boy. Ben was here a moment ago and said he's stirring. It looks like he'll be fine. I wasn't sure you'd survive the demon, but I should never doubt you, Lackland."

Huw sat in his corner, singing softly. The familiar sound of his harp and the warmth of Billy's welcome suffused Lackland with the feeling of having come home, and for a moment, he felt as if he'd never been happier.

Lady Mags sat at the table, along with Merry Kat and Lucy Blue-Eyes. Huw put his harp down and came to sit with them, demanding the tale which Julian told, occasionally interrupted by Jack. "So, now I've lost my new shirt, and my horse hates me." Julian finished telling the tale. "But on the good side, there's one less waterdemon on the road to Dervy."

"I'll just say it was a job I don't ever want to do again." Jack shuddered. "I need to get me a couple of majik amulets for handling those sorts of things."

"It might be worth the cost," agreed Julian. "Although it doesn't seem fair to the poor beasts."

The others stared, not sure they'd heard him right.

"Julian—there's no such thing as a fair fight." Mags's saucy grin lit her face. "The only thing that counts is winning." She winked at Billy and Jack. "I always win."

Lackland sighed. Bess had finally married Billy, Lucy was mad for Huw, and Merry Kat was firmly paired with Jack, which should have meant there was hope for him and Mags.

But it didn't, and he knew it. In his heart, he knew Mags would never leave the trade, despite his wistful yearnings to the contrary.

BILLY AND BESS could have told him so, as they later agreed while preparing for bed.

"She's merc to the core, Billy. She'll foster her babes out like Stella if the herbs don't work, you'll see. Julian will never have what he so obviously wants." Bess disengaged young Brand from her breast and carefully laid him in his little bed.

"Will I get what I want?"

Billy's wicked grin charmed her. "You will, you lucky sot," she said, climbing back into bed.

"I am that," replied Billy, overwhelmed by the fierce emotion his wife always inspired in him. He fervently thanked God for all his blessings. "I'm the luckiest sot in the world."

CHAPTER 6

JULIAN LACKLAND WAS now twenty-five and in the prime of his manhood. He and the other gentlemen Rowdies had spent much of the previous five summers fighting with King Henri down in the mountains on the border with Lanqueshire. Summer was the most opportune time to make war, and thanks to Lackland, Billy's mercenary knights were the best trained, but the gentlemen's absence had left him shorthanded and the ladies struggling to keep the merchants safe with scant crews.

Lady Mags had become Billy's lieutenant, and everyone acknowledged the Lady Rowdies as the best in the business.

King Henri's staid old lords wouldn't allow women soldiers into the ranks of the army, which exceedingly annoyed him. In his opinion, they would have resolved the matter in one summer, although their methods, at times, made him squeamish. Fortunately for commerce, Henri had come to an agreement with the Lanque king at the end of the last battle, and the Rowdies' crews were back at full strength.

Lackland was still in love with Lady Mags, but she'd turned away from him the previous fall. With the disintegration of their relationship, Julian was adrift. A new crop of young men and women filled the ranks of the Rowdies, including the boy he and Jack had rescued. Beau Baker had grown into a tall, broad-shouldered man of seventeen, and now had two years in the saddle behind him.

One by one, the older Rowdies who had been Julian's closest friends retired, leaving him feeling alone, despite being among familiar faces. Slippery Jack and Merry Kat were the first to leave, marrying, and starting a business in Castleton, dealing in fine gems.

Mags had not explained her change of heart toward him, which left Julian confused and wondering what he'd done wrong. A month before Yuletide, she'd gone home to her father's house. Most Rowdies went to visit family at Yule if they had any to visit. But Mags left several weeks early, departing one day and leaving him no note or explanation.

Heartsore, Julian asked Billy where she had gone. Billy was unable to disguise his surprise that Mags hadn't told him. "She returned home to care for her mother, who's expecting a child. The countess is too old, nearly fifty. It worries the healing sisters that she won't survive, and the earl begged Mags to come home. I couldn't refuse."

Mags didn't return until May.

In a letter from his own mother, Julian learned the countess had given birth to a son and then died from complications at the end of March. Mags remained absent for two full seasons, helping her father through his grief, and finding a good nurse to care for her infant brother.

She returned to the Rowdies at the end of May but remained distant to Lackland, treating him with professional courtesy. For a brief time, he'd thought perhaps she'd found another lover, but as far as he could tell, she hadn't taken another to her bed. She was unfailingly friendly and polite but behaved as if he were an unfamiliar new Rowdy she'd been incidentally teamed with.

Her behavior made him suspect the truth was more complicated than Billy knew but couldn't bring himself to ask her about it. Instead, he buried his questions and suspicions under a veneer of lighthearted banter. The last thing he wanted was for his problem to affect the rest of the Rowdies. So, Lackland took comfort elsewhere when a friend offered it to him but rarely courted a partner. He couldn't let go of his romantic dream.

Now Julian considered leaving the Rowdies permanently to return to court as the Royal Arms Master. Henri had made it clear he could have the job whenever he wanted. However, he wouldn't leave the Rowdies until either his suspicions were confirmed, or he knew what had turned Mags away from him.

The morning began as usual. Julian sat in the common room at Billy's Revenge, polishing his boots, waiting for a job assignment. The door opened and closed, and messengers came and went all morning long. Various Rowdies departed on assorted jobs, and the common room gradually emptied until only Lackland and Mags remained, the last two Rowdies available, since they were the most recently returned.

As the morning wore on, Lackland played nursemaid to Billy's children, crawling about on his hands and knees with young Brand on his back. Sisters

Cissy and Letty whooped and laughed in a mad dance, all of them having a great time.

The door opened, and a man in the king's livery hurried over to Billy. "We have a problem that requires your help." He plunked a fat pouch of gold down. "There's no one else available to handle this. The king and his men are down at Bekenberg Pass again, but now this situation has arisen."

Billy looked at the pouch suspiciously. When the customer led the negotiations with gold, it was probably a nasty job that could end with a funeral and a wake for a Rowdy. "We're a little shorthanded right now. You should have come last evening. I had a full house then."

The messenger looked around the room, spying Lackland on the floor in the corner with the children. "I'm sure whatever help you can send will be fine. It's a task in which numbers matter not but requires a certain amount of cunning and guile."

"Exactly what is the problem? The war is over. Surely the king's guards are available for a small task such as you're describing." Billy had a bad feeling about it, but the gold was real; twelve gold crowns, by the weight of the purse. "What are you asking of the Rowdies?"

"A beast is holed up in the Grimmenstock mine," replied the messenger. "We've no one to spare to deal with it because a renegade group of bloody Lanques blockaded the pass down at Bekenberg again. This time, they're charging our merchants a toll to use the king's road."

Billy's eyebrows rose. "I see. Henri wouldn't like that, I'm sure."

"He doesn't. The master miner has been unable to open the mine for half a season. It wasn't a problem until that little emergency came up, but now we're running low on ore. Our armorers can't make swords or armor without iron."

"What sort of beast are we talking about? There are many varieties of 'beast,' and they all require different methods of removal. This may not cover our expenses." Billy looked at the full pouch. "We don't do dragons. That's a job for the king's men."

"I have no idea, but it's closed the mine. This is a deposit, just to get the heroes on the road," the messenger said. "The Lord Dog Walker said you could name your price. We must reopen the mine, or we'll lose access to the Eynier Valley."

Billy nearly refused. John De Portiers was Lackland's cousin and held the office of Lord Dog Walker, King Henri's secretary. John De Portiers *never* said "name your price"—his purse was always empty, and he bargained more closely than any merchant. "I suppose I can send someone. But if this turns nasty, your deposit is forfeit." He tucked the pouch into his shirt. "I'll send you the bill when this is finished. And if it turns out to be a dragon, the fee will be quite high."

"De Portiers said it would be so. Send the bill, but rout the beast, please!" With that, the messenger turned and left.

"Lady Mags! Lackland! I have a job for you," shouted Billy. "Roust your arses and hit the road."

"You two boil the water before you drink it in those mountains, or you'll be dying from the shits," admonished Chicken Mickey, when Lackland and

Mags arrived in the stable yard. Mick was Cob John's life-partner and provisioner for the Rowdies.

"Yes, Grandma," they both replied, laughing.

"You fools can laugh, but Johnny Malone boils the water now. Ask him if you don't believe me." Mick finished ticking off the list of supplies and the two pack ponies he'd given them to carry their provisions. "Lackland, you've got more luggage on your poor beast than the entire company of ladies took with them."

"It's my new armor. It needs a saddlebag of its own." Lackland looked at his horse ruefully. "I'm not wearing it until we get there. This brigandine is much more comfortable for traveling."

"Lady Mags doesn't have as much luggage, and she has her armor in a bag with two dresses and an extra surcoat," the old man groused. "Are you leaving home? Everything you own is in those bags."

Cob John stood in the doorway, nodding his head.

Julian's barely suppressed irritation flashed. "Lay off, Mick. I have what I need. I swear you're worse than my mother." He secured his longbow over the top of everything, then looked over the list of supplies. After showing the list to Lady Mags, they both signed off on it.

Feigning a good mood, Lackland taunted, "Goodbye, Mother! Goodbye, Father," as they left, receiving rude gestures in return. The horses were eager to go, having been cooped up for two days.

Lackland and Mags kept the conversation cordial and polite, but little of substance passed between them. They joked, laughed, and said all the things they would say to any Rowdy, but it felt awkward. Still, he didn't press for anything more, although he was full of questions and desperate for answers. With the weather being fine and the horses cantering along at a good clip, they entered the gates of Castleton well before supper.

They wound their way through the throng to the Queen's Garter, the inn the Rowdies all favored. Lackland didn't blink an eye when Mags ordered two rooms, as he'd expected it. Once settled, they sat in the common room and listened to all the gossip, partaking in none.

When Fair Ellen, a lady of the mercenary group known as the Ravens, invited Julian to her room to see the book she'd just purchased, he was drunk enough to go with her, and they passed a friendly evening.

Downstairs in the common room, Mags sat, telling herself he was better off finding comfort elsewhere. All she could offer him was a shadow of what he wanted, and it was wrong for her to lead him on. Julian had never asked her to marry him. He'd never pressed her to leave the Rowdies and take up the life of a goodwife, but she'd sensed it in him. He yearned for a home and a family.

Lackland was the marrying kind.

Whenever she saw him playing with Bess and Billy's children or Gertie Smith's little ones, it cut her deeply that she would never see him play with her children. But a woman couldn't save the world or guard a caravan with a babe at the breast and two more tied to the apron strings. Lady mercs who found themselves with a bun in the oven either fostered them out or left the business to raise them.

Mags had no maternal instinct and no idea of how to care for a baby properly. Just the sight of such a tiny, helpless thing made her panic, in a way that gruesome beasts or terrible danger never did. A woman could take certain herbs, but short of abstinence, nothing was sure to prevent pregnancy from occurring.

The only thing Mags had ever wanted to do was to carry a sword. It was who she was, a lady-knight sworn to protect the innocent or even the not-so-innocent, as some of her clients were. No matter what it turned out to be, the job brought with it a thrill that was indescribable.

She *needed* to feel that pleasure, craved that sense of exhilaration that gratified her more than any romp in the sheets she'd ever had. She loved the thrill of waking up alive after a job went bad. Mags took every opportunity to rid the world of vermin who preyed on the weak and helpless. She was making a difference in the frequently bad world, making some small good happen amid the misery.

She would have said bloody Billy Ninefingers had done it on purpose, pairing her up with Julian, though she knew he had not. The rotation had simply fallen out that way.

All day, Mags had worried that Julian would try to rekindle their relationship, or at least, want to know what he'd done to drive her away.

And that was the trouble. He'd done nothing at all.

Mags had begun by not telling him the truth, and she was a coward and an idiot, but there it was. She couldn't be honest with him. She couldn't even be honest with herself.

Julian was too simple and good. He would have accepted what Mags should have told him. Then she would have had to look at him, and everyone would know she had driven the knife into his heart.

But who was she pretending to fool? They all knew it anyway or suspected.

Bloody Huw the Bard would make a ballad that would wring tears from a stone if he ever found out the truth.

Mags knew lust didn't drive Lackland, and she didn't feel jealousy as one might think she would. She felt some strange emotion whenever he bedded someone else, but even when she looked honestly at herself, she knew it wasn't jealousy.

What Mags felt so keenly was a deep and desperate sadness, both for herself and for Lackland. She was fully aware it was broken-hearted loneliness that drove him into the arms of other women.

Or men, perhaps. He'd always admitted he was attracted to people regardless of their gender and hadn't bothered to hide his relationship with Percy St. John when they were still at court. He never demanded fidelity from her because he couldn't give it.

She'd noticed Davey Leweyllyn watching him with soft eyes. She wondered about him and Davey but refused to ask because one didn't, ever. The problem was that Percy was in love with Davey, and even though they didn't have a formal arrangement, his jealousy had been hard to contain.

Trips that involved only two Rowdies on a mission for the king were the dangerous ones. Three or more on a job were not dangerous in that way. When spending long evenings around the campfire with nothing to do but talk, folks shared everything about themselves. Hopes, dreams, ambitions—everything. Often it led to sharing a bedroll.

No one said a word about Davey and Lackland. But Davey and Percy were together again, so they had resolved whatever had gone sour between the three of them.

Besides, Mags had dumped Julian and never told him why. He had a right to ease his pain however he chose.

But it didn't mean she wanted to see him go up the stairs holding hands with Fair Ellen, unconsciously smiling the killer smile that set Mags's heart to thumping. Nevertheless, she pulled herself together and pretended to read a book.

At least, she ignored it until the next morning when they were all down in the stables preparing to leave, and she overheard Ellen's smug voice describing Lackland's prowess.

That was when Lady Mags's blood boiled.

She despised her jealousy and stuffed it down. Bidding a cheerful farewell to the stable boy, she trotted out into the sunlight ahead of Lackland and his white stallion, Farroll. It was a perfect summer morning, filled with birdsong and peace, and all the while she was seething and angry with herself for suffering so needlessly.

In good weather, the journey from Castleton to the Grimmenstock mine would take five days. Since it was the long, dry, first week of July, they would most likely be there by Sunday.

There were no inns, but wayside shelters stood at intervals for the great ore wagons to stop at. Stout longhouses built of stone, they could shelter the teams, wagons, and drivers of two ore convoys at one time, although it was tight quarters when such was the case.

They entered the King's Forest and began the part of the journey Mags dreaded most. The forest was comprised of hundreds upon hundreds of leagues of wilderness. Unlike any other road in the northern half of Waldeyn, it was paved, making travel easy for the heaviest wagons. But despite how well maintained it was, the road they were on was more dangerous than any other on the continent. The deep forest was still the domain of many of the largest beasts born of majik. That made traveling the road so hazardous that no one could enter the forest without permission from the Crown.

This meant that with the mine temporarily closed, they might go days before meeting another traveler.

Lackland also feigned a good mood. His interlude with Ellen had been pleasant in a drunken way. They parted on good terms, friends but nothing more.

As he and Mags traveled, the silence stretched, and soon neither one knew how to break it. Toward evening, they stopped at the first shelter. As was usual, when anyone traveled with Lackland, he did the cooking.

Mags snared the pheasants and dressed them out, and Lackland roasted them with his own special mix of herbs. Part of what the pack ponies carried was his specialty cooking tools and spices. Everyone who traveled with him knew they were in for a treat when he cooked.

"I've brought something along, so we won't have to boil the water to drink it." Lackland uncorked a bottle of wine. "Mick was right about the trots, but I'll never tell him. The old thing enjoys mothering us so. It would take away the joy of nagging us to death if he thought we could care for ourselves." He poured two mugs for them, and though the meal was better for it, things didn't warm up significantly.

Thanking him, Mags sipped her wine slowly, careful not to relax her guard. She couldn't risk it, no matter how much she lamented her decisions. Regrets had become her closest companions, but she had done the only thing she could. Julian would find happiness elsewhere if she gave him no other option. She had to believe that.

They spent the rest of the journey in much the same way until they finally arrived in the mining town of Grimmenstock. It was a town in the sense that six or seven houses, a general store of sorts, and the barracks for the miners dotted a clearing where the road ended. Giant trees grew between the buildings, spreading dark branches over them as if protecting them from the sky.

The trading post sold the necessities; beans, bacon, cheese, flour, honey, salt, pepper, a few spices, and some other things a person might need for the long journey back to Castleton. The storekeeper also provided a large room above the store for the teamsters to stay in when they came to pick up a load of ore to take back to the king's smelters. The room contained six bunks, a small pot-bellied stove, a window, and a large, round table with six chairs. There was no common room, and the storekeeper's wife brought meals up to the guests.

The privies were clean, and a large bathhouse with one tub and a bucket on a rope for a quick shower served the entire community. Bathers hung the "in use" sign out and had to clean the tub after themselves. They also had to draw water from the well to refill the cistern that fed the water heater. But, outside of Billy's Revenge, every place was like that.

Lackland and Mags arrived at dusk, and the storekeeper, Geordy, was glad to see them. "They told us the king was sending someone, but we didn't expect you two! We'll be famous for having had Sir Julian Lackland and Lady Mags staying with us."

The master miner, a short, dour man named Colin Macre, sighed with obvious relief. "I was afraid they'd send the castle guard instead of someone with brains."

As they ate their dinner, Mags and Lackland questioned the master miner closely, wondering what sort of beast they were dealing with.

"Didn't they tell you? It's a dragon of some sort." Colin's surprise was almost laughable, given what Julian and Mags knew of court manipulations. "I told the Lord Dog Walker it was definitely a dragon. The damned thing bit poor Jakey in half! I've seen nothing like this beast, but it's every bit as most bards describe them—wings, large head, hundreds of teeth, long neck and tail, and a body as big as a house. I'm sure you'll agree it's a dragon."

"So…." Lackland's serious blue eyes met Mags's worried brown ones. He cleared his throat. "Well, this could take a while then." He looked at Mags again. She gave the slightest of shrugs. "How far into the mine has it made its lair?"

"I would say about half a furlong," said Colin. "Not too far. The workings lead out of a large natural cave. When I was a boy, they mined what they could safely reach in the cavern and then began working back into the mountain. The tunnels are too small for it to fit in, the further back you go. I have a map ready for you." He placed a scroll on the table. Lady Mags unrolled and flattened it out. Then she, Lackland, and Colin pored over it.

"So, would it be just about here then?" She pointed to a place just inside.

"Yes," muttered Colin. "It can easily come and go from there. But it doesn't stay gone for too long when it goes out for its meal."

"It has to hunt deer or miners because no one has farmed anywhere near here for years, and we keep the horses stabled," added Geordy. "Deer are much bigger than most miners, so we're not high on the menu, but since it got Jakey we don't trust it prefers venison."

"It's not too discriminating, food-wise. We saw it fly home with the biggest mountain lion last month. That was disturbing." Colin shuddered. "Anything that can kill a mountain lion of that size without shedding blood over it won't be an easy thing to defeat."

Mags asked, "When does it fly out next?"

"It flies out every three days or so to hunt, and then it doesn't budge out of there until it goes out to hunt again. So, perhaps tomorrow, after midday," replied Geordy. "The beast is a slothful creature, fond of a long lie-in in the mornings. When it rouses from its slumber, you won't even hear an insect call. Nothing will show itself when it's out and about. The birds don't fly, and even the bears take cover."

"Right. Well, then...." Lackland thought hard but came up with nothing. "We'll let you know what we'll need after we decide how to do this."

After more small talk and much smiling and bowing, the two men left Lackland and Mags to get on with planning.

"We're in for a long fight," Mags said thoughtfully. "Maybe we can poison it. Poisoned arrows, perhaps? I'll see what sort of plants we have around here."

"I don't know what sort of poison would work on a dragon." Lackland wrote another comment on his list. "And I doubt my bow could penetrate a dragon's hide. Regular arrows just bounce off dragons. It might help if I sharpen the arrowheads to a razor edge."

"Your bow may be what saves the day here." Mags peered closer, her coppery curls brushing the map. "What about a backdoor into the mine? That could be useful." After looking at the map again, they saw there was another entrance, but it was much farther to the south. It was the old entry to the worked-out part of the mines. Some shafts were marked as dangerous.

After they finished planning what they could, Lackland courteously offered Mags the first bath. They spent the rest of the evening as quietly as they had the previous ones, Mags on one side of the room and Lackland on the other. Both wore pleasant expressions, pretending to be absorbed with their own tasks.

The next morning after breakfast, they found Colin. Mags asked if any explosives were available.

"Um…I'm not comfortable with this notion. How much do you want?" His face had "no" written all over it.

"Well, you know how big he is, and I don't." She turned her best, most charismatic smile on him, a weapon few men could resist. "How much do you think it will take?"

Colin weakened under the force of her charm but didn't quite cave. "He's big enough that if you're even a hair off on how you place the explosives, you'll collapse the cave and kill yourselves too. Plus, we would be able to reach the shafts, which is the problem now," replied Colin. His eyes shifted nervously from Mags to Lackland, and back to Mags. "I don't want to be the one to go and kill such beloved heroes as you two. There must be a better way to do this."

"There is, but the king's men were unavailable." Lackland felt a trifle sour about that but did his best to hide it. "So here we are, wracking our brains trying to figure out a way to kill your dragon instead of letting the royal guard get on with it as they should be doing."

"He should fly out sometime today. If you can get a good look at it, you might see what you need to do," said Colin. "I take it you were surprised to hear it was a dragon."

"Yes and no." Lackland's sunny smile belied his disgruntled acceptance of the situation. "Yes, the messenger lied to us, but these things happen. It was no real surprise about the lie. We rarely deal with dragons, because the standard method is to keep throwing men at it, keeping it busy and hacking away at it. You usually lose five or six before the damned things grow tired enough that you can swarm and kill them. Mercenary companies can't support those kinds of losses. This will cost the king dearly, and I feel sure upon his return, Henri will take it out of the pockets of the knights who've shirked this duty."

"Oh," said Colin. Everything fell into place in his mind now. "I see why the king's messenger was less than honest with you. The real soldiers went south with the king to stop this feint by the Lanques. All who remain to guard the castle are the men of suspect bravery that no one trusts on a battlefield. Men like your brother—they won't stick their necks out for the likes of us. John De Portiers couldn't offend their fathers, but he had to do something, and so he settled on you."

Lackland smiled widely at Colin's assessment of the situation. "You're right. This thing in the Bekenberg Pass isn't a war right now, so there's no need to bring in mercenaries just yet. But it will be war again soon enough." He turned to Mags. "I guess we should sit somewhere and wait for the beast to fly over us. Maybe we'll get a good enough look that we'll be able to find a weak spot in its defenses. But the forest is too thick, even here. Is there a field nearby?"

"There's an abandoned farm, half a league from here," Colin said. "They used to supply our town, but—well, you'll see. I can set you on the trail. Though the forest has reclaimed some of it, there are still meadows. But are you sure you want to be exposed like that? What if he swoops down and eats you?"

Lady Mags replied with a glint in her eye. "Why then you must tell the king's messenger his plan failed, and he'll need to find twelve stupid lordlings to do the job properly. We'll leave the horses here. They're large enough to draw attention we'd like to avoid."

"Don't worry about us," added Lackland. "We'll make a blind as if we were hunting ducks."

"That'll do it then." Colin felt immensely better. Sir Lackland and Lady Mags were there to handle it, consummate professionals who'd never allow themselves to get eaten by a dragon.

Geordy's wife, Lena, packed them a basket with a picnic lunch. Lackland tucked two bottles of wine and their mugs into it. Lady Mags took her map case to pore over the maps, and a notebook along with a charcoal pencil for drawing, just something to do while they waited for the dragon to pass over them. Lackland had his book stowed in his pocket.

After walking the path Colin set them on for perhaps half an hour, they came to the abandoned farm. Feeling as curious as children, they peered through the cracks of the shuttered windows, but the owners had left nothing behind. No clue remained of the previous tenants. Now only birds nested in the attic, and the sky showed through places in the roof. It was sad somehow, but the farm was so far away from civilization and so lonely, it wasn't surprising they'd not stayed, whoever they had been.

A small barn leaned heavily to one side. It would collapse soon, if not this winter, then the next. They walked past the old buildings and down a long-unused path through the brush. When they rounded a corner, both stopped with a sharp intake of breath upon seeing what lay there.

A wide field of daisies was spread out before them, thick and white as snow, contrasting sharply with the deep blue sky. Overwhelmed by the beauty that lay waist-high all around them, they walked to the center of the meadow. "Oh…," breathed Mags as they looked in amazement.

"This is how I've always imagined heaven to be." Lackland's blue eyes met hers. "I say to hell with the blind. Let's enjoy the day, and the dragon be damned. We'll see it better from here."

"I couldn't agree more," she replied, awed by the surrounding splendor.

Lackland spread his cloak and courteously gestured for her to sit upon it, which she did. He rested the basket beside them and sat gazing up. The tall daisies formed green walls, and the tranquility of the field seemed to soak into him. The wide, blue sky, dotted with puffy white clouds, arched above, making them feel small.

Soon Lackland stretched out, gazing up at the sky and watching the clouds. "Look, there's a cloud shaped like a horse," he said, feeling at peace, more fully relaxed than Mags had seen him for far too long.

His golden hair shone in the sun, and his eyes were bluer than the sky. The perfection of his face and his heart-stopping smile took her breath away. *How I love him* was all she could think.

Without further thought, Mags leaned over and kissed him gently.

Julian's arms went around her, and he kissed her with all the love and pain of the last year pouring out of him. "Marry me, Mags," he said, tenderly stroking her hair. "I love you. With all my soul, I love you."

She felt the beating of his heart, felt the life pulsing through him as he held her. "No, Julian. I won't marry you. I can't leave the trade. Not even for you."

Her voice broke. "I'm so, so sorry." Tears flowed down her cheeks, and she couldn't stop them.

"Don't cry, my darling. It'll be fine. I knew you wouldn't. Nothing's changed. I still love you." Lackland held her in trembling arms. "I'll always love you, my beautiful Mags."

"Julian, I owe you a confession." Fear darkened her eyes, something Julian had never seen. "There's no easy way to say this. You'll hate me."

"Tell me. I'll face whatever it is as well as I can," Lackland knew what he was about to hear. He'd had this notion since she'd gone to House De Leon, her father's house. "Nothing will change how I feel about you."

"You have a son." She paled, and her lips trembled. "I left him for my father to raise because I can't do it. It broke my heart, but I left our baby with my father."

"I've suspected such since the day you left." He kissed her forehead and held her close until she'd cried herself out. "Nothing has changed. Only, now I know for sure why you turned away from me."

"I didn't tell you because…because…."

"You didn't tell me because I would have pressed you to marry me," Lackland finished for her. She nodded, and his arms tightened around her. Turning her chin up to face him, he said, "You're right. I would have done that." He kissed her eyes and her cheeks. "And I know you aren't the sort who can be a goodwife, no matter what I wish for us. Does your father know I'm the boy's true father?"

"Yes," she said, sniffling. Lackland handed her his handkerchief. "He said you're an honorable man, and I've done you a terrible wrong by hiding this from you. He's right. I *have* done wrong by you, and I knew it when I decided to keep it a secret." Mags's face crumpled, and her shoulders shook. "I owe you more than that."

"No, darling. Don't cry over this. What's done is done, and given the circumstances, it may be for the best. I have nothing to offer him, as I come by the name of Lackland honestly. Will your father allow me to be a part of the boy's life?"

"Father said you would ask, and I should tell you 'yes.' Oh, my poor mother. They were putting it about that she'd been blessed with a late-life child, as sometimes happens. They posted it in Bunder town, and the whole town prayed for her safe delivery. They were still celebrating his birth when she died, and they took it hard. She was so looking forward to him, and so was my father. She'd made the most beautiful swaddling clothes for him." Mags knew she was babbling but couldn't seem to stop herself. "Mother was overjoyed to have our son so healthy and strong. But she suffered from weak lungs for years. Bunder town is desolated that she should die and not get to see Jules grow up."

"Jules?" Julian felt a stab of joy pass through him at the thought. "My mother calls me Jules. It's her pet name for me."

"He's named Jules Edward De Leon IV. It's the family name of the Earls of Bunder. My grandfather was Jules Edward De Leon, as is my father and now young Jules. Our Jules is my father's heir, and no taint of illegitimacy will touch him."

"Your father is a good man to be so understanding."

"Poor father. He wished desperately for a son and heir, but all he got was me, a wild scapegrace and fallen woman, though he's long since forgiven me. Now he has our son, and the estate and title will continue in his bloodline."

"Huh. My son...an earl." Lackland grinned wickedly at Mags, "Fancy that! Here I am a poor, landless knight, and my father only a baron. Now my ever-so-snooty brother will give way to my son at court someday, all unknowing. I'll enjoy it immensely!"

"I'm sure you will!" Mags laughed, the first happy laugh she'd enjoyed in many months.

"I've missed the sound of your laughter, my dear." Lackland kissed her, and she responded, leaning into his kiss in a way that sent the blood racing through his veins and scattering his thoughts the way no other lover's kiss could.

At last, Mags pulled away, filled with sadness at what she had to say next. "We can never have the sort of relations we once enjoyed. I can't go through it again, my dear, dear man. Leaving Jules was more than I could bear even though it was for the best. I can't count on the herbs to prevent pregnancy."

"I've had the same idea, worrying about...things. Not knowing for sure but wanting to do the right thing. After you returned to House De Leon, I visited an apothecary in Castleton whom my royal cousin recommended to me." He reached into the pocket of his cape and retrieved a small, waxed paper packet, which he unwrapped. With a wry smile, he held something up. "It's a man's responsibility. I know this now. The little glove takes some joy away, but the small jar of salve helps, and it's better than risking trouble. I do exactly as the apothecary instructed me, and I feel better about things. She tells me they're made from the sap of a tree she acquired some years ago from a far-off land. Now she has a greenhouse with a small forest to make her special gloves. I stop by her shop when I'm in Castleton, and she supplies me with what I think I might need."

Mags saw what he was holding up and laughed. Throwing her arms around him and kissing him, she unlaced his shirt. "Oh, Julian, I've missed you for so long, and it was my foolishness that caused it. If only I'd talked to you in the first place, these last months could have been warmer between us."

"Not your foolishness alone, my dear. I could have gone to House De Leon and forced the issue. I nearly did countless times but was afraid of what you would say. I couldn't bear it if I forced you into marriage for the sake of convention, and then you ran away." Lackland looked into her warm, brown eyes and tenderly touched her burnished curls. "I've missed you desperately. You'll always be the love of my life."

He took a deep breath and said the words he never thought he would ever say. "I hereby set you free of any perceived contract that may once have bound you to me. I set you free to live your life the way you wish to live it. I love you, Margaret De Leon."

Their clothes were their pillow, as they lay on Lackland's cloak and held each other. Tears mingled on their cheeks, both suffused with joy they'd made things right between them.

Yet sorrow lurked, the knowledge that their story would never end the way love stories did in Huw's tales.

They spent the rest of their time that day loving and giving love with all their hearts. A poignancy tinted the overwhelming beauty of the day with a fairytale quality. There would be no happily ever after, although they would live and love each other to the fullest, taking each day as it came.

Forever afterward, that day in the field of daisies under the deep blue sky shone in each of their memories, a piece of heaven to hold in their hearts no matter where the storms of life sent them.

Near sunset, they returned to their room over the store, sunburned in delicate places but with happy smiles and lighter hearts. Holding hands, they looked like lovers, as the ballads claimed them to be. Geordy and Lena smiled at the sight of them and reached for each other's hand.

When Colin and Geordy came by to see what Mags and Lackland had discovered, they had a plan to show them. They had seen the beast twice as it passed over them, once on the way out to hunt and the second time flying back with a fat buck in its mouth.

"We'll definitely need some explosives," said Mags. "We'll give the beast a fatal case of indigestion."

Geordy said with a wry smile, "Lena told me this job needed a woman's touch. There are some jobs that must be done with finesse and finesse is woman's work."

Colin looked horrorstruck. "Explosives are not finesse!"

"I need the dynamite." Mags gazed into his eyes and offered up her man-killer smile. "Please."

Colin was no match for her, agreeing despite his reluctance.

Lackland consoled Colin. "No man has a chance when Mags wages war. Not even the king can withstand such an assault."

The next day Lackland sat on the bench outside the general store, carefully filing the edges of his arrowheads to a razor's sharpness.

Mags asked Lena for a pot she could brew medicine in over an open fire, one that could be thoroughly scrubbed afterward.

Lena fetched a lightweight enameled kettle that bore the signs of similar use. "I make most of our medicines. This seems a wise course of action and is one I would have recommended, although it may not work. You might need some water to get the consistency right." She handed Mags a skin of purified water. "A good health tonic must be of the right consistency to soak into the wooden shafts, thick, but not like jelly."

Mags went out into the forest to find a local poison, looking for a particular plant. When she stumbled onto a large patch, she built a fire and brewed the concoction right where she was. All they needed to do was get it into the dragon if the other plan didn't work.

That evening she set her pot of poison in a corner, covering it with a cloth. Lackland immediately set the business ends of his specially sharpened arrows into the bucket to soak. "If I'm successful at getting them into the dragon, the poisoned shafts will do the damage, more so than the arrowheads. But I suspect no amount of sharpening on my part will enable them to penetrate his hide. His chest is well-armored."

Mags agreed. "It's a last resort. We'll probably be in trouble."

The next day, Lackland and Geordy went hunting. In the late afternoon, the two came trudging up to the camp, wearily dragging a large, old buck. Colin's crew quickly placed it onto a handcart and carried it down to the cold-cave where they kept their meat. There it lay, ready to be stuffed and sewn back together.

Colin brought Mags several sticks of explosives, muttering all the while. "Um…this is the most dangerous thing you could possibly be doing. You'll blow us clean to heaven if you make even the slightest error." He looked at what she had done. "That's enough, please."

She added one more, so he begged. "This is enough to collapse the cavern if it's placed wrong, and we don't want that. Stop now, please." He looked at the carcass, the whites of his eyes showing. "You've enough to do the job and then some."

Mags looked at the explosives she'd packed into the buck's belly and smiled. Then she sewed it up with twine while Colin carefully backed out of the cold-cave, muttering that she was crazier than any woman had a right to be.

With everything as ready as they could make it, Lackland and Mags sat in their room, talking with Colin and Geordy.

Mags said, "All we can hope is for the dragon to snuggle up to our offering, and pray it completely ignores the hissing and sputtering fuse as it creeps toward him. But I can't think of anything else we could do that would be any less iffy. We'll have to resort to hacking and slashing eventually in this job, so if the dynamite maims the dragon even a little, that will be in our favor."

"Well, the boys and I will back you up, if it comes to that," said Colin. "We've been talking in the barracks. We think it's a dirty shame the two of you are all who were available to rout the dragon. My brother, Bart, works for the king's seneschal in Castleton Keep." He looked at Lackland. "When I went there to tell them about the dragon, Bart told me your brother is at court and wearing his armor. He's 'defending the realm' while the king is away."

Lackland rolled his eyes. "Of course, he is. He's a brave man, my brother."

Colin shrugged. "Besides, we owe the beast retribution for Jakey."

The miners' show of support was touching, but it worried Lackland. He fervently prayed it wouldn't become a bloody massacre as dragon hunts were wont to do.

The next morning, Colin and two of his men watched the entrance to the mine. As soon as the beast lumbered out and took off, flying low over the forest, everyone leaped into action. Mags and Lackland carefully pushed the booby-trapped buck into the mine, shoving the cart all the way to the beast's lair. Lackland covered their tracks with scent from the buck's musk gland, and Mags carefully unrolled the fuse on their way out.

Everyone hid once again, only this time they were armed. The miners were equipped with picks and axes and any other sharp implement they could find.

Soon the dragon landed in front of the entrance to the mine, carrying a rather smallish doe. "Good," whispered Lackland. "He might still be hungry when he finishes his kill. Maybe he'll take the bait in one bite and get indigestion. Then we can swarm him and finish him off."

Mags rolled her eyes. "Don't get your hopes up." She went to crouch just outside the entrance, peering inside.

The dragon devoured its kill in two bites before turning around three times, like a dog preparing to lie down. As it did so, the dragon let go of a rather substantial fart that seemed to linger in the lair's atmosphere.

Suddenly, the beast noticed the booby-trapped carcass.

Intrigued, the dragon looked closely at it, first with one eye and then the other, looking exactly like an inquisitive bird examining a worm in a hole. Then he sniffed at the carcass several times before he finally came to a decision and licked the buck's head, sampling the scent with his long tongue.

After farting loudly again, several more times, the dragon ate only the torso section of the buck and then licked the now-severed head once again, not noticing the fuse dangling from the corner of his mouth.

Quickly, Mags lit the fuse and darted away from the entrance. She drew her sword, taking her place at Lackland's side. "He's eaten it! But I think venison doesn't agree with him, poor thing. He's farting up a storm in there."

"Oh, that's too bad," agreed Lackland. "I don't know what they normally eat. Probably horses or cattle."

They stood watching and waiting.

For a long moment, nothing happened.

Just as Colin was getting ready to have a look-see, there was an earsplitting shriek, and a thunderous roar as the dragon exploded. The concussion knocked everyone to the ground, as bloody bits of gore, followed by flaming hunks of burning dragon, flew out of the entrance to the mine, followed by a whoosh of flame that drove everyone back. The buck's now-antlerless and blackened head rolled out of the mine like an oddly shaped ball, sucked along by the trailing edge of the explosion.

Leaping to her feet, Mags whooped with joy. "I want to do that again!" She turned a cartwheel in her excitement. "I want to do it again!" Throwing her arms around Colin's neck, she exuberantly kissed the startled man's cheek. He stared at her, aghast as she danced and shouted with glee. "That was so much fun! What else can we explode?" She looked around, disappointed to find nothing else that needed blowing up.

"She's barking mad," Colin said faintly. "She should be locked away for everyone's safety."

"You've ruined your dress, my dear," Lackland said as she capered about. "I think you've routed the dragon, though." He was exceedingly proud of her. "Let's not play with the dynamite anymore, now. You're making poor Colin nervous."

Disappointed, Mags settled down, behaving more like the competent lady people normally saw. She picked up the buck's head, blowing the cinders off it, looking it over.

Colin stared into the reeking mine, a stunned look on his face. "There're bits of bloody, burning dragon everywhere!" At last, he pulled himself together but kept glancing warily at Mags. The miners waited until the air cleared before they went inside.

"Well, our work here is done," Lackland said, looking around at the mess. "I think it was one of the more interesting jobs we've ever been asked to do. Who knew dragons were so explosive?"

"I told her she added too much dynamite to the buck," muttered Colin as he examined things. "We're just lucky the cavern is still stable." He beckoned to his crew. "Come on, lads—let's clean it up. We've got to get mining no later than tomorrow, so move your arses." Fortunately, the dragon's body had absorbed most of the initial explosion. When the other gasses ignited, the explosion was channeled out the entrance like smoke going up a chimney.

Once Colin's crew had tidied up the mess, and he'd gotten over his initial shock, he was inclined to be more charitable toward Mags. "Maybe dragons are naturally explosive," he told Lackland sagely. "I suppose we'll be able to handle our own dragons now we know what to do." He looked sideways at Mags, who was engaged in an animated conversation with Lena. "I'll go a bit lighter on the dynamite next time, though." Colin turned back to Lackland. "She's a handful, I would guess. But she'll never marry you, laddie. What are you going to do about that?"

"I'll probably go to my royal cousin and help him win the war that is surely coming," Lackland replied, with a faraway look in his eyes. "After that, I believe I will teach my nephew and Lady Mags's young brother the art of the sword. They should be just the right age for it by then. I'll stay busy."

Three weeks had passed by the time Lackland and Lady Mags returned to Billy's Revenge.

When they walked in, the crew was sitting around the common room enjoying themselves. Billy was moping, as they were suffering a temporary lull in employment. He was thrilled the beast had indeed been a dragon and immediately drafted a bill to send to John De Portiers for one hundred gold pieces.

The Rowdies celebrated their safe return, demanding that every detail of the routing of the dragon be told.

Only Huw the Bard seemed put out. "How am I supposed to make a decent ballad out of that mess? You went on a dragon hunt, for God's sake, Lackland! I was so looking forward to a really good heroic saga, and all you bring me is a dragon who farts from eating too much venison and then explodes." His head dropped to his hands, and he said in the most tragic of tones, "Why me?"

The room erupted in laughter.

PART TWO
Lackland Undone

THE YEARS HAD GONE by faster than we believed possible. On King Henri's advice, Edward De Leon, Earl of Bunder, hired the great Lackland as his arms master and his son's tutor.

In the Council of Lords, the Earl crowed about having lured a man like Lackland to build up and train his fighting forces. "All I need to do is supply them with weapons and armor, and he will ensure my men are the best trained soldiers on any field of battle."

This meant that when Lackland and the earl weren't away fighting in Lanqueshire, they and the young heir were at court for half the year and at Bunder the other half.

As the Earl's son approached the age of thirteen, he was deemed old enough to go to court to be trained as a knight, and no longer required a tutor. Julian was asked to become King Henri's arms master in charge of training the new crop of young knights who would descend on Castleton in the fall.

He agreed. However, it was only November, and that posting was nearly a year away, leaving him time for private pursuits. As it was Yule season, Julian intended to visit his family and educate his nephew, Melvin, the future Baron De Portiers. Young Mel was the image of his uncle Lackland and the same age as Lackland's other student. He was also going to court that fall.

We had endured four wakes since the previous Yuletide. My wife, Lucy, died in childbirth. Cob John suffered a fatal heart attack, and two Rowdies we had known and considered family died at the hands of highwaymen—all gone in one bad year.

Then one cold November day, Percy and I were standing in front of the stables, laughing at a joke Mickey had told when a wagon rolled into the courtyard. The merchant had brought Johnny Malone, Little Fred Scutter, and Davey back, all three of them bloody and unrecognizable. But Davey was hurt most grievously.

Bess sent for the priestess to work her healing majik to save him. By the next day, everyone but Percy knew Davey was dying.

Fred and Johnny both swore the bastards knew him. "They were screaming at him in the language they all use down there, and they were dressed like Eynier, but it felt wrong. They hated him, for what I don't know unless it was because he's a southerner who prefers men. You know how they are about that." Johnny shook his head slowly. "They kept calling him by his surname, Leweyllyn, only they were saying it wrong, calling him Dukweyllyn, or something like that, sneering it at him."

Seated in my corner, listening to Johnny's recounting of the attack, my ears perked up at hearing the mangling of Davey's name—it reminded me of something from long ago, but the shock of Davey's mutilation overwhelmed my ability to think straight.

For two weeks, Davey lingered, hovering near death, while Percy stopped eating, stopped speaking, and stopped living for anything but Davey.

At last, just before dawn one morning, Davey opened the one eye that could still see and looked at Percy. Then he heaved a great sigh and passed away.

Percy prepared Davey's body for burial, allowing no one else to touch him. We made a beautiful bier for him down in the ladies' parlor where he was laid out in state, and Billy sent the black-notice to all the retirees.

Once his last task for Davey was done, Percy spent the rest of that day holding his lover's cold, dead hand, sitting in the dark parlor, refusing to leave him, still speaking to no one, and eating nothing. Though Mickey tried to get him to rest, he refused.

Toward midnight, Percy looked up and asked, "Why, Mick? Why? Who had Davey ever hurt that they treated him so? He was the most beautiful of men, but I can't even remember what he looked like before they hurt him. All I can see is what they did to him. I can't live this way."

I found Percy the next morning lying next to Davey with his arms around him. He had slit his own throat rather than live with the memory of what the murderers had done to beautiful Davey, unable to go on without him.

Lackland had never spoken of the fact he and Davey had been lovers for a brief time when Mags had turned cold to him. Percy had forgiven him once he and Lackland had talked it out.

Lackland was aware we all knew of it since he didn't bother to hide it, but he never discussed his private life. It wasn't out of shame he was reticent in these matters. On the contrary, he had a broad view of sexual morality. His natural discretion and innate sense of politeness made him reluctant to discuss it. He believed what happened between two people should be their business and wasn't a topic for casual conversation.

Nevertheless, Billy and I knew how deeply the deaths of Davey and Percy had affected him.

With Percy's death, something became known that no one had foreseen. It fired us up like nothing else could have.

Babs Gentry and Annie Fitzgerald had taken the tragedy in an exceedingly personal manner. Both were mothers of young sons, born within two days of each other.

The truth came out, that Davey had done them a favor. The ladies had each wanted a baby, but since they shared a pillow, it would not happen. Though they'd both once enjoyed the lads, they'd cemented their own relationship and had no desire to alter it.

When both ladies reached the age of thirty-four, they realized if they didn't have children soon, they never would. Davey felt much the same way. He'd occasionally mentioned to me how deeply he wanted a child and wished he'd been created differently.

So, while the three of them were out on a little task for the king, they sat around the campfire discussing their mutual problem and realized they had a solution to that dilemma if they chose.

Davey never told Percy about the arrangement because he wouldn't have understood how badly Davey wanted a child.

With Percy dead, there was no reason to hide who had fathered the boys. The Rowdies consoled themselves with the knowledge their Davey had at least seen his children born though it had been his own secret.

Lackland was agitated in a way I'd never seen, vengeful and determined to find the murderers. He intended to get retribution for the babies, if not for himself.

He was thirty-eight years of age that year, and a man used to the ways of war. Yet he remained naïve the way men our age never were.

Excerpt from *The Life of Julian Lackland De Portiers, Waldeyn's Last Good Knight*,
by Huw Owyn, Master Bard of Waldeyn

CHAPTER 7

WHEN LACKLAND ENTERED the common room after the funeral, it almost looked as if the passing of thirteen long years had changed nothing. Slippery Jack was there, along with Merry Kat and their young ones, who ran and played with the other children. All the Rowdies were together again, and it was a miserable old time.

Toward the end of the night, Lackland sat opposite Mags, the two of them alone for the moment. Her new lad, Beau Baker, had left to help Huw carry the Friar Robert home.

Mags looked across the table at Lackland. As always, when they met casually, they kept it strictly cordial. "My father says you're his good right arm these days. Is he as well as his letters claim?"

"Perhaps he's not as healthy as he wants you to think, but not terrible. He refuses to go to court now, preferring to stay home and run his estate. This next year he'll send your brother in his stead."

Mags nodded, taking Lackland's appearance in, cementing it in her mind so she would have it to remember. His short blonde hair had gone silver at the temples, but he still wore the thin, braided mercenary tail under his left ear, despite his rejoining Henri's court. The narrow braid fell well past his waist, showing he'd not cut it since joining the Rowdies all those years before.

That tail told Mags his heart was still at Billy's Revenge with her and the Rowdies.

He was leaner and stronger than she remembered, with laugh wrinkles at the corners of his eyes. He'd grown more handsome; more charismatic. Her heart thumped wildly whenever she looked at him.

Unaware of her scrutiny, Lackland continued. "Your brother is doing well and will enjoy his time at court. He's smitten with young Rose Dragoran, who, in turn, is taken with him. Henri and your father plan a marriage between Jules and Rose when the time comes if the two children are still agreeable." His pride was clear, although he tried to keep it buried. "Henri is quite pleased with the prospect of the two families being joined."

"I sent Jules a new mail shirt. Did he like it?" Her eyes begged to hear that he did.

Lackland smiled; the boy had been ecstatic at receiving the armor she'd had made especially for him by the famous Gertie Smith. "It was all he could talk about for a month. The boy is mad for fighting, as they all are at that age."

"I'll send him Dove's next foal if it's a male," she decided. "He'll need a sturdy mount."

Julian's mind always slowed when he was in her company. At thirty-seven, a few silver threads shone in her mahogany hair, but Mags was still the beauty who had forever claimed his heart, only riper and more polished.

He wrenched his mind back to the topic. "Good. Farroll is now living his dream. He's happily employed in the service of the King's mares. My new mount is a sturdy fellow, being younger and more interested in traveling, as I must do so often nowadays." He laughed, covering his distraction.

"Where are you off to now?" Mags yearned for him to say he was rejoining the Rowdies.

"Not too far, this time. I'm headed home to House Portiers to school my nephew over the Yuletide," he replied. "The boy is the same age as your brother and shows promise. I don't want him ruined by Morty's notions of a proper upbringing."

"I suppose Morty still looks like he has a sliver festering in his arse when he smiles." To say Mags despised Mortimer De Portiers was an understatement.

Lackland grinned widely, humor at his brother's expense lighting up his gloomy countenance. "He's still himself, only more so. Also, I want to see my mother. Next fall, when the season begins, I'll return to court as Henri's arms master. You know why I've agreed, even though I have no love of the courtier's life." His voice hardened. "As much as I can without drawing attention, I'll be wherever Jules is until he is a man, guiding him and teaching him what he must know to survive. I've promised your father."

"I'm glad you'll be there when he's surrounded by idiots like Morty." Mags found it difficult to concentrate. His wry grin and the spark in his blue eyes evoked feelings she didn't dare act on.

Julian changed the subject. "Will you go home for Yuletide? It's been two years, and your father and Jules both miss you. I promised them I would ask." He tried not to sound like he was pleading with her, although he was doing exactly that.

"I will since it means so much to you. That is, if Father doesn't mind me bringing a friend." Immediately Mags wished she hadn't agreed. "I want to see them both so badly, but I've done neither of them any good. I don't feel worthy of them."

"Don't be ridiculous. Your father just wants to see you. He and Jules won't care that you have brought Beau with you. He's a good man, and they'll like him. Edward knows you'll never be anything other than his mad, merry daughter, and Jules worships his sister." Lackland's smile eased her fears about his acceptance of her relationship with Beau. She couldn't bear to be alone, and Lackland knew it.

Lackland's eyes twinkled. "In fact, your fame as the intrepid lady-hero has lent your father a bit of cachet he wouldn't have had otherwise. It's considered quite gallant to claim friendship with your father and thereby be thought to rub elbows with the famous Lady Mags." His gaze turned to Annie and Babs, and then back to Mags. "As to my travels—once the weather improves after Yuletide, Slippery Jack and I are going down south to settle up the debt for Davey and Percy."

Mags nodded. "Good. I wish I could run a sword through the bastards myself."

"If all goes as planned, although nothing is ever sure, King Henri will be down in the Bekenberg Pass, securing the last trouble spot on the border with Lanqueshire and diverting attention from us. All eyes will be on him, and that's when we'll do what we must do." Lackland fell silent, with a puzzled expression.

Mags asked, "What is it?"

"For some reason I don't understand, Davy's murder has enraged Henri like nothing I've ever seen. I didn't know he was friends with Davey, although, of course, he knew Percy well. The king plans to use this tragedy to finally settle the situation in the Eynier Valley."

"I pity Henri's enemies, with you as his weapon. I'm glad for the babies' sake you're doing this." Mags looked over at Annie and Babs, seeing the babies who looked so much like Davey. Suddenly, she froze, praying Jules still looked like her so he would not be so obviously Lackland's son.

As if reading her mind, Lackland said off-handedly, "It's amazing how much your brother looks like you must have looked at his age. Although, he's as tall as your father already and will be much taller when he has his full growth. He has your father's red hair. Your aunt tells me he is the image of Edward as a youth."

Mags smiled and nodded with relief. If he had resembled Julian, someone would eventually put two and two together.

The doors swung open, and Huw and Beau entered, making a beeline for their table. Lackland stood up and clasped hands with Beau. Unlike most mercs, Beau had never cut his thick, golden hair in the mercenary style, insisting on wearing it in a long, silky tail despite the good-natured teasing of his friends. His lush blond hair had earned him the mercenary name of Golden Beau.

Beau admired Lackland and always had since he was a boy. This, despite the knight's having left

Limpwater not long after Beau became a Rowdy. He hadn't meant to fall in love with Mags. It happened while the two were on a long, lonely job during the prior spring. But despite the difference in their ages, he'd fallen hard for her. He'd been stricken with guilt ever since, feeling as if he'd somehow betrayed the man everyone knew was the love of Mags's life.

Thus, after the pleasantries were out of the way, Beau didn't know what to say.

However, Julian soon had Beau relaxed and laughing as he told the true story of how he and Slippery Jack had rescued him from the demon so many years before.

"It sounds much worse than the way Huw tells it," Beau said, chuckling at the mental picture Lackland had painted for him.

When Beau laughed, Lackland could see what attracted Mags to him and felt an immediate kinship. His laugh held so much joy and love of life that Julian had to smile. The four of them talked all evening, finding comfort in the stories each had to tell about Davey and Percy.

All too soon, young Brand was helping his father close the common room, and Lackland went off to stay with Huw for the night. They sat at Huw's lonely table, and Lackland could see he'd changed nothing since Lucy's death.

Huw noticed him looking around. "I have a woman who cleans for me, but I won't let her change a thing. I'm not ready for that yet."

"Well, do you feel like making a trip south?" asked Lackland, with a look in his eye that Huw recognized. "Jack and I need a guide who knows the

Long Valley, and you need to get away from this for a while." He gestured around the room where everything had Lucy's touch written all over it. "Perhaps the troubles you ran from eighteen years ago have settled down. Maybe you're not known there any longer."

"If you're meddling in politics, I might be interested," replied Huw, after a moment's consideration. His bleak eyes spoke volumes, reflecting the depth of his despair and anger.

"We'll come back for you when we go south after the Yuletide," Lackland said. "Mickey said he would watch your place while you're gone."

Huw grimaced. "I'll bet he did. He'd best not change a thing, or I'll kill him."

Lackland had no doubt of it. "Waldeyn's troubles in the Long Valley are involved in this somehow. The clan war down there is boiling again, what with the young Weyllyn duchess, Gwenevere, about to wed our Prince Harry."

Huw nodded. "I advised Henri to propose arranging a marriage between Harry and Gwen when he was through here last year. He wanted my take on the situation with the Crows. It's the best way to bring peace."

Lackland was pensive. "Yes, but it's ruffling the feathers on more than a few of your Black Crows since it happens on the anniversary of the unification of Wald and Eyn and cements the crown's claims. Harry and Gwen will live in the Eynier Valley at the old family home, jointly ruling the Long Valley as governors and providing crown justice. Even before Percy's death, St. John wanted to retire as governor. And, King Henri sees it as a way for them to get the training they must have to assume the reins when he has passed on. Best of all, it gets an Eynier princess back in charge of the Eynier Valley, thus gutting the Grand Duke Grefyn's most salient argument in his bid to break away from Waldeyn."

Huw said, "I'll look into Davey's name. Leweyllyn is the most common name in the northern end of the valley. It's a clue, but I can't figure out how it fits, unless…what did Johnny say that day?" He wracked his brains, trying to remember the terrible day three weeks before, seeing Johnny Malone wreathed in bandages and hearing his description of the attack. Suddenly, a stunned look lay upon his features.

"What?"

"A wild notion…but what does Jack suspect? Why does Henri care so much that he would commit both you and Jack to this?" Abruptly Huw changed the subject. "I believe I'll need Jack on my spying mission. And don't worry. I'll make the arrangements for the supplies."

Lackland yawned and apologized. His mind was too full of thoughts of Mags to contemplate anything else.

Huw stood, saying it was long past time for bed. As he showed Lackland to the little guest room, he said, "I'll expect you back here after the Yuletide. We'll be ready to go, I promise."

CHAPTER 8

LACKLAND'S VISIT TO House Portiers began as he expected it would. He'd barely arrived, and his mother, Lady Isabela, started loudly lamenting about how he'd never found a bride.

His family held the requisite formal dinner party for the Yuletide in celebration of Lackland's return to the family hearth. Surprisingly, Julian's typically standoffish brother welcomed him home with open arms. Always looking for ways to make himself look good, Mortimer used every inch of Lackland's fame and prominence at court to further himself in the eyes of his cronies.

People surrounded the table, Morty's friends whom Lackland didn't know. Low-ranking nobles and dissolute, self-indulgent gentry gathered at the lavishly set table, all wishing nothing more than to be seen as a dear friend of Sir Julian Lackland, the Great Knight of the Realm.

Julian's old uncle, Evelyr, cornered him at dinner regarding his lack of a wife. Speaking from far down the table, he loudly asked if the problem was "…a lad-loving-the-lads-sort-of-thing. I'm sure it's perfectly fine nowadays, almost respectable." Evelyr was himself a younger brother of Lackland's father with no money of his own, who'd spent his entire life living at House De Portiers as a poor relation. Still, as Mortimer regularly pointed out, Evelyr had done the honorable thing and married well, increasing the family's wealth. Silence fell all down the table as the guests waited to hear Lackland's response to Evelyr's comment.

"I'm so relieved you approve, Uncle!" Lackland replied, equally loudly and with a wicked glint in his eye, causing his uncle to choke on his wine. Lackland's nephew pounded the old man on the back, and Lackland added, "I'll bring my lad home with me next year. Your approval means the world to us!"

Forks dropped all down the table, and his sister-in-law fainted. Lackland's mother, Isabelle, and his young nephew, Melvin, both laughed at the consternation in Evelyr's red face. As he fanned his prostrate wife, Mortimer said, "*We* are not so modern here. We have an image to maintain."

"Well, I don't. I can do as I like and to hell with my image. Besides, everyone knows I'm in love with one woman, and if she doesn't marry me, then I'll never marry, end of story." Lackland beamed a brilliant smile around the table, receiving many shocked and weak smiles in return.

"We don't approve of those sorts of jokes, Julian," said Morty stiffly.

"Oh, stuff it, Morty," replied Lackland, feeling the full brunt of his pent-up irritation. "People who ask personal questions at dinner parties should be content with whatever answer they get."

It had taken Lackland all of two minutes to realize his brother was still a pretentious ass, and Morty's wife, Letitia, was still unbelievably silly, hanging on to her fading beauty in a frantic way. Still, despite her limited intellect, Lackland had always liked her because she meant well. Daily, she begged to hear she looked as young as ever, and ever the gentleman, he obliged, treating Letitia with the courtliness the knights in her favorite romantic tales always treated the fairest of ladies.

Lackland's nephew, Melvin, was refreshingly honest, considering the poisonous environment he was growing up in. Mel learned everything as quickly as he could from Lackland, sharply aware his uncle was only there on a brief visit. He desperately looked forward to going to Castleton and having some real adventures. With the prejudice of youth, he could barely tolerate his father's posturing and abhorred the social climbing his sire took such joy in.

It was an attitude that immediately endeared him to Lackland. Thus, Lackland passed a tolerable Yuletide, and after spending five weeks suffering the company of his family, he prepared to leave during the first week of January, eager to get on with his grim mission.

As Julian took leave of his mother, he told her he thought Melvin would do well at court. She rolled her eyes. "Mortimer just half an hour ago announced he is angling to get Melvin married to Princess Rose. I seriously doubt his intelligence, no matter if he is my son."

Lackland laughed. "As far as I know, the girl is betrothed to the Earl of Bunder's heir, young Jules. Morty will have to look elsewhere to advance the bloodline. I am sure there are plenty of fine families who'll want to join with House Portiers."

"I wish you'd stayed here and done your duty." She shifted in her chair, irritably. "I can barely stand Morty's posturing and prating about. Of course, he's not going to marry the boy to a princess, it's ridiculous, but I have to listen to it day and night. It's fortunate Melvin looks like you and my side of the family instead of Morty and your father's family. At least, he has some looks to bring to the bargaining table because he'll have little else. Morty is squandering the family's fortune with his pathetic attempt to make Portiers into an earldom."

"I have no duty here. It's all Morty's duty, and he's not disposed to be charitable about it. He made it clear long ago. I refuse to help Morty out the slightest bit though I'm more than rich enough to do so. I won't put up with his noise, and he knows it." Though his face remained pleasant, his voice held a note of steel, causing his mother's eyes to widen fractionally.

Julian suddenly grinned. "Besides, if Morty dies young from his utter boorishness, I'll make sure Melvin has all the gold he'll need to keep the doors open here. And don't worry. If it looks like Morty is going to lose the place, I'll save his arse. I told Uncle Evelyr so. But my brother will dance to my tune if such a thing should happen, and he'll be polite and conciliatory about it."

Isabela sighed. "I know you care about the family. I just wish I could ignore your brother, too, but he insists on pretending to be a devoted son. He visits my rooms every morning, whining and begging for money. It ruins my day."

"You owe him nothing." Julian put his arm around his mother's shoulders and hugged her close. "Don't forget I'll have Melvin for my own for the next five years. I'll have his attention for four hours out of every day, and by staying involved with him, I'll make sure he understands how to properly maintain his estates. I'll ensure the rest of the time he is learning, rather than toadying for favor. Our Melvin doesn't need a princess to make him the finest knight in the realm. Besides, there are plenty of fine young ladies of good breeding out there for him, who'll be much more to his taste."

"You believe Mel will fall in love like you did, Julian? Small good it's done you." Isabela's voice was sharp, and she knew it, but she couldn't change the way she felt. "Everyone but your uncle knows you're pining for Margaret De Leon."

Julian's cheerful reply made his mother smile. "Well, some things can't be helped. I just live my life as best as I can and get on with things. I've been fortunate enough to make my way in the world. If some things haven't worked out as well as I wished, my life is still good. I'm richer than even Morty could dream of, and I've earned every piece of gold I own. I'm content with how I live my life. Melvin will inherit my fortune when I'm gone."

"Are you content spending half of every year at Bunder's House De Leon? Why would you do such a thing if his daughter won't marry you?" She pushed forward into dangerous territory.

Julian was on thin ice. Deciding that pressing his own attack was his only choice, he replied, "The earl is a good old thing, and I love his daughter. Edward is far better to me than my own father ever was. It's no ordeal to help him with managing his estates when I'm not at court. He needs my help until his son comes of age. Since I've no land of my own, if I were his son-in-law in truth, I would be there helping him. What's the difference?" Lackland felt he had her confused and off balance.

"Jules," she said, just as he bent to kiss his mother's cheek. Startled, he looked sharply at her, thinking she'd somehow guessed, but it was just her old nickname for him, and he relaxed. "I might not see you again, my dear." Isabela De Portiers looked at the wall instead of her son. "I'm dying."

"Why? What is it, Mother?" He knelt before her, taking her cool hand between his and looking into the blue eyes so much like his own. "Why do you say this now instead of a month ago?" Julian's world lurched to a halt.

"It's a lump in my breast, the killing kind. The priestess can't cure it, but she eases the pain. It's one of those things one can't mend, and polite society does not talk about." She exhaled heavily and said, "I don't know why I've told no one. I haven't told Morty either. I probably won't until I have no choice. It's personal." She gave him a sardonic smile. "It's my death, and I want it on my terms."

"I understand." He held her hand to his cheek, reluctant to let her go. "I would feel the same way."

"You're a lot more like me than you know, my Julian. We think alike." Isabela smiled and pressed a package into his hands, a heavy wooden box wrapped in a silk scarf. It was the scarf he'd given her for Yuletide his first year at court as an eager boy of twelve, so proud to give his mother a silken scarf from Vyennes. She'd worn it often, pleased with both the gift and the giver.

He began to unwrap the box, but she stopped him. "There's a letter. Look at it when you get back to Billy's Revenge and pick up your friends." Lackland was startled again, and she laughed. "Where else would you be going but to avenge Percy? The St. Johns are expecting it, and it's what I would most certainly do. Just stay safe, my darling." She kissed his cheek. "I want you to live to see your son married to Henri's daughter." And with that, she swept out of the room.

Lackland stood in shock for a moment, staring at the package in his hand. Then pulling himself together, he strode up to his rooms and picked up his gear, placing the box safely in his saddlebag.

He stopped by the classroom where Melvin was suffering the administering of a lesson in the speech of Lanqueshire. It was similar to the common tongue of the Eynier Valley but different in many ways. "I'm off now, Nephew," he told the boy, speaking in perfect Lanque. "I'll see you when you get to court in the fall. I'll be working with all of you young courtiers as the King's arms master. In the meantime, study hard. I'll be supervising your education and testing your skills in every aspect of the knightly arts. The ability to speak Lanque is just one. You must be able to speak the languages of all our neighbors: Lanque, Lournesque, Vyennesk, all of them, even Fornost!" Switching back to Waldeynier, he said, "One never knows where the king will send you, and you must be ready!" He winked at the surprised tutor.

"Uncle! How will I survive without you? It's absolute hell here, with only Father for entertainment." Melvin stood and bowed to his uncle, feeling rather proud of himself for having managed to use a curse word in an appropriate and defensible manner. At thirteen, he stood on the verge of manhood. Lackland was sure the next five years would be the making of him.

"If you would do something for me, I would appreciate it." Julian spoke seriously. "I want you to spend one hour each day reading to your grandmother." At Melvin's stubborn look, Lackland handed him a well-worn volume. "This is her favorite book. I read it to her for one hour every day until I went to court, and I've read it to her every day since I've been back. She's dreadfully lonely, Mel. You must take up this task."

Melvin's rebellious stance and the way he held his head reminded Lackland of another boy, one with burnished mahogany hair and warm brown eyes so like Mags's. They were the same height and had similar mannerisms. *They're so obviously blood-related,* thought Lackland, with a pang. *Maybe no one will notice. Maybe it's only my guilt that makes me see this.*

Melvin looked at the book with the contempt only youth can bring to such a venture and then looked again, shocked. "This…this is her favorite book?" His incredulity made it difficult for his uncle to keep a straight face.

"It is. It would please her no end if you'd read for just one hour each day. You'll find your grandmother is an amazing woman." Clasping Melvin's shoulder, one warrior to another, he turned and left the classroom, leaving his nephew holding a somewhat battered copy of *The Merrye Adventyures of Sir Roderick Smythe—A Tale of Wyne, Womyn, and Song.*

Melvin looked at his tutor. In perfect Lanque, he said, "I have to go now. My grandmother is waiting for me to read her a story." He left the classroom, heading straight to his grandmother's suite of rooms.

Melvin would be forever grateful his uncle pushed him to read to his grandmother, as she passed away the following summer. He read to her every day for more than one hour, starting again at the beginning when they came to the end of the wonderful book. Over the course of those months, he discovered that inside of his frail old grandmother was a merry girl who'd always craved adventure as much as he did.

CHAPTER 9

LACKLAND ENTERED LIMPWATER, leading two pack ponies heavily laden with all he owned. He'd emptied his rooms of his old treasures and would never again call House De Portiers home.

Huw was waiting for him, standing at his gate with a rake in his hand. "Jack arrived this morning. He's already at Billy's getting settled in."

Lackland looked at the little cottage. The soil was freshly tended around Lucy's grave under the apple tree, and crocuses poked up their green shoots.

Huw saw where Lackland was looking. "I planted forget-me-not seeds there just this morning.

She'll not lack for flowers this year, my Lucy Blue-Eyes won't."

After a moment, Lackland looked away, his eyes burning. "What a pair we are." Sighing, he looked toward Billy's. "I'll see you there later. I hope Billy has room for me."

"He does and always will. You know that." Huw turned to go back to raking, then added, "He knows you won't come back permanently unless Mags marries you, but she'll never leave the trade. You know it, I know it, and Beau knows it."

Lackland walked his horse down the street, entering the courtyard in front of the stables. For a moment, he felt like he'd come home. He handed his horse and the ponies off to the new stable girl. "I'll be back to get my things. I just need to talk to Gertie first."

As he walked the path to the old Bolthole, Gertie's home, he noticed little had changed since his last long stay. Behind the house, Gertie's forge was going as always, with Gertie and her husband, Clyde, pounding on something. An apprentice Lackland didn't recognize pumped the bellows, and the heat from the fire felt good after his chilly ride.

Clyde nodded at him but kept pounding when Gertie came to speak with him. "Are you still working with Friar Robert to make bespelled armor?"

Gertie said she was. "But it takes a lot longer than regular, you know. His majik is strong, but it's a slow process, as it must be done in the raw forging of the metal. And he's does require coins for his services."

"That's only fair." Julian nodded. "I need to commission a pair of bespelled shields, one for my nephew, Melvin De Portiers, and one for my pupil,

Jules De Leon. I'd like them emblazoned with their respective family coat-of-arms if that is possible?"

Gertie was more than happy to help. "Lady Mags has commissioned a pair of helms for these same two young courtiers." Gertie's eyes twinkled. "She values these two lads as much as you. I'll have them for you by the time you go to court, I promise!"

After he'd spoken to Gertie, Lackland lugged his baggage up to the room Billy had ready for him, noting he was now in the corner room that had belonged to Lucy Blue-Eyes so long ago. Unpacking his bags, he soon had everything put away. His poetry books filled the shelf, and on the mantle, he set several small silver-framed portraits. Jules, Edward, Mags, Melvin, and his mother all smiled back at him. Several delicate figurines he'd bought in Vyennes made the room his.

"It's good to be home," he said aloud. He surveyed his pictures and his family's beloved faces, then with his decorating done, he sat at the table by the window and opened the box his mother had given him. Inside was a fortune in jewelry, some of which he recognized and others he'd never seen her wear. Finally, he unsealed the letter she'd written to him.

"These are for your son to give his bride when he is married. They were my mother's. She was a St. Clair, and as you know, she was sister to Henri's paternal grandmother. I've made my will and registered it with the local office of the exchequer. They have charge of that which I set aside for Melvin and know my reasons for disinheriting your brother. It will be for you to manage as executor of my estate. Mortimer shall not squander his son's entire inheritance.

"Eight years ago, De Leon and Jules visited me. Morty was at court pretending to be a knight while the rest of you were off fighting a war. Edward and I talked, and we agree this is only right. Young Jules understands the situation, as does Mel. They're content to keep the truth close to their hearts.

"De Leon and Jules have visited me twice every year since then, whenever Morty is away. Edward writes to me regularly, keeping me informed as to all that is going on in the lives of both of my charming boys who live at House De Leon.

"I am proud of you and what you've accomplished with young Jules, who is so much like our Melvin. They both remind me of you at their age and have developed close bonds by virtue of our secret.

"Forgive me for hounding you so visibly about your marital status. It is necessary, as you well know, to ensure that your brother remains as ignorant as he is…."

Lackland's eyes filled with tears as he read the letter. It was a long while before he could go down to the common room.

When at last he did, he noticed the place was unusually quiet. A few Rowdies had returned and were either up in their own rooms or in the bathhouse. Lackland saw Bess looking harried and took Annie's son off her hands. He sat in a quiet corner, rocking the boy to sleep.

The only Rowdies there were Huw, Beau, and Brand, along with a young Lady Rowdy named Bold Lora Saunders. She was rather hard-eyed and somewhat less refined than the ladies they usually had in the Rowdies.

Brand helped his father bring up a keg, and Beau read a book in another corner. Huw played his harp softly, an old melody Lackland had always loved, and the sounds of it lulled him into a dreamlike state.

The new woman, Lora, seemed friendly enough but didn't fit in well. Her taste in clothing was nowhere near as elegant as that of her peers, flaunting her charms cheaply instead of the graceful way of the women of Limpwater. She had little in common with the women she openly despised and was overly bold in her way toward men.

Lackland remembered her father well. Tom Saunders had been a likable man though he'd never been clever. Watching her interactions with the others as they trickled in, he supposed Billy had felt some obligation to Tom when he hired her. Or perhaps he was shorthanded, but either way, she seemed like a troubled young woman.

Until that moment, Lackland hadn't really noticed that most of the old crowd had moved on. During the five wakes he'd attended in the last year, all the old faces had been there. He'd heard the right voices; the right laughter of all except the honored dead, whose passing had left a gaping wound in the life of Billy's Revenge.

He didn't really know any of these newer Rowdies. Young Brand MacNess, Billy Ninefingers's son, and Bennie Smith, Billy's brother, looked so alike they could have been twins though they'd been born three months apart. They were nearly eighteen now, immense, muscular men as tall as Billy himself, and well established in the trade. Both were the image of Billy at that age. It seemed like only yesterday Lackland had returned to teach them the skills they would need to know, though now he thought about it, three years had passed since that summer.

They were men now, proven and hardened by two years in the saddle, nearly the same age he was when he left Henri's court to become a mercenary. It surprised him to think so many years had passed since he first came to Billy Ninefingers, looking for adventure.

Bess reclaimed the baby, various Rowdies returned from their jobs, and the place became more familiar sounding. Bennie appeared infatuated with Lora Saunders, who loudly declared she was married to her sword while looking at Lackland with hot-eyed glances.

Julian sighed, seeing the interplay between Lora and Bennie. He was determined to stay out of that mess, as he wanted no ill feelings with Bennie. Even if she had been older, the girl was not to his taste at all.

As he sat alone in the familiar room that seemed so full of strangers, Huw and Billy sat at his table, and Babs joined them. His sense of not belonging vanished, almost like he'd never left.

Almost, but not quite.

"I've been off the road for a while now. Teaching weaponry differs from fighting the way we do here." Lackland looked up as Jack approached them. "I've been fighting for the king and carrying a shield for too long. I don't know if I'm up to the nasty fighting mercs must do."

Billy shrugged. "You and Jack will get back into the feel of it once you're on the road. You haven't been out of it for too long." He exhaled heavily. "You have no idea how hard it is to get good help, thanks to your efforts on the king's behalf. I suspect in ten years Billy's Revenge will be a wayside inn catering to the travelers, and the Rowdies will be a memory. I'd hoped Brand would have more of a business to come to, but there it is. The good ones are going off to help your cousin fight the Lanques because they all want to be like you, Sir Julian Lackland De Portiers. The young ones worship you. Most of the ones who're left aren't worth a damn."

"They're only in it for the money or the fame," supplied Babs, glancing out the corner of her eye at Bold Lora. "Some," she said meaningfully, "want an epic tale of their exploits told at every wayside inn on the trade road if they rescue a cat from a tree." She shifted her son to her other shoulder, but he continued fussing, chewing fretfully on his little hand.

"Well, there are still a few of us who'll take on the bad jobs," replied Lackland. "I haven't turned down a request for help yet, and I hope I never do."

Taking Babs's son, putting him over his beefy shoulder and expertly burping him, Billy said, "Well, this job you're off on now is bad. Very bad. We're keeping it close, just among those of us who have to know, on Henri's orders." He handed the now-happy baby back to Babs.

"On that note, I'll go sit with Annie. Thank you, Billy. You have the magic touch for burping babies." Winking at Julian, Babs left the table.

Lackland raised his eyebrow with a questioning look at Billy's son, Brand, who still sat with the other young Rowdies.

Billy shook his head. "Even Brand thinks you're back here, the same as you've always done, to teach arms and take a few jobs here and there for old times' sake out of boredom. As far as they know, you three and Beau are taking a long job and will be on the road for the next two months. Jack will tell you what he found out during the Yuletide. Beau knows what you're riding into and volunteered anyway. He begged to go, actually. This is going to either get you all killed or get you an earldom." Billy sat back, raising his hand in the time-honored fashion, requesting service from the barman. "I heard a tale from John Caskman over in Dervy. It seems there was this traveling friar…."

Brand promptly got up, went to the bar, and came over to his father's raised hand, placing a foamy mug of ale in it. Everyone at Billy's table was laughing over the tale, and Huw began another involving a lady and her footman.

Once Brand moved off, Huw finished his joke, and the laughter died away. Billy leaned forward, saying, "If you do manage to avenge Davey and Percy, you'll gut the opposition to Henri's claim in the Long Valley. It turns out our Davey was a lot more than a pretty face and a fancy sword. He was born Duke Dayved Weyllyn of Imrysdock. By the time he walked away from it and came up here, he was a prominent person in the Eynier Valley. When he abdicated in favor of his sister and disappeared, it nearly brought Clan Weyllyn down, because no one wanted a woman in charge of one of the most powerful clans in the valley."

"I remember it well." A brief feeling of dizziness washed over Lackland at the realization he'd been so close to the man he'd once searched for. For a moment, he had no words.

Jack said, "Huw figured it out, and Henri confirmed it. Apparently, Leweyllyn means 'of clan Weyllyn,' just as De Portiers means 'of Portiers,' and could mean anything high or low. Most thought him dead until a chance encounter with Henri when he first came up here proved he still existed."

Grief at Henri's lack of trust assailed Julian. "It explains many things I wondered about." For a moment, Lackland wasn't sure how he felt at discovering his cousin hadn't told him. Ultimately, he chose forgiveness. "My cousin kept that secret for reasons of his own, and I must believe he meant well. So—Henri is an understanding man, but that meeting with Davy must have been difficult for both parties."

Jack nodded. "It was. Still, Davy made it clear he wasn't going back. They'd have forced him to marry for the clan, you see. They don't approve at all of lads like him down there. He wouldn't leave Percy, which he would have had to do. So, once again, he gave Henri a letter renouncing his claim in favor of his sister and her children, and as far as Davey was concerned, that was that. Henri kept his secret since Madewyn rules her Duchy well and has become one of his more capable strategists.

"All the misery of the last twenty years in the Long Valley has been an orchestrated power grab by Clan Grefyn. Grefyn is once again making their move to break away and reestablish the kingdom of Eyn with themselves as the new kings. Henri will lose his seaport of Ludwellyn if that happens, and the last twelve years of fighting the Lanques off down there will have all been in vain, because the day that happens, the inconceivably stupid Grand Duke Amstyce Grefyn will have handed Eyn to Lanqueshire." Jack sipped his ale, letting Lackland absorb the facts.

For a moment, Lackland was silent. Then, "I'm well acquainted with Amstyce Grefyn." Suddenly Julian felt the full force of white-hot rage. "He's dared to reach too high."

His uncharacteristic show of anger startled the others. They looked at each other warily and gave him a moment to compose himself.

Jack sipped his mug of ale before he continued. "The Grefyn's dearest friend and close confidante, 'Lord' Gwartney, has a slight foreign accent as if he originated in Lanqueshire. He and Amstyce have what, in their society, is considered an unhealthy attachment, although they keep their wives and children visible to shield their relationship from too close a scrutiny. Gwartney has all the finer qualities of a Lournesque highwayman, without the conscience or flair for style. For the last three years, he has guided Amstyce in his quest to 'return to Royal Eyn that which is theirs.'"

Huw hadn't contributed to the conversation but snorted on hearing that. "He would restore Royal Eyn as a province of Lanqueshire, you mean."

"Likely so." Nodding at Huw, Jack grinned mirthlessly. "They've nearly decimated the high clan of Weyllyn. Only the sixteen-year-old Duchess Gwenevere, who is to marry Prince Harry in two weeks, and two young dukes remain of the true bloodline. Madewyn is their mother and guardian. Her husband, Earl Bry Dayle, was murdered only two months ago."

Lackland shook his head in disbelief. "I knew them both well. His death is a great loss to us. What of the children's safety? How are they being protected?"

Jack replied, "Henri brought them north for the wedding and for safekeeping. He's just arrived in Castleton with them. Young Harry fell madly in love with Duchess Gwen when he first laid eyes on her. In the meantime, Henri wished me to tell you her brothers will be under your tutelage along with the rest of the young nobility when you return to court this fall." Jack turned to Billy. "Billy has new orders for us, from Henri."

"Now, this is what the king wants you to do...." Billy explained the details and finished by handing a small pouch of gold to Lackland. "When you're done with this, which should be sometime in April, you're detached to help me out with training the newer lot here. That was your plan anyway and will keep you from getting bored over the summer before you return to Castleton in the fall."

Lackland looked at the pouch of gold he'd given Billy two months previously. "I'll enjoy being a Rowdy again for a while, until September anyway. I've missed the old place."

Huw said, "So, we'll leave at the end of next week. That gives Jack a chance to spend few days with his family before we have to leave. The road should be firmed up pretty well by then from the recent melt, and anyway, Gertie must get the horses re-shod in the southern style."

Jack added, "I have to go to Dervy tomorrow to get some stock for my shop. I'll be back for a day or so, as I have some business with Alan Le Clerk. Then I'm going home to see my wife and sons. I'll come back the day before we leave." He didn't seem excited about being gone for two or three months. Given the fact his boys were still young, Lackland couldn't blame him.

Huw, on the other hand, seemed eager to leave town. He said, "We want to avoid notice, so we'll travel in disguise as merchant guards going south to meet a ship. You're fluent in the language but have just enough 'north' in your accent that you won't pass as Eynierish even if we stay quiet and keep to ourselves. But, by staying on the king's trade road and traveling in a group with an obvious local, me, you'll be accepted as mercenaries." He grinned at Lackland. "Unfortunately, your hair is too light and would draw attention from the Crows even if your accent were perfect. Annie Fitz will color it dark and show you how to keep it that way until we're done. You remember what happened the last time you went down there."

Lackland shuddered. "I still don't like to go thirsty."

Billy leaned back. "Beau! Come here and tell Lackland the joke you told me about the knight and the farmer's daughter!"

With a smile that elevated him to beyond handsome, Beau came over to sit with them.

Billy knew just how to get under Beau's skin and enjoyed doing it. He said, "Golden Beau here is getting lovely dark tresses too, Lackland, so don't feel special."

Beau winced, and Lackland laughed as Billy knew he would.

"Our Beau's hair is his one vanity. He's a girlish thing about it too," said Billy, chuckling. "We've never been able to convince him to cut it into a proper mercenary's haircut."

"And I'm still not going to cut it. I just don't see myself with short hair, light or dark. I wear it in a tail, so it stays out of my way." Uncomfortable at being the center of attention, Beau shrugged and changed the subject. "I hope you'll bring your bow, Lackland. I have the hankering to learn the art myself. I'd like the ability to fight some things from a distance, instead of up close and personal. I think wood-wraiths would be much easier to fight with arrows. Of course, you'd probably have to shoot them in the eye for it to be effective, but they wouldn't be able to zap you."

"That's true, but their eyes are large, so it's easy to nail them if they don't see you first," replied Lackland. An unaccustomed sense of joy surged within him. "You're the first Rowdy to ask to learn the art of archery. I have an extra bow stashed in Billy's armory, in the hopes someone would ask. But you'll want to use one you made yourself. We'll cut a bow and begin your training immediately in the morning."

The others went off to bed, but Julian and Beau sat discussing weaponry and techniques for killing some of the stranger beasts until Billy closed the common room. Regretfully, they went their separate ways.

CHAPTER 10

THE NEXT DAY, Mags returned from her job along with a Lady Rowdy named Belle Tanner. Her parents, like most of the older, retired Rowdies, raised Belle on Huw's romantic tales of their exploits. She was a lady of about twenty-two and had been a Rowdy for five years.

She currently had no lad, and with things being what they were with Mags and Beau, Lackland was attracted to her. She was enough like Lady Mags that they could have been sisters. Surprisingly only to him, he enjoyed her company more than he thought he would enjoy a woman's company again. She was witty and well able to hold her own in either a sword fight or a conversation—just his sort of lady.

Julian tried to keep it casual, telling her at the outset that when he returned from his long job, he would only be there through the summer. Belle had no desire to settle down either unless it meant she could still swing her sword.

The next morning Lackland and Beau went out and found the perfect yew for Beau's longbow. Then they searched for the right shafts and flint for the arrowheads. Iron heads were best but weren't always available, so being able to knap arrowheads was integral to the craft.

Mags watched as the two blond men strolled past the window of the common room, laughing with unconscious enjoyment. Both men were relaxed, more so than she'd ever seen either of them in anyone else's company.

By noon, several new bows lay on the grass next to Beau. Julian gave Beau his spare leather bracers, which were still useful despite being well worn. "We'll make new bracers next, but in the meantime, these will protect your arm." Julian showed Beau how to fasten them on with one hand.

Then they took Julian's longbow out of the armory and went down to the paddock where Lackland set up two straw targets. He swore Beau had been born with the gift because he was quick in learning the skill.

Bold Lora Saunders saw herself as the most desirable woman with the reputation of having had many notable lovers. She'd boasted of her intention to add Sir Julian Lackland to her list the moment she heard he was coming back to the Rowdies.

The first night he was there, Lackland made it clear he had no intention of taking her up on her offer. She was far too young for him even if she had been to his taste. Still, she dogged him, following his every move, turning up at every corner with an open invitation to her bed.

On the third night of his return, Bold Lora slipped into Lackland's room, not an hour after he'd left Belle. Lackland woke to find her naked body sliding into bed with him with a rather surprising, at least to her, result.

Lackland was a man who'd always slept lightly, and he was, as were most of the other Rowdies, a dangerous man to surprise. She suddenly found herself with a knife at her throat.

Once Lackland realized who it was and what was happening, he got out of bed. "I'm sorry, lady, but I won't dally with you. You have an understanding with Bennie Smith, and I won't get involved. It's what makes for trouble on the road. I have an arrangement with Belle Tanner. I'm thirty-eight and am older than your father, whom I knew well and respected. Please return to your bed, and we'll forget this happened."

Instead of leaving, she lay there in his bed, smiling challengingly at him. Lackland then did the only honorable thing he could think of. He had locked Belle's door behind him when he left her, and she was sleeping, so that haven was out.

A light showed under the door of Babs and Annie's room, so he went there to stay the rest of the night, fleeing down the hall in his nakedness and carrying his clothes in front of him.

He knocked on their door, and Babs let him in with a surprised look on her face, a look that turned to anger when she saw him standing naked and shivering. "My dear, what's happened?" She pulled him inside.

Annie stood behind her, covering him with a blanket. "Julian, sit down. Who's driven you from your room?"

He dressed quickly, telling them what had occurred.

"I knew it." Annie shook her head. "That girl has got to go."

"Your arse is still a wonderful thing to look at, dear," Babs said, a sparkle in her dark eyes. "The years have been kind to you!"

He laughed.

The ladies genteelly made room for him in their bed, giggling and telling him, "In the old days, you'd have been running from the frying pan into the fire by coming to us for safety!"

He laughed. "In the old days, I would have been up to it!"

For a while longer, the three of them talked about the changes that had come to them all and then went to sleep.

The two ladies took a dim view of the whole farce, and the next morning, Annie cornered Lora. "A man is not fair game, just a trophy to hang around your neck. If it's wrong to force a woman, then it's wrong to force a man."

Billy's anger flared on hearing what Babs and Annie had to say, but he handled it quietly, freeing Lora from her contract. "I won't have trouble here. This is the third complaint I've had of you forcing yourself on a lad who declined your invitation. To make matters worse, you've been pissing off my ladies. Take your horse and don't return to Limpwater."

Annie made sure she left. "The Ravens are always shorthanded, so maybe you'll do well there. But I guarantee they won't tolerate aggression among the crew."

With her usual colorful flair for curse words, a livid Bold Lora told Bennie she was riding Bekenberg, to join up with the Ravens.

Bennie seemed unsurprised by the abruptness of her departure. He handled it well, smiling and bidding her a safe journey, then turning and walking toward the smithy with no look back.

Huw just happened to be crossing the stable yard.

Lora gave him the finger, cursing as she rode out.

Huw was unimpressed. He looked at Bennie and said, "It's not my place to say, but you're better off without that sort of trouble."

Bennie grinned and shrugged. "Yep." He heard the sounds of hammers in the smithy. "I should go help Papa Clyde shoe those horses. Pop won't care, but Ma will chew my ear for being late."

Huw laughed. "Gertie's a woman with a strong will."

"She is that." Bennie looked toward the smithy. "She and Pop made sure I have a craft and a future besides swinging a sword. I've lately realized what a blessing my family is. If nothing else, Lora showed me what a gift my brother and my parents have given me."

That afternoon, the tubs were full in the men's side of the bathhouse. Beau soaked, feeling as if his arms would never gain the strength he needed to reliably draw back and shoot a longbow. "I know why you're the strongest man in Waldeyn," he told Julian. "I don't think I've ever been this sore, not even from lugging sacks of flour for my father at the bakery."

"You'll get used to it," Lackland assured him. "I'm sometimes away from the bow for weeks. I have to get back into the right mind for it, and my muscles feel it sorely."

"I've never understood how you can shoot those things so accurately," said Johnny Malone from his tub. "Lackland scared me to death when he killed the bastard who was sneaking up on me in Feinberg that time. Julian was clean across the clearing, and the thief was right behind me!"

"I practice a lot, and still seem to have a good eye for it," Lackland replied.

"When your eyesight goes, it's best to give it up," added One-Shot George from his tub. "I'm no good with the bow anymore, but I dare the bastards to run themselves onto my sword any day!" Everyone laughed, as not two weeks before, a desperate highwayman had accidentally run himself up George's sword in his effort to escape Beau.

"That's how George got his mercenary name." Lackland laughed. "He shot one bolt at these two Lanque highwaymen who were attempting to flee in the dark with the goods after they ambushed our camp. It went clean through the first one and nailed the second through the heart! Only three of us were guarding Dolman, the wine merchant; me, George, and Alan Le Clerk. Alan and I didn't have time to string our bows, but our swords were handy. We cut four down before old Dolman could even get out of his bedroll. George nailed the other two with one shot, which was one of the finer moments I've seen as a bowman!"

George sighed. "Sadly, my eyesight has suffered. Now, if I want to shoot a highwayman, I must ask someone where to point my arrow!" Everyone laughed again.

Johnny Malone began a story about how he, George, Davey, and Percy, had surprised a pair of thieves lying in wait to waylay them on the caravan route to Fornost. "George snuck up and shot one of them in the arse. I bet he never sat in a tree waiting to ambush anyone again!"

"Yes, he came down from the tree rather quickly." George chuckled. "He finally yanked the arrow out of his arse, and the last I heard of him was his cursing as he tried to find his horse. Of course, Davey had stolen their nags."

During the following days, Mick and his new assistant got their provisions in order, and Gertie re-shod their horses. Lackland and Beau spent long hours together in the paddock practicing. Beau developed quickly as an archer, although he had many new blisters to show for his efforts.

While they waited for the roads to firm up, Belle and Lackland spent their evenings playing stones with Beau and Mags or dancing to Huw's music.

The two men quickly became inseparable, causing Belle and Mags to each feel private moments of jealousy. They seemed happiest when they were together, and where you found one, you would also find the other.

Neither lady would admit to it, nor did they discuss it with each other, but both feared the two men would find all they needed in each other's company while on their long journey.

Jack arrived back in Limpwater at the end of the week, not really excited about the journey. "Kat understands, but the boys don't. On the good side, they think their shopkeeper father is a knight in shining armor. Nothing could be further from the truth."

The next day dawned cold and clear, with the chilly brilliance that brightened January. Lackland felt as if spring was around the corner. He and Beau sat in the courtyard while Annie Fitz colored their blond hair dark.

Rowdies sometimes went disguised for various reasons as each job had its requirements. She showed them what to do to keep it black and made sure they had enough little packets of the dye to maintain their disguise for six weeks if the job should take that long.

Lackland fervently hoped it would not, a sentiment later echoed by Slippery Jack. "My half-brother is at court, and he's a good man. He'll care for Kat and the boys if something should happen. But it's not the same."

The next morning, Julian Lackland, Huw the Bard, Beau Baker, and Slippery Jack rode south, purportedly on a trip to guard a shipment of fine wines.

CHAPTER 11

AS THEY RODE out of Limpwater, Julian felt that lightness of heart that always accompanied embarking on a job, even unpleasant ones. Huw hummed a ditty, and Beau joined in. Soon the group was singing Huw's bawdiest ballads. By evening, they had passed Somber Flats and were on their way south toward Bekenberg.

They camped at a place they often did, settling in for the night. Slippery Jack insisted on posting a watch. He didn't say why he felt so nervous, but no one argued. Finally, on the third night out, as they made camp about halfway to Bekenberg, he said to Lackland, "Someone's following us. I haven't seen them, but they're there."

"I know. Beau mentioned it too," replied Lackland. "We'll just keep on as we have been, pretending we don't know they're out there and see what happens." He and Beau had been looking for material to make short bows they could shoot from horseback, working on them once they stopped for the night.

After four long days and three short nights on the road, they entered the rather gloomy hamlet of Bekenberg and promptly found the inn known as the Broken Wheel. It was nowhere near as nice as Billy's Revenge. As far as the food, cleanliness, and quality of the furnishings went, the inn was barely tolerable.

They didn't go to the Raven's Nest and check in with the Ravens, though it was much the better place. They were posing as free mercenaries heading south and hoped to blend in with the rest of the flotsam.

Sara Murtrey, captain of the Ravens, would hear that they'd been through town anyway and would know it was on business. Two of her Ravens stood quietly at the bar in the common room of the Broken Wheel, looking over each merc and merchant who passed through.

Lackland found a spot in a corner where they sat and kept to themselves. As the four ate a bowl of something billed as stew, Beau surreptitiously gave the two watchers a signal, telling them everything Sara needed to know. The room was full of lower-class merchants and the mercs who guarded them but didn't have the atmosphere of camaraderie that characterized most such places.

Jack couldn't shake the feeling they were being watched by more than just the two Ravens. It wasn't surprising he felt that way; they were being scrutinized by every merc there, the same as they were observing everyone else. He keenly felt the surveillance of one person, but no matter where he looked, he couldn't see who it was.

The innkeeper offered the four Rowdies one room to share, but after seeing it, they opted to camp just outside of town as it looked suspiciously bedbug infested.

At dawn, they were back on the road, heading for the village of Clythe. It was a dark town, one that guarded the narrow gorge and the road into the Eynier Valley. The south fork of the Limpwater River flowed to the sea through this gap, entering the valley in a series of spectacular waterfalls.

The Eynier was a long, broad valley, over two hundred leagues of verdant farmland dotted with tiny villages stretching from Clythe to the port city of Ludwellyn. The mountains to the east formed the border with the Kingdom of Vyennes, and those to the west bordered the small seafaring country of Lanqueshire. The Eynier Valley went all the way to the sea, forming a wedge between the two larger nations.

The far northern countries of Fornost and Lournes, together with the eastern countries of Harlynde and Vyennes, were eager to support Waldeyn in its fight against the Lanques. They had made new treaties allowing foreign merchants to travel freely in Waldeyn as long as they hired Waldeynier mercenary guards for their protection. They shipped their goods into and out of the port of Ludwellyn, increasing the commerce in both Waldeyn and Vyennes.

With no dawdling caravan to slow the Rowdies down on their journey through the pass, they made good time. On the fifth day out of Bekenberg, the Rowdies rode into Clythe, a small village with an inn that served the traveling merchants and their guards.

As they settled their horses in the stable, Huw said, "You won't find anyone who can claim to be a bard in the Eynier. My apprentices in Limpwater are all that's left of the craft." His features grew melancholy, as he thought of his father and the trouble that had driven him out of the valley so many years before. "I'm the last fully trained bard of Eynier still alive in Waldeyn. The people still make their music, though, and it's unlike anything you've ever heard. My soul has missed the valley more than you'll ever know."

The Green Man was a neat, clean place, as Lackland and Jack well remembered from other journeys down in the Eynier Valley. The original owner, the Bear, whom Lackland remembered, had died two years before, and Huw hoped he'd left the Green Man to his niece. "Sinean will understand and help us if she was his heir."

Their luck was running high; the new owner was the friend of Huw's youth in Ludwellyn. She had only one room for them as she was full up, but there were two beds, and she brought up two cots for them.

Sinean was overjoyed to see Huw, although she seemed concerned about the melancholy that was now an integral part of his somber countenance. Huw introduced his friends, using the names Joules, Bo, and Jaky, all respectable Eynier versions of their real names.

"I was afraid you were still saving the world down in Ludwellyn," Huw said. A genuine smile lit his features. "You regularly vowed to never leave the road until Grefyn was naught but ash, as I recall."

"Things come along that change a person's view. When the Bear died, I brought the crew up here. We stay busy enough here in Clythe. That hasn't changed." With an anxious look, she added, "We must talk privately. Your friends will excuse us, I'm sure."

Although he was clearly glad to see her, Huw looked uncomfortable and unsure of himself as they went upstairs. Culyn, a young man Sinean introduced as her son, cast a surprised and worried glance at them.

"Huw is still mourning Lucy," said Lackland, speaking in Eynier as he and Beau settled into a corner. They would only speak the local dialect from here on out.

"How he's changed," remarked Beau. "How we've all changed, even you, though I'm at fault for that." His accent wasn't as smooth as the others, but he spoke the language well.

Lackland gripped Beau's forearm. "No. I set her free thirteen years ago, and I meant it. I'm content with the way things are. Mags needs you. She can't bear to be alone, and you're the best man in the Rowdies. You're the best man I know. I feel better knowing she's with you."

Beau searched Julian's eyes and saw he spoke the truth. "I know what keeps you at House De Leon and why you left the road. She told me all about it. Nevertheless, I feel caught between the two of you in a way I can't explain."

"This is just the way it is. It affects nothing between you and me. I trust you more than any man alive."

Lackland's assurance eased Beau's guilt somewhat, though he admitted it would never completely go away unless Mags married Julian.

Julian's voice was low but firm. "We both know that is unlikely, or it would have happened thirteen years ago. It can't be changed, so don't dwell on it."

Jack chose that moment to return from the privy. Lackland and Beau kept their conversation light in his presence, touching on nothing serious.

While Huw was up in Sinean's rooms, the other three played a game of stones. The tap room had filled with locals and also a few travelers going north or south. Sinean's son served them excellently brewed ale and a superior stew. Culyn was a young man of about eighteen years of age, quietly making a name for himself in Clythe, both as a musician and a merc.

Earlier as they arrived, they'd exchanged the usual signals, so Culyn knew they were Rowdies. They fit in well and didn't stand out too much as being from up north. He decided they were up to something of interest. "Where are you off to?" he asked, as he brought them a second round of ale.

"Ludwellyn," replied Jack. "We're to meet Murfee's ship and ensure he makes it to Castleton with all his merchandise." Lackland and Beau both admired his flawless Eynier accent. It was as thick as Huw's.

"It's been a bad winter. The weather hasn't cleared, so you should watch yourselves, especially at night." Culyn glanced around the room casually as if discussing nothing important.

Jack's ears pricked up. "So, the weather has been that bad? From which quarter does it blow? Then we'll know how to set camp."

"It comes across the waters from the land to the west and blows through Ludwellyn. It's rough going as you head toward the sea right now. I would also watch the wind over the pass west of Bekenberg on your way back north. The weather up there has been fierce this year."

Jack nodded. "It's brutal there most of the time."

"Many have lost their lives in the storms that battered us these last years." Culyn's cheerful, professional smile remained in place. "I expect it will pass too. All things pass in time."

"Under the light of the sun, all things will pass," replied Jack, effortlessly answering the Eynier proverb. The speech of the Eynier was littered with them, one thing that had been endearing about Davey. Huw was not as given to spouting proverbs as Davey, but still, all the Rowdies knew the Eynier proverbs by heart from having been around the two southerners for so many years.

Culyn looked over his shoulder, seeing that no one needed his help. He pulled out a bench and sat at their table for a moment. "Is your comrade a good man? He's befriended my mother."

Lackland replied, "Huw is a good man and true. It seems they were young together and have much to catch up on. Some of his news will distress her and isn't a topic for the common room."

"I see," Culyn said. "He seems melancholy."

"He lost his wife and unborn child, along with several others dear to him this last year," said Beau. "She was the love of his life."

"I'm sorry to hear that." Culyn nodded. "At least he has friends to help him through the hard times."

Soon the men of Clythe gathered in the common room to make music, with one or another of them pulling flutes or viols out to play. Each fellow was applauded by his mates. Then, as if by mutual consent, the group launched into a rondo, playing as well as any troupe of entertainers Lackland had heard at court.

Culyn played the harp, the likes of which the Rowdies had never seen. Huw would have immediately recognized it, as he had gained his master's pin for the making of it.

The men of Clythe were superb musicians. Beau's clear tenor rose above the other voices, as he sang all the songs Huw had taught him. To the great pleasure of the locals, Jack and Lackland danced in the northern style to the pounding of the bodhrán, unable to stay still with the thrill of the music firing their blood. They danced until ten o'clock when it was time to close the tap room. If Huw had been there, it would have been the best evening they'd had since leaving Billy's Revenge.

Later, as they went up to their room, Lackland wondered where he'd seen Culyn before, a thing that nagged at him. After an hour, Huw entered their room, finding him lying awake and reading, unable to sleep. Julian saw Huw in the candlelight and realized why Culyn looked so familiar.

Huw had a stunned look about him and wasn't disposed to engage in conversation.

Lackland understood the feeling. Since Huw didn't mention it, he didn't either. He blew the candle out and promptly fell asleep.

Huw Owyn lay wide awake. His whole life had just turned upside down.

The next morning, they gathered in the empty common room, ready to go south. Huw and Sinean talked quietly in the corner behind the bar. Lackland and Beau had stepped over to the hearth to give them some privacy.

"I think it's for the best. Let him decide." Sinean's voice carried, although she spoke quietly. Huw's voice was muffled as he replied, and then they heard Sinean saying, "You need a guide, and this way, he'll know what he wants to do. It's hard for him here with the stigma of illegitimacy. Up there, he'd have a future." Huw replied something low again, and she said, "Ask Lackland then. See what he says."

The others looked at each other, somehow unsurprised she recognized Lackland. Huw reluctantly walked over to them. His expression was that of a man torn.

"What is it? Is it Culyn?" Lackland's question took Huw by surprise. "This changes things for us. We need a guide, but has she told him what you are to him?"

"I only found out last night. How did you...never mind," said Huw. "She told him after the music was done. Culyn and I talked for a while and then went to our beds to think about things."

Beau and Jack looked from Lackland to Huw, absorbing what they'd just heard. "Well, how I missed that I don't know, except everyone has black hair, blue eyes, and sings like an angel in this place," muttered Jack. "He's the image of you the day you walked into Billy's Revenge."

"What do you want to do?" Beau asked.

"I want to get to know him more than anything. He's the son I thought I'd never have," said Huw. "But I don't want to involve him in a blood feud with the black Grefyns, which is what we're caught up in here. And they *are* black-hearted, blacker than anything you can imagine."

"He seems an able man," replied Lackland. "If he's willing, we could use his help." Jack and Beau both nodded their heads. "Why are you so reluctant?"

"If it goes awry and I lose my son over murdering the Crows, I'll never forgive myself." Huw leaned close to Julian, his voice a whisper for Lackland's ear only. "I have a child, a daughter I can never claim, or it would destroy her life. She's highborn, do you understand? Her mother keeps me informed, but I can't be a part of her life. I've accepted it and wouldn't change it for anything."

Lackland nodded. Thinking back to how he'd met Huw all those years before, he suspected the Countess Dwyn was the mother in question.

Huw spoke aloud. "I've lost my Lucy Blue-Eyes and the daughter we might have had. So many deaths this year. I fear I'll go like Percy if I were to lose Culyn now I've found him. A son! I have a son, and he's everything I ever dreamed, and more." Huw's bleak eyes met Lackland's supportive ones. "I understand Percy. I know why he went that way. Some sorrows kill your soul but forget to tell your body you're dead."

Culyn came up to them. "Let me do this, Father. We'll both be better for it. All my life, I've wondered about you, believing you dead. I always knew you were a bard, but I believed you were lost with the rest of the craft in the great fire." His voice was like Huw's. He wore mail and carried saddlebags, with his sword in a well-worn scabbard. "We didn't have my childhood to share. Let's use this time and be grateful for it. Besides, I have skills you'll need."

Huw replied, "This may be more than you should be involved in. We've come to collect for our honored dead, for two wee babes of Dayved Weyllyn, whom we've all adopted."

Culyn's eyes widened. "The missing heir to the Weyllyns. We thought him dead."

"He was in the North, living as a mercenary. He saved my life when I was escaping this valley and was our brother-in-arms." Huw's worry was echoed in the features of the others.

Jack said, "We're collecting from high Grefyn on behalf of his sons. I wouldn't want my boys along for this, were they your age."

Huw nodded. "Blood will flow, a river of it. In settling up for Davey, we must carry out a task for Lackland's highly placed cousin. If we're discovered, we won't survive the hospitality of Grefyn."

"All the more reason for me to come along then," said Culyn, smiling Huw's old smile, the one that charmed women high and low, but with his own particular honesty. "I have abilities that go beyond playing my father's harp and pouring ale." He sighed and looked away. Then he said, "I have a grudge against Grefyn though I have no right to collect for my dead, as these things go. It lies festering there, anyway."

"What's your grudge?" asked Jack warily. "We're not interested in going too far afield in the completion of our task. That will get us killed, and I, for one, am not ready to leave this world." His easy smile received an answering one from Culyn.

All eyes had inadvertently turned toward Huw to see his reaction to Jack's words.

"I have a reason to live too, now," muttered Huw, feeling their scrutiny. "And more reason than ever to protect what's mine if I can." This last, he delivered to Culyn, rather gruffly.

"It's not my legal right to bear this grudge against the Crows. At least, no more than anyone who loves the valley and hates to see the destruction and murder they wreak upon us. Yet it's personal and cuts me deeply. Sit here, and I'll tell you." Culyn began his tale. "There was a town to the south of here, Maury."

"Any tale that begins with 'There was a town' is bound to be a sad story," said Huw, as Culyn fell silent, lost in his dark memory. "I remember Maury well. I grew up there."

"Then perhaps I have a right to justice in this matter. It's a sad tale, Father," he said. "Did you have family there?"

"No. My mother died when I was your age. She was all I had of the family in Maury." Huw shook his head. "But bad news travels. I've heard what you're about to say, and it's terrible."

Looking at the others, Culyn explained, "Maury was famous for their weavers and was home to the girl I hoped to marry. The Weyllyns had the town on the Maab River, with the Grefyns locked out of the cloth trade. The river powered the waterwheels, which drove the great looms upon which they wove the cloth that made Maury famous. They situated the village in a perfect place for the looms, as the Maab River rarely freezes over and is constant in its depth and speed. The looms were seldom idle, and the cloth they turned out was famous all over the continent.

"The Weyllyns are good to their people and don't tax them harshly. The Grefyns have a grudge against the Weyllyns that goes back generations, and the higher you go in the clan, the worse the grudge is until at the top there is only hate, and the desire to crush Weyllyn with room for nothing else.

"Grefyn's Crows had come twice to demand that Maury town turn to Grefyn and aid them in their effort to restore the crown to Royal Eyn by taking it from the Weyllyns and Wald. The people of Maury sent the Crows away unsatisfied, saying all such a thing would do is leave the valley open for the Lanques to plunder.

"One bright Thursday morning two summers ago, the people of the village were all occupied at their looms and various other tasks, just as they should be. As the weavers worked, a large band of masked highwaymen came into town, creeping through the shadows. Fanning out, they crept to every factory, shop, and house. They nailed shut the doors and windows and set fire to the town, cutting down any who tried to escape the flames." Culyn saw their shocked faces.

"Grefyn posted bills in the surrounding villages saying the people of the Long Valley had risen against Clan Weyllyn and murdered the traitors in their midst. Everyone knew it was a lie, but it was one more way to divide us, to make us weaker.

"Carynne and I were young and not yet betrothed. Someone introduced us to each other at the May Day Faire only that spring. I courted her in keeping with the concerns of her father, visiting her on Sunday afternoons and sitting in their garden under the watchful eye of her grandmother. We were only sixteen, and while I had the stigma of illegitimacy, which her father didn't look kindly upon, he'd found favor in me and my prospects. I don't know if we would have married. Our love was new, a possibility only, although I had hopes." Culyn finished his tale, gazing at his father with eyes older than his years. "So, I've no proper right, as our people see it, to collect for the dead, but I bear Grefyn a grudge."

The others were silent, watching the interaction between the two men who looked so alike, one man old and sad beyond his age and the other man young and yet so wise. Abruptly nodding, Huw said, "You have a right to be a part of this. We must eliminate the rats from the granary, and we intend to start at the top."

"So, let me be your guide in this extermination. I know where the Crows do business. I've had some success in other ventures of this nature and know just the way to accomplish this thing." Culyn laughed. "Besides, if I were to die today, I would die happier than I've been in my life. I know you would have claimed me had you been given the opportunity, but you know how Mother is. She doesn't do things anyway but her own."

"It was a harsh time. Sinean had to protect you. Giving you my name would have made you a target. Fortunately, I'm no longer worth murdering, so I aim to rectify the issue of your legitimacy today."

"How so?" asked Jack, smiling widely. "She refused to marry you then, and I don't see that changing now."

"It's of no matter." Huw's handsome features broke into the first truly joyous smile the others had seen since before Lucy's death. "This is a happy day. We're going to the chapel now, this moment, his mother and me. We'll re-register his birth today, and I am claiming him as I would have done." He put his arm around his son's shoulders, meeting his gaze. "You are

Culyn Owyn, son of Huw the Bard, and everyone will know it. Today you receive your true name!"

CHAPTER 12

THE TRADE ROAD to Ludwellyn was long, and rather than chance the dubious hospitality of public houses on the Grefyn side of the river, they camped alongside it. Huw discovered his son was the perfect Rowdy and a bard in the making. They fell under attack by highwaymen just after leaving Clythe, and Culyn acquitted himself well, as Lackland had suspected he might.

One week of hard riding after leaving Clythe, they arrived in the port city of Ludwellyn. Huw remarked, "It took two months of walking the back roads to get from here to Clythe when I left the valley." He grinned mirthlessly. "Most of the way, I was dodging Crows and backtracking rather than going forward."

The city was several times larger than Castleton and crammed to bursting with people. Culyn directed them straight to an inn in the poorest and most crowded section of town, right on the docks.

The Sailor's Rest was full to overflowing. Culyn proved his descent from a long line of bards when he turned his charm on the innkeeper, persuading him to rent them a certain room on the second floor, one room for all five. The landlord was no match for him, succumbing with good grace. "It means turfing out the current tenant, but I'll do it because you're Sinean's boy. What you're up to, I don't ask. You have that look about you."

"Hello, Waite," Huw said, coming up behind Culyn. "Remember me?"

"Huw Owyn. The Golden Throat—the maiden's dream come true! What's made such a melancholy mark on you, old friend?" Sharp blue eyes under a thatch of white hair surveyed Huw sadly. "You left here long ago, vowing never to return. The bastards who caused you all that grief are long gone, but we hear tales of you and your golden voice." Shaking his head, Waite looked at Culyn, then at Huw, and did a double take. "I don't know why I never saw it before. It can only be you who is this lad's true father."

"I am." Huw's pride was hard to contain. "He is Culyn Owyn, as he should have always been."

"Now I'm sure you're here on business, or your father wouldn't be along. He's made a name for himself elsewhere. But I must stay out of it, right? What I don't know can't hurt you, if you know what I mean." Waite shook hands all around. "I'm glad to make your acquaintances. It's good to have Sinean's lads down here on business. I won't have to worry about you fighting in the tap room."

The room was cramped, but they managed. The stables were decent enough, but there were no proper baths and only an outdoor privy in the tiny courtyard. However, there was plenty of water in a jug on the washstand for washing.

The windows were large, with a tall spruce tree stood outside the one that faced the alley, allowing them to come and go as they wished in the dark. "The tree is why I pressured Waite to give us this room," Culyn told them, as they stored their possessions as neatly as possible. "It's our private way in and out."

All the great families of the valley had their primary residences in Ludwellyn, enabling them to remain close to their commerce. They had originally planned to go straight to the Duchess of Weyllyn's villa, where Jack frequently guested. His business often brought him to Ludwellyn. The group would have been received warmly, even though she was away up north for her daughter's wedding. Instead, they were crammed into the rough room down by the docks, but they all agreed it was a better arrangement for their purposes.

Culyn arranged for gainful employment for the Rowdies. In the guise of street sweepers, Huw, Lackland, and Jack secretly watched the palaces of the Grand Duke Grefyn and other notables of that family. Culyn and Beau worked as stevedores, listening to the gossip, and picking up useful information.

The old city of Ludwellyn was in a dangerous mood. Women and children stayed behind locked doors, and men went out only to earn the family's living. Street corners were dangerous places to linger for any length of time. The atmosphere down on the docks and in the market was one of confusion and anger. Fierce verbal disagreements resulted in beatings when words failed to convince, and fists took over the conversation.

The Port Commander had posted notices all over town, announcing Crown Prince Harry Dragoran, and his new bride, Princess Gwenevere of Weyllyn, would take up residence at House Dragoran within the month.

Most people were glad that, two-hundred years after the joining of Wald to Eyn, an Eynierish princess would once again reign as queen, with equal sovereignty as the king. Most were happy that in the meantime, the young couple would live in the valley with them instead of in the wild, uncivilized North.

But the Rowdies heard naysayers too, strident voices whose cries of derision sounded a sour note in the celebrations. They were few but excessively loud in their dissatisfaction with "Wald's get," vociferously declaring the Weyllyns were traitors for "selling Eyn to Wald for a shiny crown."

As they went about their work, they noticed the troublemakers were most often people of a slightly different accent. The true origin of these self-proclaimed patriots, hired by the Grand Duke Grefyn, became obvious upon further examination of their daily rituals.

Culyn and Beau watched as beggars and drunks came in on Grefyn cargo ships, seeing them quickly dispersing into the crowds. Lackland, Huw, and Jack observed them turning up on street corners, trying to rouse the rabble against Weyllyn and Henri. When they were successful, they received a daily wage from the Grefyn paymaster. Beau and Culyn saw them standing in line at the pay window at dusk, the same as the other day-laborers.

Most of the Grefyn's gold was like the coin of Waldeyn but was minted in Lanqueshire. Still, it was legal tender since it weighed the same as gold coins issued in Vyennes, Waldeyn, or Lournes. In the interest of trade, all gold was acceptable in Ludwellyn and could be exchanged for Waldeynier crowns at the Exchequer's office down on the piers.

The clerk at the Exchequer told Lackland they'd noticed a flood of "bones," as they called Lanque golds. The pirates' gold coin had a ship on one side and a pair of crossed oars on the other. Long ago, a wit had said they may as well have stamped a skull-and-crossbones on it, and the name had stuck.

If they didn't gain a following within a day or two, the rabble-rousers lost their usefulness and were let go. Most reverted to their old ways of thievery and violent crime, the only employment they'd ever had in Lanqueshire. A resulting crime wave swamped Ludwellyn, slowly moving north in the form of highwaymen and gangs of thieves.

Clan Grefyn loudly blamed the upswing of lawlessness on the Grand Duchess Madewyn Weyllyn. Several times, as Lackland pushed his broom and refuse cart, he overheard disgruntled people saying that if a rat drowned in a rain barrel, the Grefyn would blame it on Madewyn Weyllyn.

Violence erupted as Grefyn attempted to counter the popularity of the prince and his bride. Their desperation, blatant deceptions, and an endless supply of armed bullies did little to gain the people's sympathy. Instead, the commoners grew disgusted with the power grab, pushing back as much as they were able.

In response to this opposition, Amstyce Grefyn declared all who disagreed with his plan were traitors. He declared Eyn a sovereign state with himself as King, but even his own clan didn't want to go that far, and he backed down, claiming it was an ill-judged joke on his part.

At the end of two weeks, the Rowdies had gathered enough information, laid their plans, and knew the layout of the streets well enough to execute them discreetly. They were at the point where they would have to make their move or go home unsatisfied.

Lackland wrote a coded note to Henri's Port Commander, detailing what they had discovered and recommending he search each incoming Grefyn ship for Lanques disguised as Eynier sailors. He signed it with his own name and sealed it with his signet ring. Dressed in his normal garb as a merchant, Jack took the letter to the dockside office of the Port Commander, handing over a slip of paper with a certain code word on it.

The clerk was nearly speechless at having the king's spymaster there in person, deferentially showing him into a private office. Within half an hour of his departure, a detachment of armed soldiers poured out of the crown armory and marched to the docks.

They boarded the Grefyn ships still in port, seizing and "deporting" Lanque infiltrators by knocking them on the head and tossing them unconscious into the harbor. Those who woke upon hitting the water and tried to swim to shore faced the gauntlet of archers who filled them with arrows.

By evening, the desire to rid the Long Valley of the hated Lanques raged in the streets. In what seemed no time at all, anyone who could even possibly be of Lanqueshire was in danger of "taking the long swim home."

That same night, Grefyns began dying all over Ludwellyn, ten in seven different houses. The first to die was one Lord Gwartney. He'd somehow garroted himself in his sleep. Though his front and back doors were well guarded, the alley and stepped chimneys had provided both the entry into his bedchamber and the way out.

Strangling Gwartney was easy, but although he'd avenged Davey and Percy, Lackland felt no satisfaction. "I thought it would ease the pain to rid the world of the creature who ordered such a horrific thing done to our Davey," he told Beau. "It just makes me feel soiled instead."

"I know." Beau shook his head. "The world is a safer place without him."

For Huw, it was cathartic. "It gives new meaning to the phrase 'a murder of crows,'" he said with a smug grin, as he crept through the window just before dawn after the first night of the bloodletting.

At breakfast, Waite advised them to keep to the inn, as there was trouble in the streets. Out of deference to the innkeeper's suggestion, they didn't leave their room by the front door and were conspicuously present under his roof while the streets were full of rioters.

Two Rowdies stood guard at Waite's front door around the clock, armed with cudgels, keeping the rebels outside, and protecting his premises. They rotated the guard duty. Lackland and Beau would go out, while Huw, Culyn, and Jack kept the innkeeper thinking they all still languished under his roof. Waite was grateful to them for saving his windows and his livelihood.

Over the next three days, the sport of murdering Crows spread all over the Long Valley. Once the first members of Clan Grefyn turned up murdered, other people took up the habit. Within days, Crows lay dead all over the southern end of the valley, so many the authorities could not lay the murders at the feet of one faction.

Assailants garroted some; those were the deaths the five could account for by their own hands.

However, a number of Grefyn nobles the Northerners had never heard of died in widely differing ways. Gangs of ordinary citizens set upon known Grefyn merchants as they went to the shipping office, overwhelming their guards and bludgeoning them to death. The mob violence disturbed Lackland more deeply than he'd thought possible. "This town has gone mad with murder—to openly wear the Grefyn badge is to sign your own death warrant."

Even more bizarrely, the newspaper reported that two prominent Grefyns, heirs to the coronet, had their throats cut by their own guards, retaliation for the losses their families now suffered on their behalf. The list of dead reported in the daily broadsheet made for surreal reading.

On the fourth night of the riots, Lackland and Beau found themselves trapped on the balcony of a once minor duke's study. They had only just scaled the wall when a group of Lanque thugs burst into the duke's study. Overwhelmingly outnumbered and unable to escape unnoticed, they hid among the foliage of the lush, potted plants while the group of around twenty angry men dealt out harsh justice.

The mob, desperate and furious at their treatment by the constable's men, held Duke William Gronwy and his terrified family hostage, demanding payment to support them on their trip home.

The duke held his hands up, offering no defense. "What do you want? I'll give it to you!"

A coarse voice snarled, "My brother and I worked for you. You brought us here, and now you must get me home!"

Peering through the foliage, Lackland saw the leader's blade at the duke's throat.

The duke sounded strangled, pleading. "The crown seized my ships. Indeed, they've impounded all Grefyn ships. You must try to go on a Weyllyn vessel, as they're the only ones still in port. I've got plenty of gold—I'll give you whatever you want."

"Yah, sure. They deny Lanques passage on any ship, no matter how much gold we offer. So, we tried to go north on foot, but the constable's men got hold of us. My brother's dead now, so you owe me his death-geld." The blade drew blood, and squealing, the terrified duke shrank away. The thug stuck his battered, bandaged face in the duke's. "I lost my eye. What's that worth to you? Eh?"

The duke gave them all his gold, emptying the drawers in his study. Even so, once they had the coins, the mob left his body lying in a pool of blood. Ignoring the balcony after a cursory glance, the two leaders of the mob demolished the duke's study, taking everything of value and then left the room.

Since the Lanques had done the task for them, albeit messily, Lackland and Beau waited before leaving their concealment, so as not to draw the rioters' attention.

Doors slammed in the distance, and the sounds of breaking furniture and glass echoed. Harsh voices shouted Lanque curses in the garden below, and occasional shouts and cries filtered to them from within the mansion but died away.

Not sure how much time had passed, Beau glanced at Lackland, seeing him pale. It had grown quiet, and he thought they might have gone. He was about to tell Julian so when a terrible commotion of men yelling and women screaming broke out.

The two men shot from their camouflage to go to the women's aid. They exited the study just as a group of six pirates emerged from a bedroom into the narrow hallway at the top of the stairwell. By the time Lackland and Beau had dealt with them, there was only silence in the mansion.

At the bottom of the stairs on the right, they came to the library. Blood in the hall and on the ornate double doors should have warned them, but they opened it anyway.

Nothing could have prepared them for the horror, a scene unlike anything either man had ever witnessed.

Gronwy's women and children had sheltered among the shelves and beneath tables, vainly hoping the thugs wouldn't search there. Picking their way among the corpses, they saw no one had survived the massacre, not even the lapdog.

The blood-crazed mob had mutilated the duchess beyond all recognition. Small bodies lay nightmarishly cast into corners or dropped and left lying in their pooled blood as the beasts worked their way through the rooms.

A choking noise from Lackland alerted Beau to his distress. "No...no...they were children. This shouldn't have happened...." Julian's words ended on a sob. Wide-eyed and white as chalk, he stood unable to move or look away from the grotesque corpses of four eviscerated children. The battle-hardened veteran stood powerless to move; his eyes riveted on the horror.

Taking him by the shoulders, Beau forced Julian away from the scene. "We can't help them. They're with God now. Come with me. We have to leave this place." Pushing Julian, Beau got him moving.

Several bodies lay further on down the hall, people who had tried to come to the family's aid. They wore bloody livery and must have been servants. In every room were other victims, all foully murdered. Beau dragged Julian past an aged woman's headless torso.

Nearly as stunned as Julian, Beau managed to keep his wits about him. He stumbled through the blood-spattered halls, leading Lackland, incredulous at the grisly scene. At last, he found his way outside, going through the dark garden.

Julian blindly followed. Hardly aware of what he was doing, he trailed behind Beau through the shadowy, deadly streets to the dark alleys.

At a point nearly halfway back to the Sailor's Rest, Beau realized Lackland was no longer with him. He quickly retraced his path, nearly overcome with panic. "Julian…Julian! Where are you?" His whispers went unanswered, and he grew frantic. His heart hammered in his chest. "Julian! Please, answer me!"

Cursing, Beau stumbled over something in the dark. It was Lackland, curled up in the blackest part of the shadows, his arms over his head, shaking with silent sobs.

Relief such as he'd never felt washed over him. Beau reached down, pulling Julian to a sitting position, and knelt beside him. "What happened? Did you fall? Can you stand?"

"We've begun something terrible," said Lackland, his voice strangled-sounding in the dark. His eyes saw only the horrific brutality of the scene they had just left. The children's screams echoed in his mind, drowning out everything else. "Listen to them, Beau…oh, God in heaven! The children are suffering for it now." A conviction that the fault was his had a grip on him, and he couldn't shake it.

"I know…but…." Beau shook his head, unable to find the words. "Julian, it's only you and me here. There are no children."

Clutching Beau, Julian's words were choked out. "How could I have thought this massacre would ease my grief? Was I mad? It was my duty to protect those babies, and I failed them. I failed them!"

Beau struggled to ease Julian's grief. Reaching out, he embraced Julian, drawing him close. "There's no denying something ghastly has begun. But you didn't cause it. Even you could have done nothing once the scale tipped in this direction. The weight of anger these Grefyns have stirred up is too great. I fear there's worse ahead, but you didn't cause this. The guilty fathers brought this massacre upon their own children. God help us all."

Julian clung to Beau, who seemed to understand, holding him until his sobs subsided. In the darkness, his strong embrace offered shelter, his voice soothing. "It's over now. We couldn't stop it. Nothing could have changed it."

After a while, Lackland calmed enough to hear the sense of Beau's words. He got himself under control. "Forgive me, please. I don't know what's wrong with me."

"You have nothing to apologize for. It's between you and me. Can you walk now?" At Lackland's nod, Beau pulled him to his feet. He gripped Lackland's arm and led him through the dark, barely able to breathe. At last they arrived at the tree that served as their private entrance.

By the time they returned to their room, Julian seemed almost normal, although exceptionally quiet, something the others noticed. Beau positioned himself by Julian's side, covering for his silence, another thing the others observed.

Beau said nothing of Lackland's breakdown when he explained what had happened at Gronwy's. When Jack asked Beau if Lackland was ill, he said only, "It was…he's a fragile man who always believes right will triumph. The world is just not that way."

When the massacre at Gronwy's became news, a stampede of lesser nobility, formerly aligned with Grefyn, erupted out of the Eynier Valley. Those minor players now called upon their long disdained Weyllyn roots, claiming the name Leweyllyn and swearing fealty to King Henri.

Fingers pointed to a young, dissolute earl by the name of Lyn Pyndrys, a man with a nasty reputation. The earl had suddenly risen to the high station of the Heir to the Grefyn Duchy through the deaths of seventeen of his more prominent relatives.

Although his good fortune had been through no action of his own, he saw an advantage, implying by vigorous denial he was the mastermind behind a power grab. Those few Crows still standing firm against the tide of public outrage suddenly saw him as a danger. His close association with Lanqueshire was much discussed.

The Grand Duke Amstyce also heard those rumors. Mad with grief over the death of Gwartney and incensed beyond reason that Pyndrys would dare to reach so high, he took an immediate dislike to his new heir.

Amstyce Grefyn and his guards appeared at the door of the upstart earl's manor on Highborn Street just before the dinner hour on Friday. Amstyce himself slit Pyndrys's throat and ordered the entire branch of the family down to the babies executed as retribution. By dawn the next day, there was no one left of the Pyndrys bloodline.

Amstyce's bold announcement of the earl's punishment took Ludwellyn by surprise.

As the Grefyn, Amstyce had cultivated a ruthless image. However, this action bordered on hysteria and shook an entire community that had become inured to things up to that point.

The retribution sickened the five conspirators. Julian especially felt horror at what their actions had brought down on the Pyndrys children, sitting pale and silent as the others discussed the news.

Huw's eyes sparked with more than anger. "What sort of man murders his own blood wholesale?"

Jack agreed, reading aloud from the broadsheet. "Only fourth and fifth cousins twice removed remain in his bloodline, and they can't flee to Henri's protection fast enough."

Now, even though Julian hadn't witnessed the deaths of Earl Lyn Pyndrys's children as he had Duke Gronwy's, they weighed on his conscience, a nearly crushing burden. That night and for several nights afterward, he couldn't sleep because his dreams were too ghastly. Visions of slaughtered children haunted even dreams that began agreeably.

Still, he continued on, and only Beau knew how disturbed he was during those nights.

Julian couldn't understand why he had broken down in the alley, feeling shamed by it, worried Beau thought less of him for it. As a soldier, he'd seen horrible things on the field of battle but could put them out of his mind, rationalizing the butchery of war as being unavoidable and knowing it could be his fate someday.

However, the deliberate slaughter of children was more than he could comprehend.

After a few days, he could sleep nearly normally again, although he couldn't completely put what he'd witnessed out of his mind.

The task had taken longer than they planned, and they'd run out of hair dye for Beau and Lackland.

As the two used their last packets, Beau told Jack, "It's time to leave. Tomorrow we'll make the final foray."

"We'll draw straws," said Jack. "I hope I win." He and Huw won the draw, which quietly pleased both.

The streets were quiet, and people were keeping indoors. The King's soldiers patrolled in aid of the constable's men, protecting those citizens of Ludwellyn who had to leave their homes for work. The Rowdies had solemnly bid Waite goodbye earlier in the day. He understood they needed to go back North, although he wished they would remain.

Culyn, Lackland, and Beau camped with the horses just outside of town while Huw and Slippery Jack slipped back through the dark streets. They crept over roofs to the home of their quarry. Scaling the drainpipe, the two men went in through the third-floor study window.

There, they found a body contorted on the floor beside his desk, frozen in a twisted, agonized pose and dead for several hours at least. The Grand Duke Amstyce Grefyn lay dead at age thirty-nine, which came as a surprise since they'd planned to slit his throat.

They looked around his study, examining everything. "Who of his close circle would poison him? It must have been someone he trusted." Jack methodically searched the desk, finding a letter Amstyce had been writing in Lanque, a desperate plea for help.

"His wife? She must have resented his love for Gwartney." Huw answered, but examined the emaciated man with a critical eye.

Jack disagreed. "She died last year. She'd given birth to a child every year of their marriage, only two of whom survived to adulthood. No sons, just the two daughters he used as bargaining chips. Rumor said the duchess was grateful for the respite Gwartney brought her."

"He looks as if he's been unwell for a long while, even though the murderer at last resorted to poison. But it could have been anyone. Even before this, he was the most hated man in the Eynier Valley."

With the last task completed through no effort of their own, they began the journey north to meet King Henri's entourage at House Dragoran. They would make their report to him and then attend Harry and Gwen's official installation as the first Prince and Princess of Eynier.

After their second bath in a frigid creek, both Lackland and Beau were back to their usual "golden-haired splendor," as Jack sarcastically pointed out.

House Dragoran was two days' ride south of Clythe, near the village of Longcham, and despite being a royal residence, it was nothing more than an average northern baron's estate. Truthfully, it was reminiscent of House Portiers. The kings and queens of Waldeyn had always summered there until Henri's father's time. The manor was small and shabby, but the rose gardens were famous all over the continent.

The mayor of Longcham asked if Prince Harry and Princess Gwen would build a palace in the style of the other notable families in the Eynier Valley.

Prince Harry looked surprised and said, "I don't see why we should waste coins on that. It's already much finer than most other peoples' homes, and the roof is still good." He paused and thought about it for a moment and then said with a self-deprecating smile, "Well, with a few new slates it will be good again. We should probably expand the stables, though. We have a lot of relatives who'll be visiting."

The people of Longcham loved Prince Harry for his unconscious humility, calling him "our Harry."

One day after the Rowdies reached House Dragoran, King Henri dealt with the problem of Grefyn. Because the Grand Duke had left no living heirs willing to claim the coronet, Henri declared that Clan Grefyn was no more.

The crown soldiers posted Henri's writ in every town, announcing the lands and properties of Amstyce Grefyn had reverted to the crown. No one complained as it granted the peasants throughout the valley possession of the property they had farmed for generations and cut the gentry's taxes in half.

During the ensuing week of celebrations, the king knighted both Beau and Culyn.

Huw sent a message to Sinean, who immediately came down to Imrysdock to see her son knighted, arriving just in time. She agreed to ride back to Clythe with them. "I plan to flaunt this turn of events all over Clythe. You've suffered for my folly in not telling Huw about you when I could have done so anytime. Now they'll just have to shut it, won't they? There's no stigma in being a knight, no matter I never married your father."

The king let the revelers assume the honors were a reward for services rendered in the Bekenberg Pass. Sir Beau Baker and Sir Culyn Owyn were both surprised and deeply honored.

Huw graciously declined the honor, explaining to Henri that too many new awards would draw unpleasant attention from any Crow sympathizers still hiding within the population. "Anyway, I have more credibility than if I were suddenly a noble. I hear more this way, right?"

"What about you, Jack?" Henri asked.

"My half-brother's a duke, and I have a string of useless titles I never use as it is," Jack said. "I'm already as noble as I need to be."

Lackland declined too. "Let Beau and Culyn be considered part of Harry's court and not connected to our presence here with you."

"Julian, you always give me good advice. I warn you, though, I'll deal with you later," Henri said. "You've become less sunny of late, my cousin. This sort of work isn't for you, is it?"

"No. I'd much prefer to face a man in the open and defeat him in fair combat," replied Lackland wryly. "This has poisoned my soul somehow. But it was necessary. It's just…it caught so many innocents, and I couldn't save them."

"I can only tell you this—the Grefyns received the same treatment they meted out for the last two Grand Dukes' reigns. Think of the bards, Julian, and the weavers of Maury town." Henri clasped Julian's shoulder. "You care about people too much for your own good, but it's what makes you who you are!"

The Rowdies arrived back in Clythe several days after the knighting ceremony. They spent their last two nights at the Green Man, making music and dancing all night long. After Huw and Culyn had played together, the entire crowd was on their feet, clapping and whistling their approval at the end of their set. Many said they thought they'd never hear the great tales told by a trained bard and thanked Huw over and over.

Culyn embraced his mother before he left her. "I don't think the Long Valley is my home any longer. My future lies with my father, helping him bring back the bards."

Tenderly holding Sinean and kissing her cheek, Huw assured her, "We'll both return at Yuletide. I'll not let the distance separate you from our son permanently."

Soon the tale of Culyn Owyn and how he found his father, joined the Rowdies, and came home a king's knight was a staple tale in the taverns of the Long Valley, though the story placed him at Bekenberg Pass, fighting for the king.

CHAPTER 13

THEY TRAVELED NORTH along the trade road to Bekenberg. On the morning of the fifth day out of Clythe, the Rowdies came upon an overturned wagon—refugees from the recent troubles in the South. Thieves had stolen everything of value, and the dead were either dragged off or scavenged. The white bones of a single horse gave mute testimony to the violence of the attack. Few people traveled without the protection of a guarded caravan, but the riots in Ludwellyn had made merchant trains scarce. It looked as if a week had passed since the ambush.

Culyn noticed several strange tracks, showing Jack. "I've never seen anything like these. What beast makes a track this big, and with only three toes?"

"This is just wonderful." Jack looked sick as he gazed at the marks. "It's a firedrake." He remounted his horse and glared at Lackland, who'd dismounted and was now rooting around in his gear. "What are you doing? Get back on your horse, and let's get out of here."

Lackland replied, "We can't leave it nesting by the trade road. Henri will return this way with his family. Others will end up like this. We have a job to do here." He hummed a cheerful little tune.

In Jack's experience, the happy little hum meant Lackland intended to be a hero whether it was smart or not, so he sat in his saddle and said nothing.

"Well?" Lackland stood with one eyebrow raised, as if Jack were lagging on the way to a tea party.

"Henri has a bloody army tagging along with him." Jack glared at the knight. "We're far less able to take care of it than those brave men who, by the way, are carrying shields bespelled against fire."

Huw added, "And who are paid to rout impertinent firedrakes that might bother the king. Which we aren't."

Jack dismounted again and squatted, looking at the tracks. "Let's go home before it finds us. These are far too fresh for my liking."

"You worry too much," Lackland replied in Eynierish, flashing his innocent smile. "This will be good, clean fun. We've been skulking around doing murder in the dark for too long, and it's poisoned my soul. I need to do something good and necessary, something I'm not ashamed to admit to. I'm not cut out to be an assassin, and you know it. I need to wash some of the blood off my hands, and this will help." He looked at the tracks with a professional eye. "This one's a youngster—maybe the equivalent of a young teenager." He grinned at the expressions on both Huw's and Jack's faces. "He's only about half grown."

Huw rolled his eyes. "So? He's still more than big enough to eat a family and most of their horse."

Culyn observed the discussion, keenly interested. He turned to Beau. "What do you think?"

"I agree with Julian." Beau's expression matched Lackland's in both its perfection and enthusiasm for such a mad plan. "This is my kind of fun. I see sense in what we did down south. I just hated the way we had to do it."

Annoyance sparked in Jack's eyes. "But you two are damned good at skulking, once you get past your silly, unnecessary scruples. This is not fun for me." He shuddered. "Prowling around in the dark is the way Slippery Jack does business. I've less chance of being eaten by some bloody creature with teeth the length of a man's hand and breath that sets my clothes afire."

Beau ignored Jack, barely able to contain his giddy relief at seeing Julian in such a good mood. He hadn't realized how worried he'd been and didn't want to examine his feelings too closely just yet. He checked his weapons and strung his longbow, his smile concealing his true motives for agreeing. "First, I'll play at bowling with it. Then we'll both shoot it full of arrows if we can. Firedrakes aren't as well-armored as dragons, but arrows most likely won't work."

Lackland agreed. "You're right. They'll probably have no effect, but these new arrowheads from Gertie's forge are sharp. We should definitely test them out."

Culyn looked from Lackland to Beau. Beau seemed to have become sunshine personified, as if the prospect of killing the beast illuminated him from within. Seeing him that way, Culyn understood why he was called Golden Beau. "What about Jack? He seems reluctant to deal with this creature."

Beau waved away his concern. "Oh, don't worry about him. He gets cranky when he's suddenly thrust into the light of day. He prefers the warm, comforting dark!"

Lackland seemed to feel Jack's reluctance was a difference of opinion between friends about how to approach certain tasks. "Once he sees us having fun, he'll perk right up. When the going gets rough, he'll be right there with you, never fear. Jack always has your back, no one better."

Beau hummed a happy song as he loosened his sword in its scabbard and settled his armor. Jack recognized Beau's little ditty as "A Firedrake in the Kitchen," a country melody everyone knew and sang. Soon Lackland and Beau were merrily singing the chorus.

"Oh, Lord. I knew it. Look who's just as bad as Lackbrains," Jack muttered. "Those two deserve each other, God help the rest of us."

Culyn and Huw both shrugged at Jack's assessment.

Culyn hid his keenness from his father, pretending nonchalance. "I've never fought one of these creatures, so this will be different. What are they, some kind of dragon?"

"They're like dragons, and yet they aren't," replied Lackland. "Usually, they're smaller, quicker, and stupider. They have a second breath that's a weapon, and they don't fly. But they can run faster than a horse, and those strange little arms with the claws at the ends are surprisingly quick."

Beau added, "Something about their breath catches fire when they breathe it at you. What you must do is stop them up, so they can't roast you."

Lackland agreed. "Mags told me about your solution to this little problem—I think it's quite elegant. I'll definitely use it myself the next time I have to take one on alone."

Rolling his eyes, Huw spoke in the tones of a man who had heard it all. "Culyn, I can't stop you, but don't get carried away by the enthusiasm of idiots. These things are bloody dangerous. Stay away from its breath, whatever you do, or you'll be well-roasted." He raised his sleeve so his son could see his horribly scarred arm. "I got this when I was your age. Two good men died that day—granted it was an unusually large drake, but still. Personally, I prefer to sing about those two fools routing the damned things."

Jack had been wracking his brains for a way to get out of fighting the beast and finally hit on one he thought sounded helpful. "Lackland...the area in front of the den is likely to be rather cramped. Huw and I will just stay out of your way unless you lads look like you're in trouble. Right, Huw?" Jack looked at the bard, who nodded agreeably. "After all, you and Beau really are the professionals in these sorts of matters, and we'd just be in your way."

"Good idea." Lackland seemed oblivious to Jack's manipulation of the situation. "They do nest in rather tight places, and the beast will be thrashing about somewhat. The three of us should be able to handle it." He turned to Beau, "Once you've plugged him up, we'll swarm him and try to get the head off quickly. Agreed?"

Beau and Culyn nodded, and Lackland trudged off down the faint path, leading his horse, with the others following him. "Be sure to stay nimble. They tend to be snappish," Lackland called over his shoulder to Culyn.

The trail led to a lake and then wound along the shore, where it turned sharply toward the entrance of a cave. Many bones of both horses and humans littered the outside. Tying the horses where they couldn't see or smell the creature, they followed the trail to the cave entrance.

Jack stood across the clearing, hanging back with Huw. Great piles of droppings randomly dotted the landscape outside the den. "This is just wonderful, Lackland. You always manage to find low-paying jobs that involve shit, or stench, or... did I mention shit?"

"I knew you'd find something to enjoy here." Lackland smiled his charming best and winked at Jack. Standing in front of the cave, he shouted, "Hey! Firedrake! Come on out and play!"

Huw whispered urgently, "Don't piss it off, Lackland. This is more than stupid enough without pissing it off."

A strange, dry rustling sounded in the cave, and as they watched, a huge shadow filled the entrance. The beast lingered just inside, as if curious about what was happening in the clearing.

"Sometimes they're a wee bit coy, and you have to woo them out," Beau said. "This one doesn't seem too hungry. Of course, he just ate an entire family and their horse, so he's probably not feeling too peckish right now. We'll need to tease him out. They can't resist snapping at anything that moves quickly. It seems to be a reflex of some sort."

Beau looked around in the debris and picked up a round stone. He bowled it at the entrance. A huge, scaly, triangular head on a long, sinuous neck darted out and snapped at it, swallowing it faster than anything Culyn had ever seen, and disappeared back into the cave. The drake made a strange gagging sound, followed by a burp.

Beau said. "Human skulls work well for this if you can't locate a good round stone, but they have to be big ones. You can usually find plenty of good skulls around a drake's lair."

The odor of burning sulfur filled the air.

"I need a bigger stone," said Beau, as he poked around the edge of the lake. "That one went all the way down, I think."

"Oh…it'll constipate the poor beast." Lackland shrugged. "Oh well, it can't be helped."

Jack and Huw looked at each other, incredulous. "He's mental," muttered Jack.

Huw fervently agreed with him.

"How about one this size?" asked Culyn, handing Beau a larger round stone.

"Perfect!" Beau bowled it at the cave entrance.

Once again, the drake snapped it up. This time, he gagged, unable to get the boulder up or down his long throat.

The distressed drake staggered out of the cave, a round bulge in the middle of its long neck. Lackland immediately fired an arrow that bounced off its scaly chest. Beau shot his arrow just as Lackland let fly a second shaft, and again they bounced off the massive chest.

The drake's head swung back and forth, and he made strange choking noises as he tried either to swallow the boulder or cough it up.

Lackland abandoned his bow. "Damn. I was hoping these new arrows would work." Drawing his sword, he ran yelling at the drake, with Beau and Culyn on his heels. Hacking and slashing, they attempted to hamstring the beast while dodging its snapping maw and whipping tail.

The three men slipped and slid in the piles of dung randomly dropped in the clearing, but somehow, they stayed upright—most of the time.

With a lucky blow, Lackland sliced half of the whipping tail off. Blood splattered everywhere, making their footing even more slippery. Strangled sounds erupted from the drake, but the stone in its throat stifled its cries.

At last, Beau cut the hamstring of one huge leg, and they had the beast crippled. It was down, but the snapping jaws continued to dart and gnash at them. Desperately they hacked at the whipping, sinuous neck, all the while dodging and sidestepping the giant maw full of sharp, knife-like teeth. Vicious claws lashed out, short little arms attempting to grab the attackers. The stump of the tail had become a brutal and deadly club.

Random blows rained down upon the beast. Most of the strikes glanced off the thick, scaly skin, although it seemed as if the firedrake was tiring.

Culyn tossed a large branch, one thicker than his arm, toward the drake's head, and the beast deftly caught it. With splinters flying, he crushed one end in his terrible jaws. Then, tossing it the way a bird does a fish, he attempted to swallow it.

The branch caught at a bad angle, jamming the beast's jaws open.

Pawing at his face with his little hands, the drake paused its attack long enough for the three to finally decapitate it. They stood looking at the immense head and then at each other.

"You have something on your shirt, Sir Culyn." Lackland stood beaming.

"You have something on your boot, Sir Julian," replied Culyn, with an answering grin. "And Sir Beau has it in his hair."

Huw and Jack stood across the small clearing, leaning on their swords, laughing uproariously. "Well, you three seemed to have it under control, so we thought we should just let you get on with it. We'll just see to the horses," said Jack, once he could speak. "Speaking of which, you'd better bathe before you come near them. The smell of drake shite makes them nervous."

Walking back to the horses, Huw and Jack chortled uncontrollably. Huw called over his shoulder, "And don't forget your bows. They're sticking out of the pile by the stump!" His snickers echoed across the lake.

Lackland said, "I suppose a quick bath in the pond would be a good idea. I should have warned you, it's messy work."

"But it was fun." Beau's radiant smile was contagious. "You have to admit; it was a lot more fun than other things we've done lately."

Culyn's laugh was an echo of his father's. "It really was exhilarating. Too bad there was only one!"

They searched the den, finding no valuables, which was odd. Beau seemed mystified. "These beasts usually keep a pile of shiny objects their victims had on them. This one has been nesting here for a while and should have a collection of belt buckles and buttons and such, at least. This is the first one I've ever seen with no pile of sparklies."

"It was young. Or possibly, the people it's been dining on lately haven't been well off," replied Lackland. "But maybe while it was away from home, someone robbed it. Some highwaymen do chance it, although it's a dangerous way to steal a living. They'd have to be desperate." Beau and Culyn nodded in agreement.

"I'm glad now I've finally seen a firedrake," ventured Culyn as he looked around the fetid den. "This was a good morning, all in all."

· Laughing and joking, they retrieved their bows and quivers and the arrows that had fallen by the way. Then they walked back down the trail away from the mucky area in front of the den. Once they reached the shore of the pond, they stripped, washing their clothes and armor and weaponry before jumping into the frigid water.

"Oh...cold...," groaned Lackland as he submerged himself. "It's better than stinking, though. At least, I think it is." He grabbed a handful of sand and vigorously scrubbed himself and his hair.

Rather quickly, they were shivering too much to continue their swim. The three gathered their possessions and jogged to the overturned wagon. Huw and Jack had a roaring fire going. They'd made camp and then gone off to collect more firewood. The three frigid heroes spread their damp clothes and armor out to dry, then hurried into their clean changes of clothing.

Finally, they stood warming themselves, grateful for the fire.

Later, wrapped in his cloak for warmth, Beau stretched out on his bedroll. He told Culyn, "Too bad Lackland couldn't bring his cooking gear on this trip. He's an excellent chef when he has the chance to do it right."

Lackland enjoyed the praise. "Thank you, Beau. I cook for the earl, young Jules, and myself whenever we travel, so I've developed certain skills with fresh-caught game." He turned his frozen backside to the fire. "I'm looking forward to supper. I seem to have worked off my breakfast."

"Killing a firedrake is a lot of work." Culyn yawned.

Beau agreed. "And that one was only half as large as they usually are."

Culyn stared. "Really. I suspect that wouldn't have gone so well, had it been an adult." He turned, seeing his father and Jack had returned from gathering wood.

Huw spoke conversationally, stacking the wood near the fire. "No, it wouldn't have. I'll give you the details of just how badly fighting one of those can go if you want. Anyway, Jack thinks we're being watched."

Beau turned on his side and leaned his golden head on one hand, leafing through a book of poetry he'd purchased in Ludwellyn. "Another beast?"

"If it's a beast, it's riding a horse shod in the style of northern Waldeyn." Jack poked at the fire with a long stick and added a log. "Possibly shod in Somber Flats."

Huw said, "Someone camped for a long time not too far from here. We found a lean-to for a horse and a larger lean-to for a person. It's impossible to tell how long ago they left. They knew what they were doing—they erased their tracks well. Jack couldn't say if it's our watcher from before or not."

"We'll post a guard tonight," said Lackland. "They may be friendly, or they may not. We were being watched when we were through this area the last time."

The next morning found them riding toward Bekenberg, where they planned to arrive in the early afternoon.

The ambush came just after midmorning. Lackland vaulted from his horse's back, his sword flashing, as did Beau and Culyn. Soon the bodies of six dead outlaws lay lined up along the road. After looking closely at their clothing, Huw and Culyn both agreed they were Lanques. "Their clothes are like those the rabble-rousers in Ludwellyn wore."

Jack rode up with six horses, some shod in Lanqueshire, and some in southern Waldeyn.

"Well, we know who was watching us," said Beau as they built a cairn over the dead men. "And this stretch of road is safer now."

Though he nodded and agreed with Beau, Jack had a nagging suspicion their watcher was still out there but decided he was just paranoid. He tried to settle his mind, but it wouldn't stay settled. "It's just the last few weeks have made me nervous," he finally said aloud.

"You were born nervous," replied Lackland. "We'll stay alert because if you're nervous, there's a reason to worry."

"Now we have some horses to trade in Bekenberg," said Huw. "This gives us our cover story. We're tracking highwaymen for King Henri." The others agreed.

Lackland said, "You're right. It's best we go openly as Rowdies now." He turned to Culyn. "We're in Raven country once we enter Bekenberg."

Culyn nodded. "Ravens used to guest at the Green Man as they did a lot of business on the Vyennes trail, and down to Ludwellyn. Not for a year, though. Not since Younger Murfee died."

Huw had worked as a Raven when he first came north and liked Bekenberg. He still had some close friendships there, although many had passed on. He explained to Culyn how the agreement that Billy Ninefingers had with the Ravens for found horses worked. "We'll hand three horses off to the Ravens. Then, if a Rowdy working down here needs a mount through accident or, God forbid, theft, they'll find a horse for him or her. The other three, we'll take back to Limpwater for a similar arrangement."

At midafternoon, they rode into Bekenberg and continued straight on through the gloomy village to the inn known as the Raven's Nest, which was outside of town on the Vyennes trade road. There they met with the ostler for the Ravens, a large, jovial, red-bearded man.

After catching up on his news, they continued into the common room, where they sat and gossiped with the captain of the Ravens, Sara Murtrey. She was a woman of Lackland's age, tall and strong from moving kegs of ale. She placed a mug under the tap and deftly filled it. "It was a bad year for the Rowdies, so we've heard." She placed a foamy mug of ale in front of each of them. "I heard about Davy and Percy. What an utter waste—but I suspect you've been settling accounts down south." She came around the bar and embraced Huw. "I'm so sorry about Lucy Blue-Eyes."

Huw's eyes filled with tears at the mention of Lucy, and she hugged him again.

Sara turned to Culyn. "But at least, you still have family. Is this man your son?"

"Yes, he is," said Huw, a smile lighting his gloomy features. "Culyn Owyn, meet Sara Murtrey, as fine a sword as you'll ever want at your side in any melee. And she cooks like an angel!"

"We love to hear your father's music in the common room," she told Culyn. "Are you as gifted a songbird as he is?"

"I would say I love music as much as my father does," replied Culyn with his charming smile, eyeing her the same way his father had always done. "I've never made my way with it as he does, though."

Huw's fierce pride was impossible to hide. "He's as good as my father was."

"That's high praise, Huw. Balen was one of a kind. I hope you and Culyn will play for us tonight." Then she looked pensively at her mug and said, "I must tell you something, Lackland, a wee bit of a heads-up."

Lackland looked interested.

"A former lady of the Rowdies, Lora Saunders, applied for membership with us at the beginning of February. We sent her out on two jobs, but while she was good enough with her weapons, she was not suitable for what we need. I think you know why. So, we sent her on to Wister. They're always hard up for help, and she could have done well there, had she been of a mind to."

Warily, Lackland said, "Go on. We're acquainted with her."

"She didn't work out well there either," Sara said. "The girl has a grudge against you. She blames you for her unemployment from the Rowdies. I feel sure she means you harm. The last I heard, she was heading west to Galwye to join up with the Wolves. Her father worked for the Wolves if you remember." A frown marred Sara's smooth features. "Lora didn't arrive there, according to my daughter, who's married to their ostler. No one has seen or heard from her for near-on two months."

"She could be dead. There was a firedrake, not two days south of here. We killed it," replied Lackland. "I'd be sad to hear that. She was young and showed promise. She could have done well, but...."

"She was a bitch, Julian." Beau's words were hard-edged.

Huw, Jack, and Sara nodded at his blunt assessment.

Lackland looked away, unable to meet their gaze. "Well, I won't speak ill of her."

"I will," said Beau. "She was loud as to her intention to add you to the list of 'famous lovers' she claimed to have had. You were to be another notch on her belt."

Lackland's face reddened. "She was far too young, a troubled girl."

Huw replied, his low voice heated. "You're too generous to her. She threw herself at every man in the

Rowdies. My wife wasn't dead two days when she came knocking at my door."

Beau agreed. "She was like a terrier with a rat in its teeth. She wouldn't stop hounding men until they finally surrendered and gave her what she wanted just to get her to leave them alone."

Huw said, "Billy made my day when he threw her out. I've wondered what triggered that." He looked at Lackland for an answer, who refused to meet his eyes.

Instead, Lackland examined his mug and said nothing.

The others' eyes met; they nodded as they saw confirmation in Lackland's demeanor of what had happened.

"All I know is she got up Annie Fitz's nose one time too many," said Jack, finally. "She seemed to believe she was the most desirable woman in the trade and thought sex with any man she desired was her right and her due, instead of a privilege between equals." Anger sharpened his tones. "She had the nerve to tell me a man can't cry rape, because 'men want it all the time, like rutting beasts.'" He looked away. "That comment got her tossed out of my room. Twice. I'm married, and I take my vows seriously, but she wouldn't listen. I had to take it up with Billy, and she found someone else to badger."

Lackland looked at him sharply but said nothing.

Jack sipped his ale. "I know what got her fired from the Rowdies—it was a private matter, and I didn't get involved. Annie was done with her shenanigans and made her pack it up and leave at once," He carefully ignored Lackland. "My room is next door to Annie and Babs, so yes, I heard exactly what happened during the night, but I won't comment. It's between them."

"Well, she could be dead if no one has heard from her for so long," said Lackland again, desperate to get them off the subject.

"It wouldn't surprise me if she went down to Lanqueshire to find work there," Sara said. "She's just their sort of woman. I like to keep the lads happy and feeling secure, and I won't allow catfights."

Soon, the Ravens' crews returned, and the common room filled. Old friends greeted them, glad to meet the newest Rowdy. Huw and Culyn brought out their instruments and regaled them with the music of Eynier. Culyn was last seen following a lovely Raven up the stairs, laughing with her over some jest she'd made.

Huw and Jack had gone up not long after Culyn, and Beau remained standing at the bar, nursing his ale. Sara closed the common room. The three of them talked as she finished wiping down the bar and Lackland asked, "Whatever happened to Fair Ellen?"

"Oh, you know how it goes. She's married to a silk merchant and just popped out her fourth," replied Sara. "The good women all go that way, eventually."

"You didn't leave the road until Matt died, and you had to manage on your own here. Mags won't, nor will Babs or Annie Fitz. They'll never leave the trade," replied Lackland. "Too bad; Ellen was a merry lass."

"My sword slowed. Matt slowed, too, and it killed him. But I miss the road." She sighed. "Feeling lonely, Lackland?" Sara's question took him by surprise. "I have a big bed, should you wish for companionship. What fun we had when you were down this way with the king during the troubles!"

"Now you mention it, I do recall your bed was definitely big enough for two," said Lackland with a smile.

"Two or three," she said, winking at Beau, who choked on his ale and looked at Julian to see what his reaction was. "I'm a woman with a large heart to go with my large bed."

Lackland just shrugged with his charismatic smile. "Two or three," he agreed, his eyes sparkling. He sipped his ale and grinned at his friend's shocked expression. "It's a spacious bed, Beau."

CHAPTER 14

THE ROWDIES LEFT Bekenberg at dawn, leading the three horses they were taking back with them. As they traveled, they laughed at a silly but imaginative ditty Huw had come up with at the expense of Lackland and Beau's dignity. It involved his take on their escapades of the previous night in Sara's capacious bed.

Apparently, although her bed was large, the walls were thin. Sara had been quite enthusiastic in her appreciation of the moment.

The two grinned somewhat sheepishly and rode along, everyone feeling a sense of relief that the long journey was nearly over. Soon they were discussing their homesickness.

"God help me, I even miss Mickey's fussing," said Huw. "He drives me mad trying to keep me from 'sinking into a decline,' as he always says. Everyone knows *he's* the one who needs worrying about."

"Since John passed away, he has no other chicks in his nest." Lackland's eyes twinkled. "He's a maternal man, don't you know."

Everyone laughed, and Culyn said, "I look forward to meeting this paragon of motherhood!"

"He's a nag." Huw's grimace turned into a fond chuckle. "But he's a good soul. For all he's near on seventy, he's in amazingly good shape."

By evening, they'd found a grove of oak along the road to camp in and settled in for the night. Lackland roasted the brace of quail Culyn had snared, along with some wintered-over potatoes they bought in Bekenberg. Afterward, they listened as Huw told an epic tale.

"I love a good romance that ends happily," commented Lackland as he bedded down for the night. He yawned and was soon asleep. The others stayed up for a while, but soon they too went to their bedrolls.

Lackland awoke in the dead of night to a sword at his throat.

"Get up. Drop the knife." The voice was quiet but familiar and hard as nails. "Drop it." She wore men's clothes, but it was Lora Saunders.

Lackland laid down the knife that had sprung to his hand. The sword stayed at his throat.

"You and I have unfinished business." Lora's voice mocked him. "Keep it quiet, or I'll slit your throat now and be done with it. Get up. You're going for a midnight stroll."

Slowly, Lackland rose from his bedroll. He reached for his breeches, slipped them on, and jammed his feet into his boots, her sword at his throat all the while.

Shifting her sword to his back, she said, "Now walk with me."

Confused and afraid, he stumbled along in the dark. Periodically he felt the stab of the sword's point as he stumbled or paused in his footing, unsure of the way. "This way," she said, as she shoved him down a faint trail. They walked for some time until two rough shelters loomed in the shadowy forest. One housed her horse.

"I followed you from the lake to the Raven's Nest. Then I figured out every place you'd likely stop on your way back to Limpwater. You men are so predictable." Her voice was harsh as she taunted him. "You picked the perfect place to camp, from my point of view. Now, take off your clothes." She prodded him again with her sword.

He obeyed, noticing several large spots of blood on his shirt. "You know, this won't make it easy to satisfy you," Lackland said wryly. "I don't work well under pressure." As he stood shivering in the cold of the late April night, it was evident he was not aroused by her style of seduction. "Perhaps a small fire would warm things up." An undercurrent of fear made it difficult to keep his voice even.

"Yes, and alert your lover you're here," she smirked. "I'll warm you well enough myself, so don't worry."

"My lover? I have no lover right now." Lackland's mystified confession drew a snort from his captor. "I've had no lover since I left Belle in January. Well, except for Sara last night, but that was just for old times' sake." His breath hissed as her sword sliced him neatly across the chest.

"You'd better get used to working under pressure, you bastard. You aren't leaving this place alive unless you do. Now lie down there." She pointed at a rumpled bedroll. Her saddle was at the head, as was usual. However, several other saddles were stacked there, along with a sack full of lumpy objects.

That struck him as odd, but he was in pain and too bewildered to think about it. Numbly, Lackland did as she said.

She stood watching him. "I saw you and Beau playing in the lake with the new southerner after you killed my firedrake. Do you and Beau talk about Mags when you're riding each other? Do you think she knows that you and Beau are lovers? Do you both ride her at the same time as you two did Sara the Fat Whore last night? I watched the whole thing through the window. I was on the porch roof."

Lackland stared at her, at a loss for words.

"Your hands were all over each other. The fat woman was just your excuse to be together." She undressed, keeping her sword on him. "I figured it out when I saw how you and Beau couldn't keep your eyes off each other when you were swimming. You could barely keep from touching each other. I rather expected you to have a threesome with the new lad, bonding over the corpse of my poor firedrake. Traynor was mine, you know. You killed him." She stepped out of her breeches.

"Your firedrake? How does a person own a thing like that?" Anxiety and confusion numbed his wits, making his speech slow, thick-sounding. A memory dawned, reminding him of her father. "You named him after your father's horse?"

"Of course, I did. I fed him, and he protected me from highwaymen like Traynor did my dad," she said. A cold light filled her eyes.

"You fed him? You mean, you hunted for him?" Disbelief intensified his confusion. "You brought him meat? Deer and such?"

"Yes, in a way. You could say I brought him meat. I brought highwaymen to him. They all thought they would lie with me and then go their merry way. When I finished with them, I led them to the lake. Traynor fed on them and their horses." Lora delivered the horror in matter-of-fact tones. "You took him away from me too." Her sword flashed, and a long line of blood appeared on Lackland's belly, deep but not gutting him. "I followed you for a while when you went south. I knew I'd get you some day, and I knew this would be the place."

For a moment, Lackland had no words, barely able to comprehend her revelations. "God in heaven...you've gone over the edge, Lora." Only now did he understand the danger he was in. "You've gone mad."

Her harsh laughter cut through the night, a sound bordering the edge of insanity. "You have no idea." She had nearly finished undressing when he knocked her legs out from under her, and the sword flew out of her hand. "Bastard!" she shouted as they struggled for the sword.

Lackland finally got control of her, holding her down, but she held a knife to his throat, her eyes glittering. "I thought you'd try something like that, so I placed this sharp little sticker where I'd be able to reach it."

She moved suggestively beneath him, spreading her legs and wrapping them around his thighs. "Go ahead. Stick it in me. You know you want to." He let go of her and rolled onto his back. She rolled with him, her face only inches from his, her knife under his ear.

"You're a right bastard, Lackland. You sleep with everyone else and refuse to sleep with me."

Her knife flashed in the moonlight, and a line of blood appeared across his throat. Several more slices made blood trickle across his chest. He gasped as thin lines of blood appeared on his thighs, horribly close to his manhood. Then the knife was back under his left ear, drawing blood. He felt the pain keenly in all his slashes. But more than anything else, he feared she would castrate him.

"This won't do," she said with a mad grin. "Why are you still struggling?"

Holding her knife under his ear, she reached into her saddlebag with her free hand and came out with a length of rope, looped at one end with a slip knot. "I can tie you up if it's what you like." Lora grabbed his right arm and slipped the loop over it one-handed, tying his wrist to the sapling that made part of her lean-to. "I've had a lot of practice at this. I knew you'd need to be tied up at some point. You lads always do."

Her knife stayed at his throat the whole time, and her eyes glittered. "If you're really good to me, I'll leave the rest of you free, so you can treat me like a woman should be." She pointed the knife between his legs. "Now get that up and make love to me. You owe it to me. I can't get work anywhere because of you." Her voice went hoarse with rage. "You owe it to me. Make love to me and tell me I'm the best woman you ever had, or I'll be the last woman you'll ever have."

"What makes you think it's my fault you can't get work?" He clenched his jaw, refusing to cry out as Lora first moved to lie on top of him, and then straddled him, holding the knife at his throat.

The wounds on his thighs and his belly burned and stung as she lay on him, tearing them open. Still, he gasped out the truth. "I've never spoken to anyone about what passed between us, other than Annie and Babs. They've told no one. They respect me too much to tell my secrets." Pain such as he'd never experienced drew tears, burning his eyes, yet he refused to give in to them.

"I've been run out of every crew I've been with since that night, you bastard. You left me alone in your bed like I was dirt. Then you jumped straight into the sack with those two old hags. You had the strength to do the two of them, but none to spare for me. I have nowhere to go. I have no home. I have no one! I have nothing and no one, thanks to you."

Lackland flinched as she drew blood across his throat again.

"Annie said I tried to rape you. Men can't be raped, everyone knows that. It was a lie! You can't rape a man! Men are in rut all the time. They always want it."

"You don't have to do this, you know," Lackland said. Regret that he would die in such an ungraceful way was overlaid with deep sadness that it had come to this point. "I'll give you what you want." He tried to get more comfortable, but he was in agony and lying on a rock or a root or something. The cuts on his back tore open each time he moved. "Let me get more comfortable. There's a stone killing my back." With her still straddled across his lap, getting into the better position was painful. Lora made it as difficult as she could, grinning her insane smirk all the while, holding her knife at his throat.

Finally, he was sitting up, leaning against her saddle. He felt a little more comfortable even though his right wrist was still tied to the tree. "You want me to be your lover tonight." He tried not to sigh, desperate to give her no reason to cut him again. "All right, I'll do as best I can. Don't expect much from me, though." Lackland made his voice conciliatory. "I'm sure I can make you happy."

"And you'll stay with me," she said fiercely. "You'll stay with me, and we'll go down to Lanqueshire and get work there." She wrapped her legs around his waist, leaning her head against his bloody chest and holding the knife under his arm. "Promise me you won't try to escape! Swear it!"

Lackland was silent, unwilling to commit to such a thing.

"I know you won't break a promise. You're far too noble!" Lora drew blood under his arm this time.

"I'll do as you say." Lackland felt a terrible weakness coming over him. Blood-loss and the near-freezing cold of the mid-April night took their toll on him. He thought he must owe her something...he could have done something long ago to change her life when she was a child, and her father was away so much...something...but it was too late. His mind was clouded; fuzzy. For some reason, he couldn't think well. Unable to argue, he agreed. "I won't try to escape. I promise."

"Promise you'll stay with me forever and never leave me alone." Lora's voice was almost like a child's, lost and afraid.

Lackland nodded reluctantly. "I'll do as you say, but this is cold and loveless. Where is the romance in this, Lora? There isn't any affection binding us, only your pain and suffering and my debt of friendship to your father."

She hadn't heard him. She only heard him agree to her wishes. Lora hugged him and kissed his unwilling mouth joyfully. "I knew if I could just get you alone, you'd understand! We'll go down to Lanqueshire. No one knows us there. We can hire on to a crew of mercs, and we'll be together. Think of it! Bold Lora Saunders and Julian Lackland, together and living happily ever after. We'll be famous!"

Lora laid her head on his bloody chest, with her knife at his ribs. Lackland unenthusiastically put his free arm around her, deciding to just get on with it and, at least, perhaps get some warmth in the night's chill. Nothing mattered; he would bleed to death before they could leave there. He felt hopeful at the idea. The night and Lora and the darkness of the forest—everything was too surreal, a dream he couldn't wake from. Lightheaded and trembling with cold, he just wanted to get on with dying.

"I love you, Julian! I'm going to make you so happy. You'll see." She set the knife down beside them and leaned back, reaching between his legs to fondle him, still astride his knees. As she did so, a bolt transfixed her, piercing her heart. Behind an oak, some fifty feet away, stood Beau, nocking another arrow.

Lora clutched her chest, where the arrow had protruded through from her back. Gasping for breath, she tried to stand but fell forward onto Lackland's chest, her hands still clutching the arrowhead. Beau lowered his bow when he saw she'd collapsed.

Lackland's free arm went around her, cradling her, his eyes wide with shock.

"You promised…." Her eyes were those of a lonely, scared child as they glazed over. Julian held her with his one arm, dazed by the turn of events.

Beau lifted the dead girl away, laying her to the side. His eyes widened as he took in the bloody wounds crisscrossing Julian's body. Fresh blood welled from the countless cuts and slashes on his thighs when he removed Lora's body. Beau's breath hissed as he saw what she'd done to his throat.

"Oh, God." He swallowed. "God in heaven." Anxiously, Beau cut his arm free. "Julian…what has she done to you?" Blood covered Lackland's legs and loins, but in the dark, it was impossible for Beau to see the extent of his injuries. "You're bleeding to death." He tore his shirt into strips to bind Lackland's wounds, wrapping his throat, trying to cover the deep wounds as best as he could. "I've got to get you back to camp. Then we'll get you stitched up."

Lackland had no words. A ragged sob escaped him, and mutely, he clung to Beau as a drowning man might cling to a branch.

"Julian? Are you all in one piece?" Beau waited until Lackland could get himself under control.

"She cut me up, but not too badly, and nowhere important. She had plans for that part of me," Lackland finally said. He wiped his eyes with the back of his hand and looked at Lora. "Oh god, Beau! I held this child on my knee when she was a toddler." His voice broke. "She was the sweetest little thing, all dark curls, and big eyes. I don't know what went wrong that she should have come to this. She was trying to find some way to feel loved." Julian's face crumpled, and he bit back his sobs. "I don't know why she chose me."

"Shh…save your strength." Beau held him tightly, trying to warm and calm him. "We'll talk about this later, I promise." Worry made his voice rough. "It's a good thing we still have that brandy your royal cousin gave us. You'll need a good swallow or two. You're in shock."

Lackland tried to put his clothes on over his bloody bandages, but Beau ended up having to dress him as best he could. With his teeth chattering, Julian explained most of what had happened. He didn't tell Beau what Lora had said about the two of them. "I must have owed her something," he finished. "It was because of me that Billy sent her away from the Rowdies." He tried to hide the raw guilt and self-loathing poisoning his soul.

"You owed her nothing. She tried to rape you that night, and she was raping you tonight." Beau rubbed Julian's arms to get the circulation going, avoiding his wounds. "She would have killed you. She had to know you'd never have left with her."

"I promised her," Julian said, miserably. "She knew I wouldn't break my promise." Tears ran down his face. "She made me swear."

"Oh, Julian. In some ways, you're the most innocent man. You always believe the best about people. They're never as good as you think they are." Holding him close one last time, Beau's voice was fierce. "We need to get your wounds fixed up and get you warmed. I'm afraid tonight's work will be your death."

Beau offered Lackland his hand to pull him to his feet but had to lift him off the ground. Once on his feet, Julian could walk, though he was lightheaded.

Beau found Lora's cloak and around them both, hoping to get him warm. "I heard what Lora said about you and me," he said as Julian tried to get his balance.

Julian froze, dizzy and struggling to pull his fractured thoughts together. "She wasn't right in her head, Beau. I don't want her words to turn you away from me. She was spying on us with Sara."

"I know. I heard her, and she was right about some things." Beau chuckled and placed Julian's arms around him. "Hold on to me, so you don't fall. Let's walk now. We need to talk seriously later, I promise." He gently urged Julian to walk, and he did, although he was slow and couldn't manage well. Hoping to make Julian laugh, he said, "She was nuts. We've never once discussed Mags, although I eyeball your arse regularly. I had a lovely view of it last night, bad boys that we are. It's one of the finer arses I've ever seen."

Julian laughed weakly. "People keep telling me this." He was unsure if it was relief or loss of blood that made him so giddy.

Beau half-carried Lackland back to the camp. The other three were so shocked at Lackland's appearance, they could hardly speak. Undressing him again, Jack and Huw did the best they could to clean his wounds by lantern light while Culyn stitched him up.

He was generous with the medicinal salve as he wrapped Julian's throat, deciding not to attempt suturing it. The brandy helped Lackland, both as an antiseptic and to ease his pain. Beau forced him to drink several good tots, hoping it would settle his nerves.

After they had finally gotten Julian to sleep, Beau insisted he would guard him while the others buried Lora. They brought her horse and a stash of saddles and loot back to their camp. The lumpy sack by her bedroll contained all the trinkets that should have been found in the firedrake's den.

The four of them talked over the events of the night until dawn. Beau told as much as he knew of what happened. "I heard her whisper, so I followed." He described how he'd been unable to shoot her until she laid down the knife and leaned away from Lackland. "I feared the bolt would go through her and pierce Lackland too, or her sword would slip, and she would kill him." Misery, anger, fear—raw emotions burst from him in a torrent of words.

By the time Beau finished, Huw was enraged and ready to dig Lora up to kill her again. Culyn watched in amazement as his usually quiet and reserved father paced back and forth, describing the hell he hoped Old Grim would put Lora through, astonished to see his father so livid.

Eventually, they settled down and got some rest before they left that place.

They all agreed Lackland needed a healer, the sooner, the better. There was no healer in Bekenberg, so they had no choice but to get him to Somber Flats. They broke camp after a few hours of sleep and began the trek north. Lackland's wounds made it difficult for him to ride, and it was soon clear he wasn't healing well.

After two days of riding, he was feverish and sometimes incoherent, although they washed his wounds with brandy at every stop. Huw was afraid he had wound-fever.

Beau said, "It's only half a day's ride now to Somber Flats. Whatever it takes, we must do it." They tied him to his saddle, knowing he was in terrible pain, but also knowing only a healing priestess could save him.

They rode as hard as they dared, but when they arrived in Somber Flats, the chapel infirmary was closed, and no one knew where the priestess was. Mary was behind the bar at the Powder Keg, and she told them several babies were due on the local outlying farms. Most likely, the priestess was helping with a birth, so it could be two days before she returned.

After a quick discussion, they agreed Julian didn't have two days. They had no choice but to continue to Limpwater, generally a four-hour ride. Traveling in the rain and darkness through a treacherous part of the trade road, it became a seven-hour journey. They took turns holding the reins and leading Lackland's horse. Riding by the light of a lantern, they finally arrived in Limpwater. At dawn on the fifteenth day of April, they rode into the courtyard behind Billy's Revenge with Lackland tied to his saddle, delirious and raving.

Sister Leona immediately came and used her healing majik, removing the infection and healing the many still-open wounds. Then she turned to healing him of pneumonia. Once he was at last sleeping peacefully, she told Beau and Mags that Lackland would survive his ordeal. They stayed at his bedside until he woke.

Sister Leona couldn't keep his wounds from scarring him, as he'd gone too long on the road before her healing. She praised Culyn's skill at suturing the worst of Lackland's injuries, telling him he had likely saved Julian's life.

She whispered instructions to Beau, who hovered over Julian's bedside. "He'll bear many scars from this ordeal, and the ones you can see are the least. He's in for a long, troubled time, but he'll recover physically in a few days and have his full strength back in about two weeks." She held Beau's gaze, her words solemn. "You love him. You must encourage him to talk about whatever is on his mind. It will be hard for you, but don't press him to talk, and don't try to comfort him physically until he tells you he's ready. Do you understand?"

Beau nodded. "I think I do." His gaze turned out the window. "I'll make sure Mags and Belle understand too."

The next morning, Lackland woke and was, as Chicken Mickey put it, "sitting up and taking nourishment." Mick then clucked over him like a mother hen until Julian got out of bed just to get away from his mothering. With nothing else to do, he went down to the common room to sit alone by the hearth and read, taking his book but staring at the fire.

Culyn Owyn was promptly accepted as a Rowdy. He was the kind of fighter Billy was looking for, smart, calm-headed, and deadly. He immediately earned the merc name of "Fair Culyn," as he was easily the most handsome man to join the Rowdies since Davey Llewellyn.

Culyn agreed to send a letter to his mother in Clythe to see if any others wished to come north. "Though if any do, they'll be folks like me, with a stigma of some sort. The valley isn't kind to lads who love other lads or ladies who wish to swing swords. Any stigma is hard down there. But they will fight the harder for you because you accept them."

Huw finally made several good ballads out of their adventures, although nothing resembled the actual events. "Lackland and the Witch of the Woods" became popular, despite having only a tenuous basis in truth, the way Huw told it. Lackland enjoyed it when he heard the ballad but wondered who it was about. Regardless, it was dramatic and made a great romantic tale.

"The Murder of Crows" chronicled the events of the demise of Clan Grefyn, but pointed directly to Earl Lyn Pyndrys, Duke Amstyce Grefyn, and Gwartney of Lanqueshire.

The hysterically bawdy tale, "Rowdies Bouncing on the Raven's Bed," rather dismayed Beau. Though it named no names, only two gentlemen Rowdies were "fair-haired lads with eyes of blue." The crew cast many a knowing glance his way while they hooted with laughter and thumped the tables in appreciation.

Despite his having healed from his wounds, the ordeal had changed Lackland; the difference in him was clear to everyone. He avoided being alone with any woman, especially Belle and Mags. The only person Julian felt comfortable with was Beau, although he maintained a steady banter of nonsense and fluff to cover his depression. Huw and Culyn did their best with him, but they knew he would be a long time getting over what Lora had done to him.

Jack returned to Castleton and his life with Merry Kat as soon as it was clear Lackland was back on his feet. "Don't let it kill you," he told him, speaking in Eynierish, as he sat on his horse in the courtyard. "Don't let what she did destroy you. Kat and Bess know what you're going through. They've been through hell too. You can talk to Bess."

Lackland nodded, unable to look Jack in the eye, but he smiled and replied, also in Eynierish, "You're getting to be as bad as Mickey."

Jack rolled his eyes and rode off through the rain.

Looking up at the windows facing the rear of Billy's Revenge, Lackland had the sudden urge to get on his horse and ride as far and as fast as he could. But where would he go? His mind followed him everywhere, and he couldn't escape it.

Seeing Mickey headed in his direction, Lackland turned and quickly walked up to his room, shutting the door and locking it behind him.

CHAPTER 15

LACKLAND HAD JUST returned from guarding a shipment of casks to the cider mill in Dervy, a pleasant job taking perhaps half a day. Belle and George rode ahead of Lackland and Huw on the jaunt back to Limpwater and Billy's Revenge. High in spirits, the banter among the three elicited many smiles and chuckles from Lackland. He was noticeably quiet but enjoyed their witty quips.

It was his first job since he'd returned gravely injured from the Eynier Valley two weeks previously. Billy feared it was too soon for Lackland to be going out, but the knight had insisted. His temper flashed to the surface as it was wont to do. "I'll go mad if you don't let me get away from Mick. He's mothering me to death. There's no escaping him!"

Billy wasn't the only one who'd noticed how unpredictable Lackland's moods were. He'd become exceedingly reserved. Belle didn't know what to think, so she maintained a professional distance from him.

Lackland thought he could see her drifting toward Culyn but couldn't muster the desire to stop her. With his mind so twisted over things he couldn't change, he felt it would be for the best. Culyn was a good man, wiser than his years. Belle deserved that kind of man in her life.

Beau and Mags, along with Culyn and three others, were off on a trip to Castleton with a silk merchant and would return before supper. All the other crews were due back that afternoon too.

Lackland settled into a bathtub full of steaming hot water, unable to avoid looking down at his new scars. The heat of the water helped him sort through his muddled thoughts. He would have to talk to Belle some time but didn't know how to open the conversation or even what to say.

"Lackland, can we talk?" George soaked in another tub. He was the oldest Rowdy still working, being fifty-two. He'd been off on a long job when they brought Lackland home and hadn't heard the complete story of Lackland's kidnapping.

Lackland nodded, resigned to the fact George would meddle where he shouldn't.

"We've been friends for a long time."

Lackland winced. George had always been the master of stating the obvious. "Yes, we have," he replied, smiling brightly. "I've also noticed that."

"Look, I know something happened while you were away on that long job with Huw. I heard some of it, but you're doing yourself harm, holding it in as you are. You need to talk to someone."

Lackland shrugged but said nothing. He knew George only wanted to help but could never confide in him. He was as bad as Mickey.

"You were so quiet today. You might as well not have been there."

"But I was. I had your back, just like always. I had nothing to add to the conversation. That's all." Resentment surged, and Lackland attempted to bury it.

"I know you had my back. I wouldn't doubt it for a minute." George's offended tone made Julian smother a grin. "It's just you're as silent as Huw and as jumpy as Mick. It's not like you. I'm concerned."

Lackland's smile faded, anger sparking in his eyes. "I'm sorry. You're right. I am jumpy, and I'm not in the mood to talk. When Beau decides it's time for me to purge myself of the horrors, we talk. It's as much as I'm comfortable with, so don't press me for more. Huw and Culyn know what happened and will explain it if you ask them." He abruptly got out of the tub. "I'll be fine, you'll see. I was sick with pneumonia, and you know how it affects you for a while afterward, so...thank you anyway, George. I'm just not in the mood to discuss it."

As Lackland dried himself off, George got a good look at the myriad red welts that now crisscrossed Lackland's chest and throat, the long ropy scars on his belly, and the smaller ones under his ear that his mercenary's tail usually disguised. His thighs were a disfigured mess too.

When Lackland turned his back, George plainly saw the scars where he'd been prodded. "My dear old friend...who tortured you so? Was it the bloody Lanques?"

George's horror and angry concern were more than Julian could endure. "Ask Huw, Beau, or Culyn what happened. They were there. It's over, and I don't want to talk about it. But thank you for caring." He threw his clothes on and ran out of the bathhouse as fast as he could, heading up to his room.

Julian lay on his bed, too worked up to rest, thanks to George's well-meaning concern. He couldn't think about anything except how he could have done things differently with Lora. *I could have fought back more. I could have grabbed the knife and turned it on her any time. Instead, I let her do this to me. Why?* His mind wouldn't stop, wouldn't let up.

A quiet knock on his door followed by Belle's voice asking to come in got his attention.

Sighing, he got up and opened the door. "I'm not really well right now. Maybe I tried to do too much too soon. I just need to rest," he said politely and tried to close the door.

She pushed past him and sat on his bed. Patting the spot beside her, she smiled reassuringly at him.

"I see. You're not taking no for an answer," said Lackland as he closed the door. "Would it make a difference if I said I'm not fit for companionship of an intimate nature?" His charming smile had a slightly crooked quality as if he were working hard at maintaining it.

"I'm not here for that, my dear friend," she said. "Sit here beside me. I won't pressure you in any way, and I promise I'll go downstairs for dinner with my hair un-mussed!"

"That will surely ruin my reputation," he said with an attempt at humor that fell flat, as he gingerly sat next to her.

"Julian, what you endured that night in the woods scarred you in more ways than the obvious. I saw what you looked like when they brought you back. Culyn told me Lora cut you up on purpose. I know you don't blame me, yet you can't relax around me or any woman. But I care for you as a friend." Concern filled her dark eyes, but she didn't reach out to touch him.

"We had an understanding, and it meant a lot to me. You've been avoiding me. Don't cut me out of your life, please. I want to help you."

Lackland was silent. His shoulders shook, and he was unable to speak for a few moments. "I don't know how to tell you what happened. You must ask Beau. He'll tell you."

"He did," she said solemnly. "Julian, you did nothing wrong. You didn't deserve what happened to you. You're killing yourself with guilt, trying to tell yourself you could have stopped her." She reached for his hand.

Instinctively, he drew his hand back. He looked at Belle, seeing only honest concern and then turned his eyes away. "It's not even the torture that kills my soul. I let her do it to me, don't you see? I let her do this to me because of who she was. She was Tom Saunders's little girl, the joy of his life." Guilt was stark on his face though he tried not to show it.

Belle nodded, encouraging him to continue.

He sighed. "I know I could have done more to stop her when she started cutting me. But it was my fault she'd gone mad."

Belle hid the shock she felt at his misconception, realizing it was part of the trauma. "Julian, she was verging on madness before she ever laid eyes on you, if we had only known it then. The signs were there in the way she behaved toward all the men, treating them as if they were her personal stable of stallions and refusing to take 'no' for an answer." Belle thought for a moment. "Maybe you could have stopped her that night, but you had an attachment to her. You knew and liked her father, and you kept thinking it was all going to go away. That she would be normal and let you go if you were just polite and nice to her."

He began to relax, speaking almost to himself. "Yes! You understand. I thought exactly that. I was sure she would decide she'd scared me enough and let me go. But after she said she had been luring highwaymen for the firedrake to feed on, I knew a madness of some sort had taken her. I fought back then, but she had a knife hidden. That gave me most of these." He raised his shirt. "They aren't the worst. You should see what she did to my legs. But in a peculiar way, I'm glad she cut me."

"Julian, why?" Despite her dismay, Belle didn't reach out to touch him, knowing he couldn't stand it. "Why did you deserve such punishment?"

"Because I rejected her and then the world abandoned her. Believe me, I've thought about this long and hard. I think I finally know why she went so badly astray. When she came here, she had nothing. She just wanted to be important to someone. She thought if she were famous, it would fill the emptiness."

Belle started to speak, but Lackland said, "No, listen to me. What band of mercs is more famous than the Rowdies? Of course, she decided to become a Rowdy. But her clumsy attempts at gaining fame failed, and they sent her away from here. She couldn't keep a job because of her instability, and then the only friend she had was a firedrake. And then I insisted we kill it, not knowing it was her pet. You see? I took everything away from her, leaving her with nothing, no one, and nowhere to go."

He looked out the window bleakly, not seeing the view. "What's even more cruel, I didn't have the slightest idea of what I'd done to her. Once she left Billy's Revenge, I forgot all about her. I dismissed her from my mind as completely as if she didn't exist."

Lackland's eyes turned from whatever inner landscape he'd been seeing, and he looked earnestly at Belle, trying desperately to convey to her what he now understood. "But she did exist, Belle. She existed, and she was a human being driven into madness by my actions, which meant nothing at all to me." He ran his fingers over his throat, feeling the ropy welts. "The scars remind me to be kind to people. You never know what they might have lost."

For a moment, Belle was speechless, trying to understand the complicated grief that gripped Lackland. Finally, she said, "We aren't busy tomorrow, so Mags and I asked Billy if we could picnic by the river if the weather is as pleasant as today was. You can be with me with no strings attached, and I'll protect you from people asking questions." She patted his hand and stood as he reluctantly nodded agreement. He would much rather have stayed in his room while the others went without him, and she knew it.

Smiling, Belle said, "You'd better come down for supper, or George and Mickey will be up here wanting to know if they should send for Friar Robert to give you the last rites. Mick swears you should still be in bed, and George agrees with him. If they see you with me, they'll assume you're back to normal."

"Oh God, not Mick and George together— please not that. Kill me now." He followed her down to the common room.

They sat with Beau and Mags, chatted about silly nothings through the meal, and then played a game of stones, which Mags won.

After dinner that night, Billy announced the next day would be a proper day off for every Rowdy in town, and there would be a picnic by the river. He was covering for the fact that there was no work for the next few days, which worried him, but a picnic would keep folks from fretting about the temporary lack of jobs.

They went upstairs, and at Lackland's door, Belle kissed his tensed cheek. To his relief, she resumed walking to her own room. Confused and worried about feeling such a reprieve, he shut the door behind him. Then he lit the lamp and added more coal to the fire in the hearth, as he couldn't stand to be in the dark. A part of him knew it wasn't normal, but he thought if he just learned to live with it, it would get better.

Sleep came fitfully as it always did now, and he woke up off and on, thinking he was still in the forest. Sometimes, he couldn't tell if he was dreaming or not.

He couldn't stop thinking that although Lora didn't cut his manhood, she might as well have. His reflection interested him, the mirror revealing the lattice of scars. He worried that his fear of intimacy meant he was mind-touched. No matter how he tried, he could find no way to change it. Every night since he woke from his illness, he found himself in front of his mirror, staring at his scars, wondering how to get past his problem.

Billy Ninefingers was up at dawn, as always. He swept the floor near the great hearth and nearly jumped out of his skin as he came upon Lackland sitting in the corner. The knight held a book but stared into the fire. "God Almighty, Lackland! You gave me a turn," he said, his eyes wide. "I wasn't expecting to find anyone sitting there."

"I just felt the urge to read," replied Lackland, knowing it was a weak excuse. "You know how it is."

"Well, no, I don't, actually. I read a bit after supper, like normal people. But, if you say so." Billy bustled back to the kitchen, where Bess was in the middle of the day's baking.

He closed the door behind him. "This little plan of Lady Mags's had better work. Lackland almost gave me a heart attack, lurking in the dark by the fire like that. If getting him off to the river for a frolic in the reeds with Belle doesn't help, I don't know what will."

"Billy, you don't know what it's like to experience such a thing. Neither did Julian until it happened to him. No one ever does." Bess worked her dough and turned it on her floured board. "That girl destroyed his sense of who he is. Don't be surprised if their plan doesn't work." She gave her dough a good thump. "You made me whole again. But think how long it took." She met her husband's gaze. "Five years, Billy—all that time we could have had was wasted while you struggled to save me from my demons."

"Not wasted, love. Never wasted."

Bess smiled. "Lackland just needs time and understanding. He can do his work just fine, so don't worry. It's his personal life as will suffer."

"I loved you the minute I laid eyes on you when I was a new merc of sixteen summers. Then, after my injury I was lucky you would give me the time of day, poor crippled lad that I was." He pinched her plump bottom as he put his arms around her.

"Crippled lad, my arse," replied Bess, love illuminating her flour-dusted features. "Bastard John, God rest him, wounded your hand, but your wits were as sharp as ever. Besides, the difference in our ages doesn't seem so much now."

"You're a good woman, Bess." Billy hugged her again, as flour puffed in little clouds around them.

"Well, get out of my kitchen and let me get on with my work, silly man, or there'll be no food for the picnic today." Bess kissed her husband, whose embrace had become too confining. "Shoo!"

Only Billy Ninefingers and Chicken Mickey remained behind to keep the doors to the inn open. Gertie Smith and her husband wouldn't leave their work in the smithy, but Bess took their young ones as always. Bess was every child's mother while their parents worked, and she loved them all.

CHAPTER 16

LACKLAND FOLLOWED the others out past Gertie's forge. The sounds of hammers ringing in the morning echoed, a rhythmic counterpoint to the songbirds in the orchard.

Bess and Gertie's youngest children ran on ahead, laughing and chattering while Annie Fitz and Babs carried their babies. All the younger children wore sunbonnets, making their little faces look like flowers, touching Lackland's heart in a way he couldn't identify. These children would never suffer what Lora or the children in Ludwellyn had, and he would give his life to ensure that.

The four older children, all around nine years old, but not yet old enough to attend school, attempted to behave like proper young Rowdies in their wide-brimmed straw hats. The procession looked like a flock of merry butterflies running down the path, with everyone wearing their summer finery.

Among the adults, sun hats also abounded, gaily bedecked with flowers and scarves for the ladies. For the gentlemen, simple flat-brimmed straw hats shaded faces that had seen little sun so far that year.

Soon they had passed through the hilly field where sheep grazed, and finally, after walking down the steep path to the lower meadow, they arrived at the river's side. They quickly spread blankets on the grass, each staking their claim to the best spots in the shade. Full of energy, the children ran, tossing several beanbags amongst themselves.

Though the river was still running high with the spring melt, the meadow was dry from several days of good weather. Seemingly overnight, the shade trees had burst with bright green leaves. The day promised to be warm, a harbinger of the long-awaited summer.

The adults lounged for a while in the morning's warmth and then began their own game of toss-the-beanbags. Laughter echoed, as toss-the-beanbag became hide-and-seek, which became a game of chase-and-tag.

At last, exhausted, they rested and chatted a while before enjoying the picnic lunch Bess had prepared. After they had eaten, full stomachs and the warmth of the day lulled the adults to nap in the shade with the babies and younger children, while the older ones ran off exploring.

"Don't go too far," called Bess. "Stay where you can hear us, and we can hear you. And don't go near the river!"

Four heads nodded earnestly, saying, "Yes, ma'am," before running off to see the bird's nest young Eddie MacNess had found in a crabapple tree.

Lackland lay beside Belle on a blanket spread under a maple tree near the brush marking the riverbank. They were apart from everyone else, which he rather enjoyed. Gazing up at the sky through the leaves, he listened to the river and the children playing, unable to sleep, and not at all in the mood to talk.

Belle drifted off to sleep. Julian gazed at her peaceful face, feeling a peculiar sadness as he did so. He ignored the lingering fear that he would never be able to make love to anyone ever again, forever soiled by the memory of Lora and what she'd done to him.

The children's voices grew nearer, and he could hear their conversations. They seemed so happy and secure, and indeed, they were. With Bess and Billy taking care of them while their parents worked, they had a loving family and security. Not the sort of life Lora had, handed from family to family after Tom's death.

Eddie MacNess had apparently climbed onto a fallen log and was trying to impress Estelle Smith with his ability to balance on it. Their laughter tugged at Lackland's heartstrings; it was so innocent and free.

He was almost dozing off when he heard Estelle say, "No, Eddie! You'll fall in!" followed by a splash.

Leaping to his feet, he quickly shucked his boots and ran to where Estelle frantically called, "Grab the branch! Grab the branch!"

As he ran, five-year-old Mary MacNess met him. "Lackland!" she screamed when she saw him. "Eddie fell in, and the river has taken him!"

Beau was on Lackland's heels as they arrived at the riverbank. Eddie clung to a floating branch that carried him swiftly down the river. The two men dove into the fast-moving water, gasping as the cold sucked the breath out of them.

While the Limpwater was not an unusually wide river, it was deep and frigid, originating in the snow-capped mountains to the north. Ignoring the chill, they pressed on, swimming as fast as they could.

Both Lackland and Beau were strong swimmers, and they soon caught up with the branch, just in time to see the terrified child lose his grip and sink beneath the surface of the river.

Adults lined the bank, running along, following their progress. Bess called to her son hysterically, while Mags and Johnny Malone forcibly restrained her from leaping into the river. Both Beau and Lackland dove under, searching. Finally, Lackland spied Eddie, and grabbing his shirt, he pulled the boy up to the surface, coughing and choking.

"Don't fight me! Don't fight! Just let me take you to your mother," Lackland said urgently, as the panicked boy struggled. "Don't worry, I have you safe. It'll be fine, you'll see." Fighting the cold, he finally got the boy to the bank and into his brother Brand's arms. Lackland rested, clinging exhausted to the bank.

"Where's Beau?" Mags's anguished cry made Lackland turn and look back at the river where there was no sign of him.

Something snapped in Julian's chest. His eyes turned to the branch Eddie had clung to, seeing something odd tangled in it. With no further thought, he turned and swam for it.

Shouts of "Beau's gone!" and "Lackland, you fool! You'll die too!" came to Julian as people ran along the bank, following and calling to him. Strength came from somewhere, and he followed the huge branch, traveling downstream with the current of the river.

Racing as hard as he could, he swam until he reached the strange thing he'd seen. There it was— Beau's hair, tangled in the branch.

Pulling his knife from its sheath, Julian cut Beau's hair free. He let the knife fall to the bottom of the river and grabbed Beau, pulling him up, getting his head out of the water. He didn't hear the cheers and whoops as he struggled to drag Beau to the bank. His lungs burned. Desperately Julian gripped Beau's shirt with numb fingers, vaguely wondering if he would make it.

Just as he thought he was finally done for, he felt Culyn at his side, helping him swim the last few yards, helping him to bring Beau back.

Johnny Malone and Bennie Smith reached down, pulling Beau out and helping Brand drag Lackland and Culyn out of the icy river.

"Get the water out of his lungs," shouted Huw, running down the bank toward them as they turned Beau over. "Press the water out of his lungs!"

Urgently, Johnny Malone pressed on Beau's back, trying to force the water out. "Breathe," Julian urged him as he knelt gasping beside them. "Breathe!" Johnny kept pressing and pressing.

Nothing happened.

Disbelief and desolation swept over Lackland, but he refused to accept what everyone else was saying. "Don't stop pressing, Johnny! No…no…don't die, Beau! Breathe! Please, God, make him breathe. Please!"

Suddenly, water poured from Beau's mouth and nose. With a choking gasp, Beau, at last, began to breathe on his own again, lying on his side and coughing, spewing more water out. Johnny let him cough it all up while Julian clutched his hand, willing Beau to keep breathing, hardly able to breathe himself.

At last, Beau could speak, asking about Eddie. "He's safe, lad. You don't need to worry." Johnny's rough voice reassured him.

Beau struggled to recover himself, unaware of anything around him. His lungs burned, his stomach kept turning itself inside out, and he couldn't see or hear anything.

Lackland knelt next to Beau's shivering body, listening as he puked his guts up. A riot of emotions bewildered him, making it impossible to pull his thoughts together. He refused to hear anything except Beau's gagging and gasping for breath. Focused on Beau, he trembled uncontrollably.

All he could think of was the horror of how close he'd come to losing him. When he felt a blanket being wrapped around him, he looked up and saw Mags; her face full of gratitude and love and myriad emotions she had no words for.

Seeing the mute, distraught look on Julian's face, she knelt, putting her arms around him, holding him close. "I love you. You saved them. Everyone is safe."

"Oh, God. We almost lost him, Mags, my love!" He sobbed uncontrollably as she held him. "We almost lost him. I love him. Don't let me lose him."

"Shh, love, shh. He'll be fine." Mags held Julian as he shuddered and sobbed away the grief and guilt of the last few weeks. "You'll see."

Julian clung to her and wept until there were no tears left. Words spilled from him; everything he'd kept pent up, all his hurt and insecurity. The truth fell out, what Lora had said and done to him and how terribly responsible he felt for his own inability to stop her. He confessed what Beau really meant to him, everything that preyed on his mind. "I love Beau as much as I love you, but he doesn't know it. I haven't told him. I've lost you—I can't lose him too."

Through it all, Mags held him, comforting him as only she could do. "It will all work out, Julian. I know somehow it will work out. Beau's alive, and Eddie's alive, and that's all that really matters."

At last, Julian recovered himself. Eventually, Beau sat up and gripped both Julian's hands. He was silent, but tears streaked his face, still breathing raggedly and occasionally coughing.

The others had discreetly drawn off, and Belle stood guard, making sure they had the privacy they needed.

In the comparative quiet, Lackland heard a little voice worriedly ask, "Mama Bess, is Lackland dreadfully hurt?" and then Bess's voice saying, "He was hurt terribly, Estelle, but he'll be better now."

Beau finally had himself under control. "Are you well enough to walk now?" he asked Lackland, his voice hoarse from the near-fatal encounter with the water. "I feel the urge to sit by the fire and count my blessings."

"I feel compelled to do the same," replied Lackland, with some of his old sparkle returned to his eyes. "I hope I'm well enough to walk. I'll most likely have to carry you, and you're no lightweight, you musclebound moron. Who told you to go swimming in May?"

"Moron? Look who's calling me a moron, Lackbrains," replied Beau. "I'll most likely have to carry your old bones as usual." As they walked back to the meadow bickering back and forth, they each sounded like their old selves, to everyone's relief and great joy. They ended up leaning heavily on each other and on Culyn and Brand but were much improved by the time they arrived back at Billy's Revenge.

The men gathered in the bathhouse. "Do you think we should tell Beau what Lackland did to his hair, or should we let him find out on his own?" Culyn's eyes sparkled with mischief as he looked at Huw, who just shrugged and smiled knowingly.

"He'll be finding out soon enough," said Johnny Malone, chuckling wickedly. "Why should we spoil the day by mentioning something trivial like Beau's amazing new hairstyle?"

They all snickered, relieved that whatever else had happened, the incident had snapped Lackland out of his melancholy, and no one had died.

After his hot bath, Beau stood before the mirror to shave, shocked by the way his hair looked. "Good lord, Lackland! Don't take up hairdressing, whatever you do!"

The rest of the lads laughed hysterically.

Annie Fitz trimmed the ragged mess up. "I've been telling you for years, Beau. Most mercs don't wear their hair long, no matter what they'd like, but I never knew why. Who knew long hair could kill you?" Laughing, she cut it as short as the other Rowdies' hair, leaving the long tail under his left ear.

"I shall heed your wisdom, ma'am," Beau replied, fingering the thin braid that was all that remained of his golden mane. "Somehow, I don't feel quite as vain about my hair this evening as I did this morning."

The din in the common room was nearly unbearable. Most of Limpwater had descended on Billy's Revenge to celebrate the lives saved that day.

Young Eddie rapidly grew tired of being grabbed and kissed by random adults and anxiously looked for someplace to hide. He didn't even fuss when he was sent to bed before the grownups had finished their party. The realization that Beau had nearly died in the attempt to save him was more than his nine-year-old mind could handle.

Huw had immediately made a tale out of the day's ordeal, and after regaling the crowd with *The Rowdies' Picnic*, he and Culyn soon had the crowd dancing and singing, making the party that had so nearly been a wake into a joyous celebration of life.

When he finally made it into his own bed, Billy lay silent for a long while, unable to sleep. He felt his wife's arms go around him, comforting him.

"What's the matter, love?" Bess's sleepy voice was soft, near his ear.

"We almost lost Eddie today, along with two of my closest friends. I didn't even know it was happening." He felt mystified that such a thing could occur without his having some knowledge. "The river nearly took our son, and two good men almost lost their lives saving him. While all this was going on, I was doing the accounts and wondering how we would stretch the wintered-over potatoes until the new crop is ready for digging. I never had an inkling anything was wrong until you all came back. I wasn't there when our boy needed me. I wasn't there, and I didn't even know. I should have known!"

"You don't have the gift of second-sight, so how would you know? Lackland, Beau, and Culyn did what had to be done. They saved our boy, and Culyn surely saved Lackland and Beau. I don't think Lackland could have reached the riverbank without him." She hugged Billy reassuringly. "Besides, since we're low on potatoes, we'll make dumplings more often. Everyone loves dumplings, and we need to use the flour before it sets weevils, anyway."

"How can I send Brand or Bennie out on a job? I'll fear every moment now, wondering if I've sent them to their death." He was silent, staring at the dark. "It'll be like my dad…I wouldn't know until it was too late."

Bess was silent for a moment. Billy rarely mentioned the day his dad had gone out on a job and come home tied across his saddle, dead. "Nothing has changed, love. It's always been this way, and it's happened our loved ones have not come back alive. What's changed is you. Now you have children who want to take up the trade, and you're worried about them." Her voice sounded sleepy. "Brand will be fine and so will your little brother, just as we were. Eddie and the girls will do well when it's their time too, I know it. You worry too much."

"At least, Cissy had the sense to marry an apothecary, boring, chinless lad that he is," he muttered. "Letty wants to take up her sword this year as a Rowdy, and I don't have the right to stop her."

"No, you don't. She'll find her way as they all do. Anyway, Lackland will be here to train her and the rest of the youngsters this summer, and the Ladies have been working with her. You can't ask for better than that." She kissed his cheek and said, "Well, since you have me wide awake, I think you should take advantage of your good fortune!"

Billy's eyes gleamed in the dark, as did his smile.

Beau lay awake, staring into the darkness. Mags lay next to him, also unable to sleep. A space as wide as a canyon lay between them, and the conversation had drifted into dangerous territory.

He asked the one question he'd vowed to himself he'd never ask. "You love Julian. Why aren't you with him? He has never stopped loving you and would have you back with him right now with no recriminations regarding me. I love you, Mags, as much as Julian does. But you're part of his soul. You want him, not me. You love him the way he loves you."

"Not true! I love you that much, as much as I do him. I love you both with all my heart. But I can't give him what he wants. I can't leave the trade." Sadness colored her voice. "I'm the worst person he could be in love with. I've done him terrible wrongs, things no other man would have forgiven me for. You know what I did and how I lied to him. I'd still be doing him wrong because there's no place for a lady like me in polite society. Men who're good with the sword can be knights, and it's all perfectly fine. Everyone loves a good knight. Women who can wield a blade aren't discussed, though they're no longer considered abominations. Still, there's no place for me at court. I love my life too much to change it. And yes, it makes me terribly sad to know I've hurt you both so much."

"Mags."

Something in the way Beau said her name made her look sharply at him, wondering what he'd been holding back that he wanted to tell her now.

"I love you deeply and with all my heart. But I'm that much in love with Julian too. He's far more than a brother to me. I fight better and think better with him. He has part of my soul, and I can't live without him." He felt the sudden, sharp intake of her breath and laughed the low, sexy chuckle that always sent a thrill through her. "I've shocked you. It's not just a lad-loving-the-lads sort of thing though it is that. I want him, and I want you too. Is that so terrible? I'm being honest with you about this, as you've always been to me. This is love like I've never experienced it before." Beau smiled sadly as he watched her confusion turn to comprehension. "Something outside my control ties my heart to him as much as it does you. I don't want to part from you, but when Julian goes to court in the fall, I'm going with him unless he tells me to stay behind."

"He'll have you, never fear. He's in love with you too. He said so today on the riverbank while you were still puking. It's been clear to everyone for a while. I'd hoped that loving you meant he would stay here with us. But he'll never abandon Jules, not even for me."

Wretchedness threatened to burst from her, a torrent of pain at the thought they were both leaving her. "If anyone ever knew about this sad triangle, they'd weep. I find it hard to accept that you and Julian can live happily ever after, but I must lose both of you because of my own folly. It should be the three of us together if life were fair." Mags hated the sound of her own misery. They lay there in the dark, not touching one another, wondering what to do about their peculiar situation.

After a long, silent moment, Beau turned to face her. "You could come with us, Mags. We would make Henri let you be a knight." He applied as much pressure as he knew how. "You could have everything you want, and Julian could have you the way he needs you." He found himself begging her. "Please believe me when I say he needs you, now more than ever since that bitch cut him up so badly. Julian will never be the same. Now he's fragile and broken in some strange way. He'll accept Belle for tonight, but he needs you. You're his strength."

"I know. I know this better than anyone. But I would be an oddity at court. You know he must be there for Jules, and that's my fault! This whole mess is my fault." Mags gave in to the rage, helplessly angry at herself for having so little courage. "Conversations would stop when I walked into a room. The ladies of the court wouldn't want to be rude to me because of my high birth, but they'd have no idea how to treat me because of my famous lovers and equally famous sword. I have a place here and the respect of my fellow Rowdies. I'm given jobs that fit my abilities and make me work to grow, and no one doubts I have their back. I'm not brave enough to go to court and lose that. The only knights who would trust me behind them would be former mercs. Perhaps Henri would, but no one else."

Helpless sorrow silenced Beau for a moment, and then he said, "I wish you'd change your mind, but I accept you won't." His sadness was for Julian as much as it was for himself. Tears stung his eyes as he lay there. "I love you, Mags. I really do. It should be the three of us forever."

"At least we'll have the summer together. The three of us, like you say." She turned to him. "You nearly died today, and you aren't really as well as you pretend to be. Your voice is still raw, and you couldn't sing tonight. Are you feeling well enough for a little comfort?" she asked, her voice soft and vulnerable. "I need comfort. I'm losing everyone I love because I can't change the way I am.

Beau gave her his answer in his embrace.

Belle traced her finger along Lackland's perfect profile, looking at him in the flickering light of the candle he'd insisted on having, a little embarrassed to admit he was afraid of the dark. She committed him to her memory. He slept peacefully, and she suspected it was the first restful sleep he'd had since his ordeal in the woods.

I'll miss you when you leave me, my beautiful man, she thought. She was still in awe of the day's events and stunned by the terrifying knowledge that had come over her during the aftermath.

Despite her best efforts to the contrary, she'd fallen for Sir Julian Lackland De Portiers and didn't care if his heart was squarely wedged somewhere between Mags De Leon and Beau Baker. He loved her a little too, and that was good enough for her.

He'd allowed her to make love to him. He'd consented to her tentative invitation to her room with a vulnerability that was touching. He was unsure of himself now, and there was a part of him he held back, unable to completely give all of himself to her as if they were only a brief encounter.

To be honest with herself, she supposed they were. Nevertheless, she was glad for what she'd had with him, knowing she would wake up alone. This would be the last night she would have with him, a kind of farewell, a blessing of sorts. A sixth sense told her that tomorrow and forevermore, he would be with Beau and Mags.

It didn't bother her the way it might have. She loved Culyn too, in a different, more sure way. He loved her and didn't hold Julian against her. He seemed to understand that she needed this one last night with Julian, and then she could move on.

The events of the day had changed her. Life was so fleeting. Now she longed to have a child, some kind of immortality, and Culyn was a good man, the marrying kind.

No matter what the future held, she would have the memory of having loved Julian, a man who was so much more than just a good knight. He was a good man, still innocent despite everything.

Despite the scars.

PART THREE
Redemption

IN SOME WAYS, Lackland never recovered from his ordeal in the woods.

I confess I wondered about the Great Knight's sanity at times. He had always believed his horse talked to him, but this seemed different. This, I believed, was more akin to the madness that occasionally cropped up in the closely related noble families.

After Julian and Beau went to Castleton, Mags took a string of young lovers, none of whom ever took the place of Lackland or Golden Beau in her heart.

On Mortimer's death, Lackland had paid his brother's debts. Although his nephew had a long task ahead of him, Julian ensured that Mel had what he needed to bring the fighting forces of House Portiers up to a proper standard. Legally an adult now, Baron Melvin De Portiers had become a handsome, well-loved knight, as had Lackland's protégé, Jules De Leon.

Thanks to Lackland and Beau's training, the young generation of lords knew what it took to ensure their armsmen would be competent and properly kitted out when the next war came along.

Lackland was still stronger than any man half his age. His skills with weapons remained unsurpassed. King Henri made him his Lord Commander, despite his lack of lands. All the mercs in Waldeyn, including myself, had sworn to serve him, giving him the largest, best-trained cavalry to field. Not even the most difficult of the old lords raised a complaint. Every young knight at court and every old lord still leading his own men followed him slavishly, for no man knew how to wage war like Lackland.

We knew Beau was his right hand, and I suspected he kept many secrets, feared he concealed an unpleasant truth that at some point could make Julian unfit to command. I didn't want to contemplate what that could mean for Waldeyn.

Six years after Lackland and Beau left Billy's Revenge, King Henri requested my journeymen and me to entertain at his youngest daughter's wedding. Princess Rose was to wed the Heir to Bunder, young Jules De Leon.

Excerpt from *The Life of Julian Lackland De Portiers, Waldeyn's Last Good Knight*,
by Huw Owyn, Master Bard of Waldeyn

CHAPTER 17

AT LAST, THE DAY had arrived for the much-anticipated wedding of seventeen-year-old Princess Rose Dragoran to eighteen-year-old Lord Jules De Leon, the heir of Bunder. Now in his mid-sixties, Edward, the Earl of Bunder, was gradually stepping back, leaving Jules in charge of running the estate under Lackland's watchful eye.

King Henri had put on a most extravagant wedding party for his youngest daughter, and his jovial commentary made it known to all the guests how pleased he was to have joined his family to Bunder and the House of De Leon.

The marriage ceremony was held promptly at noon, as was most auspicious. After the traditional dances, they served the afternoon banquet. Everyone rested, wetting their throats.

The post-wedding celebration was in full swing. Huw Owyn, now the Master Bard of Waldeyn, sat at the main table with the groom's family, as did Julian Lackland and Beau Baker. Huw had brought the best of his journeymen from the Bard's College in Limpwater to provide the entertainment.

Lackland's nephew Melvin, who was the groom's best mate, had toasted the bride and groom, and with that out of the way, Huw's journeymen bards played the most popular of the new romps and galliards, bold, modern dances imported from the southern half of Waldeyn.

The food and drink continued to flow, and those who didn't dance were well into toasting the most minor of guests. The bride and groom circulated, chatting and making sure everyone was well-fed and comfortable.

Huw had one ear on his journeymen's performance and the other on the conversation. The groom's sister, Lady Mags, and her new lad danced to a galliard, much to the jealous dismay of the proper ladies of the court. Lackland and Beau were courteous, partnering the more daring ladies while Huw kept the frail Edward De Leon company.

As always, Huw found small things he could put into a ballad or comic song here and there without offending the noble concerned. It occurred to him that Old De Leon was more like a father to Lackland and Beau than a friend. He watched them caring for his needs, seeing how the old man relied heavily on them for companionship now his son had grown. For the previous two seasons, any time Huw needed to contact Lackland or Beau, he would find them at Bunder with the earl.

The galliard ended, and the two knights approached the table bearing drinks. Julian served Huw and turned to walk around the table to serve Edward De Leon.

As he did, four flashes of lightning lit the windows, followed by the thunderous roar of an explosion. It shook the hall, raining dust, glass, and bits of rock over the stunned assembly. Glittering shards and smoky dust filled the air, as a gaping hole appeared in the western wall of the great hall. Daylight filled the room, and blocks continued to fall. People ran for their lives. Finally, the rumbling of falling debris stopped, leaving a pile of rubble where forty people had been sitting. The wall had collapsed on one of the two long tables where members of the royal family sat, and onto the end of the main dais where several foreign envoys were seated.

Dumbfounded, Huw barely registered the odor of gunpowder. Disbelief paralyzed him as he realized the earl, who had been seated across from him, was gone, buried; and the table between them crushed. Had Julian made it to that side of the table with the Earl's drink, he would be dead too.

The bride and groom raced to the rubble, lifting stones and timbers. Chaos ensued as the wedding guests frantically called for their loved ones.

Lackland took charge, marshaling everyone into crews and shouting orders. "Guards, to the king! The rest of you use the beams to shore the wall up! We'll lose more people if what's left of that wall collapses!" As screams and cries from those trapped in the debris began to penetrate the dust, Lackland turned to Huw. "Get your journeymen to evacuate the elderly and the children from this place. Take everyone to the little reception hall and small anterooms. They must keep them there and entertain them as best they can. Then you come back. We'll need you here."

Huw turned to do as Lackland commanded, observing the king's spymaster, Slippery Jack, accompanied by his eldest son and four of his noble protégés, disappearing over the rubble and through the great hole in the wall. The look on Jack's face said he meant to do murder when he found the person responsible.

Toward sunset, the dead were all accounted for, and the survivors had done all they could. Prince Geoffrey, Henri's second oldest son, was dead, his infant son's corpse still in his arms. Earl Edward De Leon, the groom's father, was also dead as were thirty other guests, many of them children.

Weary in soul and body, by midnight nearly everyone had gone to their beds, except King Henri. He sat at his old worktable in his private rooms, too busy to sleep. Opposite Henri sat his spymaster, Slippery Jack. Beside him, his secretary, John De Portiers, silently took notes of the meeting.

On the table between them lay a shoe, a tiny carved box, and a fur-trimmed hat. Jack spoke, and the king listened. "The damage is bad, but it's nothing a mining engineer couldn't have done better. The engineers tell me it's definitely the work of an amateur."

"I see." Henri sighed heavily. "A hell of a lot of damage for an amateur."

Jack nodded. "Our killers lingered a while to see what sort of havoc they'd wrought and nearly got caught. Footprints in the muddy garden show how two men, one of whom is about my size and missing one shoe, ran toward the Knights' Garden, where they parted ways. This shoe matches none worn by the guests. We found it stuck in the deep mud. The owner lost it running away."

Jack picked up the hat, turning it over in his hands. "An overgrown bush snatched this off a much larger man's head as he scaled the hedge. The culprits didn't dare tarry long enough to retrieve their possessions, as I was hot on their heels. In his haste to escape, one of our killers dropped this little box. I suspect it was the nobleman."

"The style of this hat looks familiar." Henri picked it up and examined it. "The shoe as well."

"The hat could be from any of our northernmost provinces, as it is a tribal style of garb. The fur is ermine, common in the northernmost provinces of Waldeyn. It's more common in Lournes and Fornost, but too rare and costly for the average person to wear any further south than Marionberg. The shoe and the wooden box are of the style of Lournes and are of high quality, a nobleman's possessions." Jack handed the shoe to the king. "See the embroideries here on the shoe's upper and the silk ribbons? It's a courtier's shoe and cost more than a laborer could earn in a year. The hat, the box, and shoe are of Lournesque origin."

Henri looked up from the embroidered shoe. "But to leave behind something like this—the whole thing seems so clumsy. This isn't something King Aethelwyrd has sanctioned." Henri was confident in his conclusion. "He and I have had a good accord since his father's death. Yes, the explosion was bad and did us great harm, but it didn't have the effect I, as a king, would expect if I had financed such an expensive endeavor. Aethelwyrd is far too savvy to endorse something this clumsy. His own ambassador is dead. All those deaths and they didn't get me. If they were trying to force a change of kingship, they didn't even come close. It damaged only one wall, and the royal engineers tell me the rest of the building is still sound."

"My lads are looking in all the places where travelers from the north might halt between here and the border with Lournes," said Jack. "I would have liked to speak to the Lournesque ambassador, but…someone in his retinue will be able to shed light on whose possessions these might be."

"How do you open this?" Henri turned the box in his hands, holding it up to the lamp, searching for a catch.

"It's a Lournesque puzzle box," replied Jack. "Here, let me do it." With three quick moves, Jack had the box open. A quantity of snuff lay concealed inside. "What an idiot. This is a Vyennesk affectation and isn't too common among the Lournesque nobility. This will narrow the field of suspects considerably."

For a moment, the two men were silent. The only sound was the scratching of John De Portiers's quill as he silently took notes.

A knock sounded on the door, and a messenger entered, handing a note to Henri. He read it and handed it to John De Portiers, who read it and sighed. John said, "I feared De Neve's injuries would kill him. How many more will die tonight?"

Tears welled in eyes Henri thought he'd wept dry. "My poor Rose. What a hell of a wedding day. Her brother…her father-in-law…to lose so many is…. Damn the bastards to Hell! When we find the men responsible for this, there *will* be retribution."

CHAPTER 18

JULIAN FOUGHT TO RUN through shadowy, forbidding undergrowth, chased by mad things that gained on him with every step. An oppressive darkness shrouded the forest, and the thick canopy obscured the moon. He faltered, unable to find his way.

A branch caught his sleeve. He struggled to pull himself free but wiry vines grasped his arms and legs. They gripped him, as strong as iron and pulling him firmly against a tree. His struggles were for naught—the coiling vines bound him to the trunk like chains never could. He felt something heavy piled around his feet and looked down, moaning in horror and denial.

Hundreds of tiny corpses gazed back at him, their dead eyes condemning. With his every frantic move, the pile of bodies trapping his feet shifted. Prince Geoffrey's battered face stared reproachfully at him, arms still clutching his infant son.

A rasping sound alerted him to another presence.

Looking up, he saw Edward De Leon's corpse bound to a tree, visible in the shadows behind the madwoman, Lora Saunders. Raising his skeletal arm, Edward pointed at Julian. "You failed us."

"No! No! I didn't. It wasn't me this time. I swear it wasn't me!"

The madwoman's laughter drowned out Julian's pleas. A knife flashed past his face, and blood colored his vision red. Lora raised her knife again. "You failed us all." A ray of moonlight shone through the branches on the rubble surrounding him, ruins that once had been a great hall.

He lifted his arms to fend her off, but the knife fell again and again. Once more, Julian screamed.

Beau's arms went around him, a haven from the confusion of the dream. "Julian, you're sleepwalking again. Come back to bed."

The forest faded, but the darkness remained. "Beau! I couldn't find you. She had me." Tears streamed down Julian's face. "Lora…. Oh, God! Poor Geoff…the babies…."

"You're having a nightmare." Beau embraced him, his familiar voice comforting. "Are you back with me now? Come to bed." He turned Julian toward the bed. "I was afraid this would happen, what with all the uproar. It's been a while since we've had to deal with this affliction."

"She's right. I failed them." Julian stumbled. "Where are the children?" The darkness in his mind loomed despite the lamp Beau had lit, his eyes wild, unseeing. "Where did she take them?" He clutched at Beau. "She has them. See? There they are!" Julian pointed to the shadowy corners of the bedchamber, at some terrible thing only he saw. "How could she be so cruel? Oh god, they were babies!"

Stricken by the cold stab of fear, Beau soothed him. "Shh…shh…there are no babies. It's just a dream." Despite Beau's words, Julian remained in the grip of his madness. Beau tried again. "Lora's dead, remember? She was evil, and she's dead."

After some struggle, Beau got Julian back in bed. He opened a drawer and retrieved a packet. He tightly contained his panic, carefully measuring out the powder and stirring it into a glass of water with shaking hands,

"Here...let me help you sit so you can drink this. I'll stay beside you. She can't hurt you. I'm here." Supporting Julian's shoulders with one arm, Beau held the glass to his lips. "You'll be better tomorrow." It was a prayer, a ward against the rising fear that this time.... "Drink this. It will help you forget your dreams." He kissed Julian's forehead tenderly, and obediently, Julian drank the medicine. Beau repeated, "I'm not going anywhere. It's safe for you to sleep."

Julian lay back down, confusion stark in his eyes. "She has them. She has Geoffrey and Edward. Why did she take them too? I could have done something. I missed something...some clue that could have prevented it."

Beau sat next to his lover, trying to keep him calm as he struggled against sleep. "She doesn't have them. Edward and Geoffrey are with God now. He'll keep them safe. And no one could have known. Even Slippery Jack didn't know, and he knows everything." At last, Julian lost the fight against the drug. Beau smoothed his silvery hair. "I love you." His whisper shook as he fought a multitude of emotions.

With the powder having taken effect, Julian would sleep dreamlessly for at least eight hours. Beau finally slid down to lie next to him. Haunted by his own nightmares, he couldn't sleep, although he was desperately tired.

The horrors of the day had taken their toll on him, and he grieved deeply. Losing both Prince Geoffrey and Edward on the same afternoon was devastating. He had drilled with the prince every day for six years. His one task had been to make sure Geoffrey and the other young princes and nobles knew how to live through a battle.

All so he could die under that wall.

Life wouldn't be the same without Edward De Leon's dry wit. Beau exhaled heavily, a ragged sigh that was nearly a sob. His thoughts took him to dark, fearful places he never wanted to analyze. He had to speak to Sister Anne to see if she could work her majik again. But she had said there would come a day when she could no longer keep Julian's demons at bay.

And Jules...rage rose up once again, fury that someone would commit such a heinous crime, deliberately ruining the most important day of Jules and Rose's lives. Beau had to force himself to stay in bed.

He could do nothing about it now, and Julian needed him. Wasting his energy on murderous intent was stupid. What he had to do was calmly plan his next task.

Protection. Henri and his children needed protection. Thinking how to arrange that diverted him from his wrath.

Beau finally dozed lightly, his arms around Julian. If he stirred, Beau would know it.

Two hours later, Beau woke and sent a messenger down the hall to the rooms occupied by Julian's nephew,

Melvin. The note asked him to come and sit while his uncle slept, saying it was family business.

Mel suspected what was wrong and came straight away. With him keeping watch, Beau sought Sister Anne, who immediately came to examine Lackland. Afterward, she accompanied Beau to the king. In a private audience attended only by his secretary, John De Portiers, they told Henri what had happened during the night. The king still sat at his battered worktable.

"So. He's had a bad turn. Truthfully, I don't blame him," said Henri. "I don't know how I'll ever sleep again after what happened at my daughter's wedding. But this brings us back to our conversation of the other day. I have to know Julian is sane." He held Beau's gaze. "Is he stable enough to handle his command? If not, I will give it to my son, Harry, or Duke Bryson Weyllyn."

Beau chose his words carefully. "Both men are adept as tacticians. Both can act in that capacity if it comes to it. The problem is their youth. Neither man has earned the respect of the older lords the way Julian has. Julian leads, and men follow."

Sister Anne said, "Lackland will be in full possession of his wits when he wakes. He needs to stay occupied, as work will be the main cure for him."

With the king's concerns mostly satisfied, she left to tend to her other patients. Henri and Beau continued talking, finalizing arrangements for the extra guards on the royal family, which Lackland would have done had he been able. Beau handed Henri the list of men and women he felt would do well. "The Rowdies' captain, Billy Ninefingers, will confirm my recommendations. No window or door is to be unguarded, and sentries will patrol the gardens. I also want extra people in Prince Harry's household down in the Eynier Valley, as he is your heir. Huw's son, Culyn, was down there recently and knows which southern mercs will be right for the task."

Henri looked at the list, nodding. "I think you've got us covered well, now. We won't be able to fart without a guard for company. That will piss my children off, but it's too bad." Henri exhaled heavily. "You will keep me informed about Julian's every mood?"

"I will. You may be sure of that," vowed Beau. "His welfare comes first."

"Jack may have found proof of who set the explosives—a shoe and snuffbox. He needs one final piece of evidence, but when he has it, I will see my son's murder avenged." The king tented his fingers, framing his words carefully. "I must devise a test before I place as great a burden on Lackland's shoulders as war will be. I have an idea, one that should solve two great problems. But first, we have many loved ones to bury. Once that's done, we'll have retribution for this heinous act and discover for sure how stable my cousin is. At least this debacle has given Julian's son the earldom I wish I could have given him. It's always offended me how tradition enabled his wastrel elder brother to inherit the entire De Portiers' estate, leaving Julian a pauper."

A smile lit Beau's drawn features. "I know, but Melvin is a good man, and he'll soon have the estate righted. Julian is content to be known as Lackland. He claims a lack of property has made him who he is."

Beau left the king's study. He turned down the corridor to his and Julian's suite of rooms, intending to relieve Mel and hoping to sit quietly and think. He'd only gone partway when Slippery Jack and Huw the Bard silently emerged from an alcove where they sat, apparently waiting for him.

"Are you looking for Henri? He's finally gone off to bed."

"No. We want to talk to you in private." Drawing him into an empty chamber and closing the door, Jack got straight to the point. "What's going on with Julian? He hasn't been right since Lora cut him up so badly all those years ago, but toward the end last night, he made me wonder. Rumor has it he may have a war to run next summer. Is he fit for it? My sons will be riding with my brother's armsmen, fighting that war. I won't allow Lackland to risk their lives if he's not completely right in his mind."

Beau resented being ambushed but answered. "He had a bad spell, but he's well now. You can't imagine the guilt he suffers over what happened to the children of Gronwy and Pyndrys." He met Jack's gaze. "You were in Ludwellyn, but you didn't see what we saw. The massacre at Gronwy's preys on his mind. Now this mess at the wedding—finding Prince Geoffrey's infant son mangled beneath the wall along with the others and losing Edward De Leon affected him. I dealt with it, and Sister Anne saw him. She said he'll be right as rain."

Huw's mocking voice was quiet, barely above a whisper. "You would say that. Well, there are lives on the line here. You'll be putting your life in his hands, Beau. As will my son, Culyn. I don't want him in danger because you see Lackland through rose-colored spectacles and think he can do no wrong. Am I clear?"

Rage flashed, and Beau chose not to contain it. "Shove it, Huw! Sister Anne reports directly back to King Henri, as do I. She and I just finished talking to him about this very thing. What kind of man do you think I am? Do you honestly think I would put Julian in such a situation if he were too ill to command? How would that benefit him? The moment I think my old lad might be unfit, I'll inform the king, and he'll give Julian's command to one of the young lions coming up in the world, either Prince Harry or the young Weyllyn duke."

"That's good to know, but what about now?" Huw rarely allowed himself to get angry but was impossible to reason with once he did. "He says some daft things at times. Things that worry me."

Beau's exhaustion made him appear far older than his years. Arguing with Huw was his least favorite occupation, which showed in his clipped tones. "Yes, I keep Julian pulled together and don't allow the nightmares to get a grip on him. I admit that. But wait until he's truly lost it before you kick him aside. No one knows war like Julian. He must lead if we are to win. He's already working with the Lord Admiral regarding sneaking the fleet in, a plan to squeeze the pirates between two forces. It will require precision and timing. The Lord Admiral won't listen to anyone other than Henri or Julian."

Huw refused to let go of his animosity. "It has to be Lackland then, but he'd better have all his wits about him. If anything happens to Culyn because Lackland has lost his mind, I'll never forgive you."

"God! You honestly believe I'm stupid." Despite his anger, Beau kept his voice low. "There's no reasoning with you. You're convinced I'm besotted, and Julian is barking mad. Get out of my way! I feel like hurting you." He pushed past Huw, saying, "Go home, since you have so little faith in me." He opened the door, intending to leave.

"Beau," Jack's quiet voice called after him. "Come back. Let's bury this now. I wanted to hear what you had to say because I'm a father. I worry about my boys."

Beau closed the door and returned to Jack and Huw. Forcing Jack to look at him, he said, "Do you think Julian and I don't care about our family, about Melvin or Jules? We care deeply about all the young men we have trained over the last seven years. And their wives and children, more than you'll ever know. We also care about you old idiots. I don't want your blood on my hands, along with everything else!"

At the mention of Jules, Jack relaxed. "I know I can trust you to do the right thing. So does Huw, but he's a grumpy old bastard." He nudged Huw. "Right?" When Huw refused to answer, Jack said, "Come on. You know Beau has too much honor to jeopardize Culyn or anyone, much less Jules De Leon. Beau loves Lackland's son as if he were his own."

Beau reached out and grabbed Jack by the throat, lifting him off the floor, his face dark with outrage. "Never mention that again! Never, ever mention that again." He punctuated his words by shaking Jack as if he were a rag doll.

"It was unforgivable. You've every right to kill me, but please don't." Jack's hands clutched at Beau's, his strangled voice pleading. "I'll never speak of it again, I swear."

Beau abruptly let go of Jack and rounded on a thunderstruck Huw, putting his face just inches from the bard's. "If that bit of information turns up in a rumor, much less a ballad, I will know the source and will kill you with my bare hands. Make no mistake about it."

Holding his hands out in supplication, Huw said, "Peace! I swear by my hope of heaven; your secret is safe with me. I have my own skeleton to hide, one not so different." Huw lowered his voice. "The heiress of Dwyn is my daughter. Jack knows, and so does Henri. Please, I'm your true friend, Beau. I have always been, and I always will be."

His face still livid, Beau said, "I accept your word. This conversation never happened." Nodding curtly, he turned and stalked back to his rooms, seething.

Huw stared after Beau's retreating figure. "Well, this explains many things. Lady Mags…Lackland…I remember when she left the Rowdies for nearly half a year. She went home several months before her brother was born. Mags's mother died soon after, which lent credence to the tale that the old dame had died bearing a late-life child, as sometimes happens. We thought her death was complications from childbirth."

"It was pneumonia. I thought you knew all along. This is King Henri's secret as much as it was Edward De Leon's," muttered Jack. For once, the man was completely thrown off balance. "I allowed my personal concerns to destroy my career. If you care at all about Lackland or me, you must never speak of this, not to Culyn or anyone. Beau has every right to hate me for what I just did. Henri would kill me."

"You know how Beau is. He's a hothead, but he'll be over it by morning as if it never happened. He won't tell Henri or Julian because he knows I'll carry his secret to the grave, and you will too." Huw's eyes narrowed, as he considered the many small things that had puzzled him for years, things he had never connected. "Bunder is crucial to Henri's plans. Of all the Waldeynier lords, De Leon has the largest, best-trained, best-equipped force to bring to the front in Lanqueshire, better than any duke or prince's army. In his role as Edward De Leon's arms master, Julian himself has seen to that, and now Henri has married his daughter to De Leon, cementing the young lord's position."

"Arrogance rides high before a fall from grace, as you frequently tell me. I fell, like a green lad new to the business." Jack stared into the shadows of the room, wondering what he could do to salvage the situation. "Thank God we picked that quarrel in private. It was more stupid than anything I've ever done. The events we just lived through are no excuse. I'd murder one of my lads for such gross ineptness."

"So—you're only human, after all. You worry too much," said Huw, clasping his shoulder. "Anyway, I'm less concerned about Julian getting out of hand now. As Beau said, this conversation didn't happen."

CHAPTER 19

TWO WEEKS HAD passed. The funerals were over, and people had finally returned to their homes. Julian's nightmares resolved themselves back to his normal night terrors. Despite the dreadful losses of the wedding day, life went on as it had always done, much to Beau's relief.

Slippery Jack's sources in the far north confirmed Prince Maldred had paid for the attack. He was the younger brother of King Aethelwyrd of Lournes, and unpopular in his country. Henri's first wife had been their half-sister, but neither brother had cared much when she was executed for treason. Aethelwyrd had sent Henri a thank you note along with a cask of ice-brandy.

At first, Henri thought he had no recourse and would have to live with it. However, within days a messenger arrived bearing a letter from Aethelwyrd, written in his own hand. The monarch was furious upon learning of the actions of his younger brother and livid at the death of his ambassador. He offered Henri an opportunity to resolve the situation.

Henri discussed the matter with Julian, walking in the privacy of the Queen's Garden. "Aethelwyrd has requested my help in ridding him of a problem. He can't do it himself because the problem is his brother, Maldred."

Lackland nodded. "The prince with a nasty reputation."

"Indeed. But he's owed favors by certain nobles at the court of Val Halle who don't want to see a princess on the throne. Aethelwyrd's son was always a sickly child, and he died a year ago, leaving Princess Attallia heiress to the throne. The old king signed a royal decree that cut Maldred out of the running completely, so his only chance at the power he seeks is to control whomever Attallia weds." Henri grimaced. "I really don't want Maldred in charge up there. The people of Lournes don't deserve that. Aethelwyrd is a good ruler, and his daughter will be too when she succeeds him, which we must ensure."

Julian sorted through what he knew about the Black Prince. "Maldred is feared by the merchant class. The nobles there consider him cruel and unjust."

"All true," Henri replied. "King Aethelwyrd wants me to devise a way to remove his brother and his treasonous cronies. Since Maldred and his henchmen murdered my son and ruined our children's wedding, I'm more than happy to help." Pent rage flashed through his eyes, immediately buried.

Lackland felt the same hot, helpless anger, but answered calmly. "My friends up there tell me that when a plan goes awry, his former conspirators sometimes disappear, only to be found in an untidy state of disembowelment. This is common knowledge, so perhaps it's a weakness we could exploit."

"I'm giving you the task. Put together a plan and bring it to me by tonight. Decide who you need to take with you, but I want you to leave in three days."

Lackland knew exactly who he would need. "Slippery Jack does a lot of business in Lournes, through his family there. He'll provide our cover. Beau and I and two other former Rowdies will be his hired guards. I'm sure Billy Ninefingers will provide our credentials and papers for the border crossing. He'll be happy to help, as rumors of what happened at Princess Rose's wedding are flying all over the country."

"I couldn't get along without the Rowdies and the other mercenary companies. They do the real work of guarding this kingdom." Henry shook his head. "Jules wants to go with you, as does your nephew Melvin, but I've just sent the two of them home, demanding they get their own estates in order. Rose needs to get away from everything, and she doesn't need to worry about her husband's safety."

"Good. I don't want Jules and Melvin poisoned by the sort of job this will be, sneaking around in the dark." Lackland refrained from sighing. "It's bad enough that it has to be done. It's best done by those of us already destroyed by this nasty life we live. Beau and I will take them on a better adventure when we come back, something noble and good."

"I'll save one for you." Henri laughed.

The hissing of rain on frozen fir trees heralded a false thaw. Faintly creaking leather, the quiet jingling of harnesses, and the plodding steps of the horses broke the silence of the winter forest. Lackland and Beau, along with Slippery Jack, and the two bards, Huw and Culyn Owyn, rode their miserable horses north from Castleton.

They slogged through snow heavy with slush, splashing through myriad puddles as the snowy landscape of the northern winter slowly melted under the assault of rain. Swathed in heavy winter cloaks, their breath steamed in the chill morning air.

Since his gem business was the cover for his mission, Jack traveled under his real name and occupation, Johan Fitzmarion, a dealer in fine gems. One of many illegitimate sons of the late Duke of Marionberg, Jack had been raised in the Duke's court. He'd also maintained close ties to his maternal family of Lournesque traders, spearheading the family's small merchant empire.

The others enjoyed being Jack's hired men, easily falling back into their old roles, wearing their armbands with Captain Billy's blessing. In some ways, it felt as if the years separating them from their old life had never happened, except the merchant they were guarding was one of their own.

Culyn said, "I'd forgotten how much I hate these forays. It may take some doing to make a decent ballad out of this. I miss the babies' howling already."

"You'll get used to the peace and quiet soon enough," said Beau, laughing. "And you'll invent a fanciful tale for them that'll make it seem like a wondrous, noble quest."

Huw tried to hide his grandfatherly pride under a gruff demeanor, but the sparkle in his eye gave it away. "If it were only the twins, it'd be loud enough, but add in the three- and four-year-olds, it's mayhem in the Owyn household." His wry comment made them all laugh. "And if Culyn hasn't told you, I've another grandchild on the way." He rolled his eyes, and his son grinned, an expression of utter contentment brightening his features. "Perhaps we'll have a granddaughter for me this time."

Lackland couldn't hide his surge of happiness for Huw. "Beau is right. You two always make these miserable undertakings into something unrecognizably noble. It feels good to get out of Castleton, though. I think Beau and I have been at court too long this time. Six years is far too long."

After riding along in silence for a while, Beau began singing an old song, and Culyn joined in with him. They rode and sang all morning, and as the day cleared, they progressed from singing to telling bawdy jokes. By sundown, they were lodged in the Velvet Purse, a tiny but decent inn gracing the village of Ebensberg.

They spent the next two nights camping along the road, but at last, the five weary men entered the northern border town of Marionberg, the most northern of the Waldeynier towns. This was where their pleasure trip ended, and the work began. All five men burned to get down to business.

They stayed at a local inn despite this being the home of Jack's half-brother, the duke. Lackland knew the duke well, as did the bards, but it was a border town. In his work as a spy, Jack had gained his best information by traveling as an ordinary merchant and listening to the gossip in the common room.

He sent a message to his brother, letting him know he was passing through on the King's business. The duke had been at the wedding and would suspect what it was about.

They were put into one room, as was normal in the lower quality inns. At supper, they sat at a corner table in the smoky taproom, rolling the dice. They exchanged small sums with each toss of the dice, five men intent upon their game. All the while, they listened to the Lournesque travelers sprinkled throughout the crowd. The conversations that went on around them were mostly innocuous, all but one.

At a table adjacent to Jack's, a heated discussion ensued, carried on in whispers and low tones. A thin, older merchant accompanied by his sons attempted to eat despite the inability of his three sons to keep their conversation strictly in safer waters. Rumors regarding the murder of an acquaintance of theirs had upset them, making them edgy and unable to sit quietly.

"I hear what you're saying. But what they did to Master Larsson was evil. They slit his throat and gutted him." One of the younger sons spoke in whispers, his posture stiff and angry. "Everyone knows who was behind it. Gutting is his signature. No man should pay with his life and property for refusing to offer his daughter to a man she doesn't want. You know it was the prince—he demanded her, not Thorgürd. Thorgürd does as he's told, with no room in his head for a thought of his own."

The older merchant's face darkened at the mention of the prince's henchman. Quickly looking over his shoulder at the other guests in the common room, he hushed his son. "We'll have no more mention of them at this table. If the wrong person overhears such talk, we'll all end our days in our own beds with our bellies slit and God knows what else."

Beau's eyebrow rose, and he looked at Jack, who nodded.

Later, in the privacy of their room, the five men quietly discussed what they had heard and, more importantly, what they had not heard. Jack said, "It tells me the list of Maldred's cronies the new ambassador gave us is most likely still accurate. We'll need to spend a few days in the market in Val Halle to confirm the rest."

"We kill only the ones who need killing," Lackland said, abruptly. "No one whose guilt is in doubt, even if they are on the list. No women and no children."

The others stared at him. "What are you saying?" Huw's low voice was rough with suppressed fury. "I've never killed a woman who wasn't swinging a sword or a knife against me. I've never killed a child."

Jack spoke hard on the heels of Huw's indignation. "Good God, Lackland."

"Forgive me, please." Lackland held his hands up, warding off their anger. "I didn't mean to phrase it so badly. I know you take no pleasure in killing and don't kill women and children. I know that. It's just...I don't want this to go like things did the last time." His face had a sickly cast, and he looked away from them, staring into the fire. "I'll never get it out of my mind. Things got out of hand in Ludwellyn. It went way beyond what we planned and turned into a bloody massacre. I can hardly live with the guilt as it is. I can't bear any more."

Culyn glanced at his father and Jack, then attempted to smooth over the situation. "There are many differences in this venture. The people of Val Halle aren't on the edge of revolution the way they were in Ludwellyn. They're prospering under their king and have no desire to topple him. This won't go beyond what Henri has asked us to do."

"I promise it won't go bad." Beau spoke from the shadows, where he sat keenly observing Lackland's mood. "We'll pull out if it even looks like it's turning into another Ludwellyn."

Jack and Huw saw the anxiety in Beau's expression and exchanged meaningful looks. They turned back to Culyn and nodded, reluctantly. Jack pulled something from inside his shirt. "This is the list of people King Aethelwyrd wants dealt with. In Lournes, an eorl holds the same rank as an earl does in Waldeyn." Unfolding the paper, he read, "Eorl Thorgürd, known to be Maldred's right hand. If Maldred wants a task done, Thorgürd does it. According to our information, Thorgürd is our uninvited wedding guest. He brought the explosives and the incompetent mining engineer."

The others nodded.

Jack continued down his list. "Next to Thorgürd in Maldred's clique is Eorl Söder. Söder is Thorgürd's tool.

"After Söder are the Eorls Freygard, Higurde, Daggurlund, and the least intelligent of the lot, Eorl Ranveg Olgurde. The new envoy tells me that what these henchmen lack in intelligence, they make up for in enthusiasm. They call themselves the Black Watch." The fire flared as Jack tossed the list into the fire and stirred the coals, briefly illuminating his somber face.

Culyn snorted. "That's ridiculous. Do they even know what they are styling themselves after? If I remember my history, the original Black Watch was a band of Waldeynier nobles from the borderlands, employed in disarming the Lournesque sympathizers during the reign of Herrold I. Their task was to bring criminals to justice and remove rebels and traitors inhabiting the disputed borderlands of the kingdom. Am I correct?"

"You're right. They got carried away, massacred a village, and went to the gallows themselves," replied Huw. "It figures these less-than-smart eorls would choose a name for the glamour of it, neglecting to research the truth. There's a certain justice in that."

Lackland agreed. "Henri and I've come up with a plan we think is doable, but it will require a certain amount of groundwork, of the sort you're highly adept at, Jack. Beau and I have special attire for this job in our luggage, garments for us all." He handed Jack a letter and waited while he read it and handed it around to the others.

After they had committed it to memory, Jack burned it, saying, "It's a good plan, Lackland. But it will require us to live the part, as we did in Ludwellyn."

"It will indeed," Lackland agreed, his features somber in the firelight. "Which is why Ludwellyn is on my mind. It must be done in the open, but in such a way that no one discovers it involved an outside agency.

We'll have vengeance, and King Aethelwyrd will have fewer thorns in his side."

"I should have known you had a plan." Huw was awash with misgivings about Lackland's stability but hid it beneath his handsome smile.

Jack's grin concealed his own qualms. "I like this plan. It plays to my strengths."

The next morning, before they left, Jack spoke quietly with several of his older acquaintances. Discreetly asking how the weather was in Val Halle, he explained he had been in the South for nearly half a year and was concerned about the northern climate affecting his family's profits. Their responses were phrased carefully.

Once they were on the road, Jack explained what the merchants had essentially said. "Their cautious words tell me Maldred has found a way around the little issue of incest. It's a capital offense in Lournes, making it impossible for Maldred to wed the princess himself, should he manage to kill Aethelwyrd. Olgurde is the weakest of Prince Maldred's supporters and is, therefore, the best choice as a puppet king from Maldred's point of view."

When they passed over the border, Jack had the papers ready, all signed by William MacNess, commonly known as Billy Ninefingers. The crossing went smoothly, as the Rowdies were well-known and highly respected. The guards were polite, waving them across and wishing them a good day.

After five more days on the road, they arrived in Val Halle. Jack directed them to a modest house in the Merchant's Quarter. "This is House Fitzmarion. Merry Kat and I bought it when we first left the Rowdies, but we're seldom this far north anymore." Jack shrugged. "Our business is such that she can't leave our shop in Castleton."

The housekeeper, Hilda, greeted them at the door, bowing low. She led them through an arched doorway into the great hall. A table flanked with benches, big enough to seat ten large men, stood in the center of the immaculately clean chamber. A fire burned merrily in the large hearth, warming the stone-and-timber room.

But what caught the guests' attention was the woodwork. The woodcrafters of Lournes were legendary, and looking up, they saw that even the massive beams of dark wood above them were ornately carved.

So too was the grand mantel above the enormous fireplace. Two opposing armies fought a great battle, with many warriors and horses lying dead on the field, trampled beneath the hooves of the victors' horses. Everywhere one looked, the exposed wood in the room was heavily engraved with warriors or busty shepherdesses who watched over impossibly fat sheep or danced with handsome young men of heroic proportions.

Near the large windows, benches offered places to read or do needlework. The corner near the fire, known as the inglenook, was an intimate area with cushioned benches set against the walls. Lournesque families frequently spent the quiet hours of the evening in the inglenook. On the far side of the hall, a broad, intricately decorated stairwell led upstairs.

Jack's wry tones fell into the astonished silence. "And the woodwork in my home is nothing compared to the wealthier merchant's lodges here in Val Halle."

"It's amazing. I've never seen such wonderful attention given to a beam or stair rail." Lackland spoke for the others.

Beaming with pride, the housekeeper said, "Master Johan, I've prepared the rooms for your men. They must share two to a room, as happens when you have more than two guards, but none will have to sleep before the fire in the hall." She bowed to the four as one would to equals, and they bowed in return. She was a pleasant woman of about forty, wearing the black of widowhood.

"This is Hilda, our housekeeper. Her husband gave his life for me. I owe her and her daughter far more than I can possibly repay. She keeps this place all year round for us and kindly allows us to stay here in comfort when we're not away on business." Jack turned to her. "Don't worry, these guards are new to us but not to their work. They're used to sleeping under shrubs."

"Two to a room will be a luxury, Fraue Hilda," asserted Huw, bending low over her hand, intent on charming her. "I am Huw, in the Northern language, Hugh. I'm at your service. If you require help, an extra hand in the scullery, more firewood, anything, you have only to ask."

Huw's delivery of the formal Lournesque language in so polished a fashion with his southern accent and darkly handsome charm caught her off-guard. Openly eyeing him up and down, Hilda giggled, causing Jack to stare at his housekeeper in shock. "We serve supper at five bells. I've firewood aplenty, so you men have time to warm by the fire after you take your things upstairs." She looked at the others, recognizing from their clothes they were all from Waldeyn. "My daughter, Ingrid, will bring jugs of hot water for you to clean away the travel dust. I've heard you men of Wald love to bathe even in the winter, unhealthy though it may be. Mistress Katryn told me that in your homes, you each have over-large washtubs you fill with water, and then sit naked in them, with water up to your chin."

Her eyes were round as the four men nodded.

"You must be crazy to do such a thing. Everyone knows the steam-hut is better for your health and cleanses the body inside and out." Hilda turned to Lackland. "But you look quite healthy for an old man, still fighting as you apparently are." She took in the terrible scars on his throat. "Indeed, you're a fine, handsome, strong old warrior. You have seen many battles. These young heroes are lucky to have your wisdom."

Jack laughed at Julian's surprised expression. "Yes, they do bathe naked even in the winter, and they're all healthy, even this incredibly old man. Thank you for your thoughtfulness, Hilda. We will avail ourselves of the steam-hut tonight."

"Well, you will never live long enough to see your grandchildren if you insist on tempting the gods with bathing naked and all that sort of foolishness. Now off with you all. Master Johan will show you to your rooms, and I must see to your supper." She bustled off in the kitchen's direction, leaving them alone in the hall.

Lackland still looked nonplussed. "Who's an old man? I'm only forty-four. If my hair's gone silver, it's your fault, Jack. It grows whiter every time I get involved with you." His blue eyes twinkled at his own vanity. "I'm the same age as you and Huw, for the love of God."

Beau's grin lit up his features. "Did you see that? Huw had her nibbling from his fingers. I'll wager a gold crown Culyn will have a room to himself tonight."

"I'm not stupid enough to bet against you," replied Jack with a knowing grin. "You and Lackland have the luck of the gods. Besides, our Huw will have every ounce of gossip she ever heard out of her before midnight and leave her smiling in the morning."

Huw shrugged, but his eyes danced as they all snickered at his expense.

Hilda's daughter, Ingrid, was a shy woman of about twenty-four, and she brought their hot water. She was quite plain to look at, and although not ill-favored, she was large and strong, of sturdy peasant stock. Hilda had resigned herself to her daughter's permanent state of spinsterhood.

However, she did frequently mention to Jack how Ingrid would make an excellent wife for a lonely merchant, saying pointedly that he should bring his unmarried cousin, Kharl, around more often.

CHAPTER 20

THE NEXT DAY, Lackland and the others went with Jack to his warehouse and offices down on the wharves. His cousin, Kharl, ran the Lournesque side of the family business.

Crime, when it happened in Val Halle, was quick and violent. Criminals had developed the trick of dressing in garb no different from anyone else. A group of thieves would emerge from the crowd, swarm the victim, and then vanish back into the crowd. This meant that guarding a trader in Lournes involved adhering to a certain protocol. Prosperous merchants were favorite targets.

Huw and Beau walked ahead of Jack, observing everything and everyone who might pose a threat to their charge. Lackland and Culyn walked behind, all four men with their hands resting on sword hilts, fully alert and on guard for any attempts on Jack's life.

A burly armed guard stood beside the warehouse door, bowing. "Master Johan! Welcome back. Master Kharl is expecting you and your men." He leaned forward, whispering, "Everything here is just as you left it. Master Kharl is an astute merchant. You taught him well."

"Thank you," replied Jack. "We will visit several merchants later, delivering procurements as ordered. I must go south again in several weeks, but it's good to see you looking so well, Gustave."

Lackland observed Jack closely. He found it interesting that when his old friend was in his role as a gems dealer, he looked nothing like King Henri's chief ferret. He became the simple, prosperous man his employees believed him to be. After thinking about it, he realized that Jack fit equally well into the role of a Rowdy, appearing to be nothing more than a common street tough. *Which was the real Jack,* he wondered. *All the roles or none?* His old friend was a man of many layers.

The guard looked disappointed. "Will you be leaving us again so soon?" Worry lines were deeply engraved into his solemn features. The waxed points of his lush mustache curved upwards in a broad smile, providing a humorous counterpoint to his gloomy expression. "It's dangerous to travel in the wild countries as you do, with no magician to charm the beasts for you or guard you against curses. These men carry mighty swords and are much braver than I, but even they can't prevail against some things lurking in the barbarian wilderness of Waldeyn."

"We must have merchandise, and sadly, the best goods come from far away. But don't worry—these men guard me well." Jack entered the door the guard held open for him, bowing. The four guards each bowed as they went in behind Jack and stepped to either side of the open office door, standing silently, swords at the ready, still on guard.

Kharl, Jack's portly cousin, rose from behind his desk. "Johan! Welcome, welcome! Were you able to acquire the opals for…?"

Jack entered his office, closing the door behind himself, cutting off the conversation.

Several clerks, two of them women, sat on high stools at tall desks positioned before the large windows where they had good light for their work. The occasional noises of wagons and passersby drifted in from the street through the windows, along with the scratching of the clerks' quills broke the silence of the room.

An hour or so later, Jack emerged. After bowing their goodbyes to everyone, the five men left the warehouse, making deliveries to certain nobles and wealthy merchants. Jack struck up conversations with every trader he met, intent on gaining as much information at his various stops in the market as possible. He was adept at reading the mood of a person, gauging how to pry information from people who believed they knew nothing.

Lackland admired Jack's skill, seeing a master at work. He asked questions and innocently phrased his responses in such a way that quiet speculations began traveling all over Val Halle market, whispers implying the eorls of the Black Watch had perhaps failed Prince Maldred in some unspecified way. Once again, gossip regarding what had happened to Master Larsson and his daughter made the rounds, combined with other dark whispers, traveling faster than the wind.

By the time they returned to House Fitzmarion, they felt as if they had bowed to nearly every person in Lournes. "And I'm such an elderly fellow. My ancient spine isn't up to all this politeness." Lackland's wry joke elicited chuckles all round.

That night, they chatted with Hilda and her daughter over a meal of heavy, dark bread, a delicious stew, pickled vegetables, and sharp cheeses. Digging for information about the layout of the homes their quarry might live in, Huw's artless questions enchanted the housekeeper. "This is a luxurious home, very different from where I come from. Our homes are much smaller. Does everyone live in a house like this?"

Hilda eagerly explained how every Lournesque home, large or small, was laid out the same way as Jack's. "Oh yes, it's traditional to have the kitchen to the north and the great room to the south. Bedrooms are always upstairs so that if you die in bed, you are nearer to God. Following tradition assures good fortune to the householders. Lournes holds to the old ways firmly. Furniture crafters earn a good living in Val Halle, and even the poor can afford well-made furniture."

"It is stoutly made," agreed Huw, who had noticed the lack of easy chairs with some chagrin. "Very solid. Even the king's lodge is like this?"

"Our king's house is identical to any other man's lodge, except it's much larger and more ornately decorated. Oh, and it's surrounded by ramparts upon which Aethelwyrd's personal armsmen keep vigilant watch of the entire countryside. We are ever alert, we of the North."

"Your king must be a good ruler. All the people we've met seem happy." Huw was curious from a professional standpoint.

"Oh, my! He's a good man, very popular. On Mondays, anyone can go to the fortress and speak to the king and tell him our problems, if we have any, which is seldom. So, we can see how he lives like any other man." Hilda nattered on, giving details about every aspect of Northern life, all of which they filed away, knowing it would be useful. "But, other than the furnishings and size of the house, there is no difference between the rich and the poor here. Every home will be like this house here, although perhaps not as nice. Master Johan was not stingy when he furnished this house." She grinned smugly. "Some homes may have golden platters, and others have platters of wood, but everyone has food and platters to serve it on." Her pride was clear. "And we have no servants here in Lournes. Widowed women earn a good living cooking and cleaning and doing laundry for the wealthier people. It's only right to pay for services others do for you.

"We don't own slaves in our country either. We hire people for many services too," Lackland said. "You're right to say it's only fair."

"Noblewomen like our princess may have several women come in to help if the house is very large and her husband has many guards, but we're not as soft as your southern ladies. Why, my sister goes to Lord Olgurde's large, magnificent lodge every day to cook his stew and bake his bread, but she is home at night to care for her own husband. Lord Olgurde is cheap too. He has four bedrooms, but only furnished one. The great hall stands empty and his poor uncle must act as his manservant and sleep in the kitchen." Hilda snorted. "Although, it's rumored the Black Prince has many people who clean and cook for him all hours of the day and night and who must wait on him like servants."

Hilda's contempt made Huw and the others smile. She spoke so fast and delivered so much information in her torrent of conversation that the five men were nearly dizzy from trying to follow her changes of direction.

After Huw had gone with Hilda to the kitchen, ostensibly to help her bring in wood, Lackland looked at Beau with a quizzical expression, his eyes twinkling. "I wonder if she would think southern women were soft if she'd ever met our Mags? Merry Kat is no fainting lily either."

The others agreed. "None of the ladies we know are weak," said Jack. "I don't think Hilda realizes my wife isn't from Lournes."

Culyn pressed his fingers to his temples. "These people love to gossip. I've never heard so much about so many people in all my life. My head is full to bursting. In the market, they vied to tell the latest news about the most minute of matters."

"They won't say certain things, though," replied Jack. "They won't discuss anything that could bring them to Maldred's attention. Consequently, I must ask questions carefully."

Huw had returned from the kitchen. He asked, "What do you make of these other rumors we hear, whispers of children disappearing off the street? The people in the market seem upset by this, but I heard no theories as to their fate."

Jack's brows drew together. "That concerns me. If these disappearances happened in Ludwellyn, one would only have to look in the workhouses where overseers force kidnapped children to do the dangerous work that requires small, nimble hands. But Val Halle is not that sort of city. Child labor is strictly forbidden, and kidnapping will earn you a beheading."

Lackland pursed his lips, staring out the window. "Something else is going on here, but I can't see how it relates to our task."

Huw and Jack's eyes met. Huw said, "The task at hand is the important thing."

"It is, indeed." Lackland nodded, still thinking.

The following day went much as the first, as did the following week. While walking around the market and paying visits to Jack's customers, they learned which lodge was the home of each man on the list.

Just beyond the market was the Way of Ealdormen. At the foot of that winding street was the Church of St. Anan. Attached to the church was a nunnery and House of Healing. Beyond the church, lining the cobbled street and rising toward the top, were the homes of the nobility.

The Rowdies were pleased to find the Black Watch gathered about Maldred's feet like the loyal dogs they were, strung along the highest circle of the Way of Ealdormen, below the large, ornate lodge occupied by Prince Maldred.

Even better, from Lackland's point of view, was the fact that, for all the paranoia affecting the merchants and the large middle class of Val Halle, there was smug complacency among the Eorls of the Black Watch. They apparently felt secure, guarded only by two or three sentries. Each lodge had several lazy, overfed dogs, whose aggression had been trained out of them to keep the neighborhood quiet at night.

The five men made friends with the dogs along the way, handing out bits of dried meat to every canine along the length of the winding Way of Ealdormen.

"What is the point of having dogs if they train them not to bark?" Lackland's disapproval made the others grin. "This is wrong."

"You really are the barbarian, to think like that." Jack's eyes twinkled. "Thank God your indoor plumbing and comfortable cottages haven't bred all the aggression out of you."

When the five men arrived home on the afternoon of their sixth day in Val Halle, Hilda had gossip waiting for Huw, rumors Jack himself had started. That evening, they sat warming themselves in the inglenook after supper.

"Tonight, we will visit several taverns, and then meet Kharl and Gustave at the Sailor's Knot," said Jack. "I haven't yet taken you gentlemen to the lager houses near the harbor." Hilda and her daughter were in the kitchen, but he used the agreed-upon code so neither Hilda nor Ingrid would inadvertently overhear anything incriminating. "The Sailor's Knot is a pleasant tavern. It's where we conduct most of our business."

"I like your northern lager. It's quite different from the dark ale we're used to," Lackland nodded as did the others.

Just when the town was settling down, the five men slipped out, shrouded in garments of black that Julian had brought for the purpose. Cloaks the color of deepest midnight covered them, and dark scarves hid their faces. Blending into the shadows, they stole through the poorly lit streets, silent and unseen.

They each drew lots to select the eorl he would murder. Jack said, "We have two hours to accomplish this, or we'll miss Kharl and lose our alibi."

Lackland agreed. "You each know the house you're going to. After we've finished the first part, we'll meet at the sewer-catch in the alley behind House Thorgürd. It's unlikely anyone will be emptying chamber pots at this time of night, but there are plenty of shadows to conceal us while we wait for everyone to finish."

Each man carried water skins to sluice away blood and other evidence from their hands and faces, along with a large, dark bag containing clean garments to change into when their task was complete. They stashed these in the darkest shadows behind a wall, one more indistinct pile among the trash heaps. The bloody garments and knives would all go down the sewer-catch when the night's work was finished.

The first lodge on the street, just beyond the church, House Daggurlund, was sparsely guarded. A lone guard stood half asleep at the front gate. He was soon dispatched, his body hidden under the hedge. Silently, Huw scaled the rough stone-and-timber wall. The bedchamber window was open for air. Gently pushing the opening wider, he entered the room occupied by the sleeping eorl. The connecting door to the countess's room was slightly ajar, but only an inch. He negotiated the route to the eorl's bed quietly. Placing his hand firmly over the man's mouth to stifle his surprised exclamation, he slit his throat. When Daggurlund was dead, Huw gutted him, to make it look as if the same person who assassinated Master Larsson had masterminded the murder. He then covered the body with the finely worked counterpane before he left, in accord with Lackland's instructions.

Soon Huw knelt in the deepest shadows where their gear was hidden, waiting for the others.

Lackland had drawn the second lodge, House Higurde. It was slightly better guarded, but the inattentive guard posted at the gate was quietly disposed of, as was the man outside the door. He left their bodies in the dark shadows of a yew hedge. Lackland slipped back to the portico and swiftly climbed the ornately carved pillar, entering the house through the window of an empty room.

Noiselessly, he crept to the room next door and found the eorl sleeping alone in a drunken stupor, a tankard of stale mead on a bench beside his bed. It took little effort for Lackland to send Eorl Higurde to kneel at God's throne. He left the body as the others were. Barely able to breathe until he was at last free of the house and in the alley, Lackland crept silently through the dark to the meeting place.

Three lodges up the street from House Higurde was the home of Eorl Söder. Beau found no guard at the gate, but a light glimmered inside the front door, and a shadow moved within, walking back and forth. Silently, Beau climbed the stepped-stone chimney and slid a window open, entering the lodge.

He was dismayed to find he'd entered through the nursery. An infant turned in his cradle but didn't wake. The door to the room where the child's nurse slumbered was open, but she slept deeply and didn't stir.

Beau crept down the hall, holding his breath. He found the right room, but the eorl was not sleeping alone. His painfully young wife also lay in the immense bed, as far from her husband as she could possibly lie.

Beau did what he had to, covering the man's mouth to stifle any cry, and making it quick. The eorl died without a struggle, never having woken. Remembering to make the artistic statements, Beau did it without disturbing the countess. At least, she didn't appear to wake or stir.

Minutes later, Beau went back through the nursery, pulling the window closed behind him and making his escape down the stepped chimney. Once on the ground, he stood thanking God Julian hadn't drawn that place. He couldn't quell his nerves. If Julian had entered and seen the child in his cradle….

Beau pitied the countess when she woke next to her husband's unlovely corpse. Seeing how far to the edge of the bed she kept herself, she may not have been too fond of him. But to wake next to such a thing…he hated that sort of work.

It was a long moment before he could calm himself, but finally he made his way down the alley toward the meeting place.

Culyn had drawn House Freygard. Eorl Freygard posted a guard at the gate, but the man had dozed off and never knew what happened. In no time, Culyn had hidden the corpse in the shadows. The eorl apparently lived alone, and Culyn found him sleeping before the fire in his large hall, two empty bottles of wine near to his hand. A fat dog sleeping near the fire looked up as he entered, his tail thumping a welcome before he settled back into his dreams.

Culyn left Freygard's bloody corpse seated at a strange angle, covered by a colorful lap rug. Surveying the scene, he had the urge to laugh, which he stifled. He met up with Beau, and the two made their way back to the sewer-catch.

Looking in the windows of the house he'd drawn, Jack saw Eorl Ranveg Olgurde was unguarded except for an older man, who slept on the floor before the fire in the kitchen. Remembering that Hilda had said the eorl forced his uncle to sleep in the kitchen, Jack quietly opened the front door. Patting the dog and giving him jerky, he went up the stairs, passing several empty rooms until he found the one occupied by the slightly piggish-looking eorl. In only a few minutes, Jack had finished, meeting everyone at the sewer-catch.

"We have one more task, and then we can get rid of these garments." Lackland's whisper was barely audible, but the others all nodded. This was the one they had all been looking forward to.

Eorl Thorgürd's house was nearest the Black Prince. Huw and Lackland silently slit the throat of the men standing watch by the gate, dragging them into the shadows. Culyn did the same to the sentry by the door. Through the windows, a guard could be seen, pacing.

"The door is locked, and I don't dare try to pick it, or the guard inside will rouse our quarry." Jack's whisper floated back to the others.

"You four stay here, and I'll let you in," replied Lackland. "I saw a cellar window when we scouted this place."

"Let me do it." Beau's words went unheard by Lackland. Before he could stop him, Julian had vanished in the darkness. Beau's heart pounded, but he remained outwardly calm. He whispered to Jack, "I know the window he means."

Four pairs of eyes met, consternation stark in all of them.

"What now? He's likely to get us killed." Huw's whisper sounded behind Beau.

Jack said, "Thorgürd isn't like the others. The place could be full of guards. We have to follow him." He moved through the shadows, with the others on his heels.

Fortunately, the eorl hadn't wasted coins by putting glass in a cellar window. Lackland inserted the blade of his knife through the crack between the shutters, sliding it up and lifting the bar. The shutters swung out, leaving the unglazed window open. He entered, careful not to dislodge the assortment of indistinct objects on the ledge below as he climbed down. In the faint light cast from the open window, he could see the shape of a lantern on a shelf. Feeling around the ledge beside the lamp, he found the striker. In a few moments, the harsh light illuminated the cellar.

Lackland was completely unprepared for what he found.

An iron-barred cell occupied one corner. It was a bizarre gaol. Someone had placed a few toys on the floor, and a pair of tiny clogs such as the poorer children wore during the winter were next to a low cot. As he came closer, he realized the cell held a small child, not much more than a toddler, lying bundled on the narrow bed. A little girl, she hadn't stirred at his entry, nor did the light wake her. She lay so quietly, Lackland feared she was dead.

He raised the bar and entered her cell. Her small chest rose and fell with soft, shallow breaths, but though he lifted her, she didn't wake. Smoothing her baby-fine hair, he could see she was around three years old. A cup sat on the stand beside her cot. Raising it to his nose, he smelled the telltale scents of poppy and other herbs. Lackland realized the eorl had drugged her, but why? The answer came quickly—to keep her quiet.

Looking around, he restrained himself from crying out. There, on the shelf below the window through which he had entered, were four small skulls, displayed as if for decoration.

A sound at the window made him look up. Jack appeared, framed against the darkness. Quickly making his mind up, Lackland said, "I will hand you a baby. Take her to the Orphan Gate of the church at the bottom of the street, now." His tone brooked no argument. Shocked to the core at finding so small a victim there, Jack nodded. Swiftly, Lackland carried her across the cellar and handed her up. "Wrap her in this blanket. Ring the paupers' bell, so the nuns know someone is in need. Then leave her on the steps and come back here. We'll wait until you return."

The others entered the cellar, and while they waited, they examined what could only be described as a theater. In the center of the large room, someone had placed several benches around a strange, long table. They were obviously for onlookers to sit on while viewing… what? The table was fitted with restraints, as if for holding a person immobile. A bench near the table held a carved chest containing surgical instruments. Noiselessly exploring the cellar, they found more children's skulls.

Sick to his stomach, Huw whispered, "I don't want to contemplate what Thorgürd has been doing here."

Lackland clasped his arm, steadying him. "Evil, Huw. He's been doing evil, and this is obviously the place where all the members of the Black Watch meet to indulge. We're putting a stop to it." His gaze was clear and deadly cold. "This is why we were put on this earth, to protect the innocents from monsters like these men."

Huw merely nodded, unable to get past the sight of the surgical instruments and what they must have signified.

Jack appeared at the window again. "I left her on the steps, in the lantern light. A nun came out right after I rang the bell but didn't see me. Now what?"

Lackland said, "You three go around to the front and wait. Beau and I will take care of whatever guards may be inside and then let you in. Give us ten minutes." Lackland turned, leading Beau through the cellar to the stairs.

At the top of the stairwell, Lackland slowly opened the cellar door, finding it led into the kitchen. The sentry seated beside it had fallen asleep. His throat was slit with no fuss or noise. The guard inside the front hall was a little more trouble, having turned at the right time to see he wasn't alone. He opened his mouth to call a warning, but Lackland's hands shot out. His iron grip over the man's mouth held him silent.

As cold as death, Julian said, "You know what your master is up to in his basement. Someone brought him orphaned children. Was it you?" At the guard's guilty, terrified shrug, Lackland slit his throat and lowered the body to the floor.

Opening the front door, they let the others in.

Culyn whispered, "I wondered what was keeping you." He looked askance at the livid handprint on the dead man's mouth, visible in the candlelight.

Beau grinned. "He wanted to chat, but Julian felt he should be silent."

Lackland took a candle from the stand near the door, leading the way up the stairs. Quietly, they looked in each room, all of them unoccupied. At last, they found Thorgürd's bedchamber. Once inside, Lackland set the candle on the mantel.

The eorl woke. Seeing the five masked men looming over his bed, he struggled. Jack put his hand over the eorl's mouth, stifling him while the others held him down.

"Lie still, my lord. I've just come from your cellar," Lackland said, his eyes glittering.

Shock and horror filled Thorgürd's eyes.

Lackland continued, "You left these in the garden at the wedding when you departed so abruptly last month." He held up the shoe and snuff box, seeing Thorgürd's stunned recognition. "We're here to return them." He set them on the mantel beside the candle and turned back to the struggling eorl. "Let's discuss the children."

The eorl's efforts to escape were for naught. Huw and Beau gripped him tightly, pressing his shoulders firmly to the bed while Jack and Culyn held his legs securely. "We must put you and your ilk down for the good of society. The punishment will fit the crime." Lackland's long knife flashed in the candlelight and fell as he disemboweled the man, who howled and thrashed, begging for mercy through hysterical sobs.

"What mercy did you show the children whose lives ended in your cellar or those who died, crushed to death under that wall? This is for the children whom you'll never again be able to hurt. Here is your mercy." Lackland's blade flashed again, stabbing Thorgürd through the heart, twisting. The eorl's agonized cries became choking, gurgling gasps, which at last dwindled away.

Lackland looked down at Thorgürd's countenance, frozen forever in a grimace of horror. "I believe he has paid for his crimes. May he enjoy the heat in Old Grim's domain." His gaze was clear and resolute.

Huw shuddered. "And his master will suffer the agonies of the damned when these murders become known tomorrow. The prince is involved up to his neck in the horrors that went on in this man's cellar. We still have his reward to look forward to."

Back in the alley, the five men silently stripped off their blood-soaked clothes and rinsed their hands and faces. Dropping the garments down the sewer-catch, they dressed again in clean breeches and shirts, covering themselves and their mail with their regular cloaks of felted wool.

A thick fog had set in, shrouding the night in murky darkness. Continuing down the alley and silently passing the Orphan Gate behind the church at the foot of the street, they saw the toddler was gone from the steps. A lamp burned inside, and the silhouettes of two women paced, one carrying a child who slept against her shoulder. Lackland watched them for a moment, then followed the others through the shadowed streets until they reached the docks.

There, they took to the main street and entered the Sailor's Knot, one of the more reputable taverns. It was filled with merchants and clerks and their guards, dicing, and playing cards. They arrived just as Kharl did, guarded by the ever-faithful Gustave. Two hours later, the six men left the tavern, laughing and behaving like any other men returning home from a night spent around the keg.

As they made ready for bed, Beau steeled himself, prepared for Julian's madness to surface. All Julian said was, "We did something good and noble tonight. We did it for the children." To Beau's surprise, Julian immediately fell asleep, and the rest of the night passed peacefully with no nightmares.

CHAPTER 21

THE NEXT MORNING began as it always did. The five men sat in the great hall, breaking their fast with a meal of substantial dark bread, fresh from the oven, and sharp cheese, along with dishes of pickled fruits. They sat, slowly sipping tankards of mulled cider, discussing small, inconsequential things. Abruptly, Hilda entered the great hall, leading a woman who was visibly in shock, unable to stop shaking.

"It's horrible! My sister, Greta, found the most disturbing thing at Eorl Olgurde's house today." Hilda's eyes had gone wide with shock. "Someone murdered him! Gutted him in his bed!"

Jack looked alarmed. "But this is terrible!" Immediately the five men stood, and Jack seated the distraught woman at the table, in his spot nearest the fire. She sipped hot cider from a tankard held in trembling hands, trying to pull herself together. Patting her shoulder, Jack comforted her as best he could. "Fraue Greta, you must be shocked beyond words. Tell me what you found. I must know before I go to the market." He looked up, his expression dark. "This will affect commerce today."

"Oh, Master Johan!" Greta raised tearful eyes to Jack. "I went to House Olgurde this morning as I have always done. And as occasionally happens, I thought my lord had overslept. I went in to wake him, and that's when I found—oh, the poor man! I didn't like him, and he was unkind to old Hanse, but he didn't deserve such a fate." She sobbed for a moment while Jack patted her shoulder. "I heard the Black Prince was unhappy with him, but to do such a dreadful thing—it's terrible. Just like what happened to poor Master Larsson. I've told the captain of the city watch everything I know, and the king's men have taken his body." Greta hiccupped and then said, "But at least my lord's uncle, old Hanse, won't have to sleep in the kitchen anymore. The poor old thing will be able to live like a decent man. Perhaps he will find a bride, now he's the eorl, frail as he is. He must have a few good years left in him."

"At least old Hanse will have you to come in and care for him," said Lackland consolingly. "He's a fortunate man to have a good-hearted woman such as you to see to his meals and care for him. We old men value such kindnesses."

"I do care for him, poor old dear. His whole life has been hard, being the poor relation, making his way in the world with a clubfoot. Your wisdom comforts me, elder warrior," replied Greta, wiping her tears away. "I must return and see to cleaning his hall and making his dinner. Hanse will need me. Despite Ranveg Olgurde's cruelties, Hanse hoped his nephew would marry well. Family is everything to Hanse." She suddenly brightened, looking at her niece. "Ingrid, today *you* will come with me. You must ensure Hanse's comfort while I work. Perhaps you can mend his clothes and keep him company while I make his chamber fit for him."

"Yes," said Hilda, her mind turning over the possibilities. "He's a kind man and needs a wife. My Ingrid needs a good husband. Hanse is no older than Hugh, and *he* is certainly able enough!"

All eyes turned to Huw, who just grinned and shrugged.

The rest of the morning was spent as always, going to the warehouse, and then calling on clients, but as the day progressed and more assassinations among the Black Watch came to light, it became impossible to conduct business. By midday, the town was agog with the sensational murders of so many nobles in one night.

The manner of the killings and the close relationship of the murdered men to Prince Maldred were remarked on. Oblique comments compared the way the men were found to other recent murders. The mood in the market became ominous when rumors of a gruesome discovery in Eorl Thorgürd's cellar surfaced.

"Now we know where the poor children who sometimes vanish have gone. But why?" The prosperous middleclass citizens of Val Halle shook their heads, whispering darkly, casting many looks toward Prince Maldred's lodge, and keeping a close eye on their own children.

Maldred himself was distraught and horrified at the deaths of his loyal friends, most especially Thorgürd. He loudly demanded an investigation into the murders, despite knowing what would become known if the eorl's lodge were searched too closely, convinced his position meant he wouldn't be implicated.

The Countess Söder and the families of the other murdered lords beseeched the king to find the killer and avenge the slayings. King Aethelwyrd agreed, promising swift punishment to the perpetrator of such a heinous, cowardly act.

Aethelwyrd had been expecting some unique thing to fall into his lap to be rid of his brother. He listened to the report of the murders as given to him by the captain of the city watch, inordinately pleased by the neatness of the trap holding his devious brother ensnared.

Carefully hiding his pleasure behind a frown, Aethelwyrd heard the evidence the captain reluctantly laid out before him. "Much of it is hearsay, sire. But there is a terrible coincidence here because none of the dogs along the Way of Ealdormen barked as they would at a stranger. Therefore, it must have been someone these canines knew, an assassin who knew the murdered men's routines. The night of bloodletting was well-planned, and the merchants are troubled. The rumors of treason cannot be ignored."

"Treason? My own brother…?"

The captain said, "I'm sorry, sire. But there is worse."

Aethelwyrd read the paper the captain handed him. "Dead children? In Thorgürd's cellar?" His amazement was unfeigned.

The captain nodded. "Yes, sir. At this point, we have found the remains of possibly fifteen."

"God in heaven. Surely my brother couldn't have been…but the evidence is compelling." Aethelwyrd stared down again at the paper in his hand then looked up, horror turning to determination. "No man is born above the law, prince or peasant. A trial will decide the truth."

Aethelwyrd immediately ordered Maldred arrested, locking him in the grim and forbidding prison, Greyhame Tower. He personally escorted his brother to the infamous tower of no return, throwing him into the darkest cell. "I can't prove you had anything to do with the deaths of those innocent children, but there is ample proof of your other crimes."

At the mention of the children, Maldred fell silent, an odd, knowing look flickering in his wary eyes.

"You knew about them. Your silence shouts your guilt." Aethelwyrd turned way, unable to look at his brother. He said to the guards, "Put him in the darkest cell and chain him well. Let no one speak to him other than the advocate, if we can find one who can stomach him."

No advocate would represent Maldred, so the prince was forced to speak for himself. A trial was convened, and Maldred was unanimously declared guilty by a jury of thirteen lords of the Eorlred. Before his head had even stopped rolling in the tower yard, his name was stricken from the histories of Lournes. His estates and possessions were divided among the families of the murdered men as recompense for his crimes.

The following week, Jack wound up his business dealings, taking orders for rare gems. The market began buzzing again, this time with the news that, at the ripe old age of forty-one, newly ascended Eorl Hanse Olgurde had found himself a young bride. Ingrid had made an outstanding, if sudden, marriage and now had a home of her own. Jack would need to find a new housekeeper, as Hilda would be helping in her daughter's household and would be too busy to care for his empty house. However, her sister was available for the task, for a small fee, of course.

Jack assured her his second oldest son would bring his bride to House FitzMarion and take up residence there in June, where he would continue working in the family business. "I have to manage our shop in Castleton, as it is our source of rare goods to supply to this city. My daughter-in-law will appreciate Fraue Greta's help in the household, as she is a trained jeweler and will be an asset to our business here."

The others hid their smiles when Hilda agreed he should pay more attention to his own shop instead of leaving it to his poor wife to run when she had far too much to do as it was. "But we women are stronger than you men, so we get things done. Safe travels, Master Johan! We will miss you!"

An unexpected precursor to spring occurred in late February, which meant the journey home passed quickly and in beautiful weather. After reporting to Henri, they left Jack in Castleton. King Henri admitted he was glad the men responsible for the death of his son had suffered for their crimes but was shaken to the core when he was told just what those crimes entailed. Privately, he was pleased with the way Lackland had dealt with it, telling Beau he felt confident Julian could handle the duties of his position.

Lackland and Beau continued to Limpwater with Huw and Culyn. They planned to return to Castleton to begin preparations for yet another war with Lanqueshire but had a proposition for Lady Mags. Entering Billy's Revenge, they found she wasn't there.

Billy Ninefingers greeted them warmly. "Mags will be back this afternoon. She and the other ladies made a short trip to Dervy this morning." Other than his sandy hair turning silver, Billy hadn't changed much. He was still the tallest, largest man in Waldeyn.

Huw presented him with a fat purse. "This is from King Henri, with a bit thrown in from King Aethelwyrd, as a token of their gratitude."

Billy looked surprised. "But I didn't do anything other than sign the paper for the border guards saying you were Rowdies."

"Nevertheless, here you go. We've already been paid."

Billy grinned. "This can go directly to the Widows and Orphans Fund."

Huw nodded. "I knew you'd find a good use for it. You've always taken good care of your own. But now I'm going to go home. I'll be back to play for the evening, as usual." A hint of disturbance lurked in his eyes as he turned to Beau and Lackland. "I have an urge to see my grandbabies, to make sure they're all right."

Lackland clasped his arm, consoling him. "After what we found in Lournes, I would feel the same way."

Billy's wife, Bess, left her kitchen to come out and embrace the two knights. "I'll make your favorite jam tarts for dessert, Lackland. We don't get to see enough of you two." She squeezed his arm. "We're more of a roadside inn, nowadays, but all the old Rowdies are still our family."

Lackland and Beau sat chatting with Billy, catching up on the local gossip. Neither man was surprised to hear Mags's new lad had returned to his noble family's hearth with a broken heart after her brother's wedding. "Mags can't take much coddling," Beau said. "She wouldn't take any help from us either."

They brought Billy up to speed with how the foray into Lournes had gone. In the end, Billy could only shake his head in disbelief. "Just when you think you've heard of every evil thing in the world, something new comes along to give you nightmares."

The side door opened, and Mags entered, along with several other Lady Rowdies. Lackland and Beau rose to their feet, crossing to the door. Enfolding her between them, they kissed her soundly. She returned their kisses, first Julian, and then Beau. "You're still the two most handsome men in Waldeyn."

"And you're still a blatant flatterer," replied Beau, kissing her hand. "Not a day goes by that we don't miss you, woman."

"What brings you here?" Mags's elation was written in her bright eyes. "I've wondered what you two were up to since Billy mentioned you'd gone north with Jack."

"We resolved the problem of what happened at Jules's wedding. Along the way, I made right a few of my own sins." Lackland's joyous smile was a throwback to the old days, before Lora Saunders and the terrible night in the forest.

Mags laughed. "I knew you wouldn't let my father go unavenged." Drawing them close and throwing her arms around them again, she whispered, "And our son can get on with building a good life with his wife."

Fearing she would refuse his next request, Beau said, "We came here first. We want you with us when we tell Jules and Rose how we settled things."

A moment of indecision passed through her eyes, but she put it aside. "Billy," Mags called. "I'm going to Bunder for a day or two to visit my brother and then to Castleton for a visit. I'll be back in two weeks. We're leaving tomorrow. And I'll have two guests warming my bed tonight, so don't worry about finding them a room."

"You're leaving just when I had my crews all organized. Now I'm shorthanded again." Billy sighed. "Oh, well. You're entitled to take whatever time you need."

"Bring your things up to my room, lads, and help me get packed." Mags turned back to Billy. "We'll be back down for dinner." Arm in arm, the three of them went up to Mags's room.

Huw came in through the side door as the trio went upstairs. Mags called a greeting to him as they disappeared. He opened the case holding his pipes, setting them near his favorite stool, then stood at the bar. "There goes a love story if ever there was one."

Billy nodded. "They do have a romance, but she'll never marry either one of them. She's a merc, through and through."

Huw shrugged. "They know, and they don't care. They love her anyway, and they love each other. As Lackland always says, they just live their lives the best they can."

Billy nodded. The door opened, and a merchant entered. Billy went to serve him, leaving Huw to consider what he knew about Beau, Lackland, Lady Mags, and Jules, the young man the world believed was her brother. *A romance indeed* thought Huw, smiling.

"Let's have some merriment. Play us a song, Huw," called the merchant, who was a former Rowdy. "You've been away a long while. You must have met a woman."

The thought of Hilda made Huw smile, and he buried his wistful longing for her earthy, sensible company beneath a roguish grin. "I did, indeed. And what a woman! I was sorry to leave her, but even she couldn't entice me away from Billy's ale for too long." The crowd laughed. "How about *Firedrake in the Kitchen*? If I must play, you must dance." Soon, music spilled from the open doors at Billy's Revenge, enticing passersby to stop in and spend the evening.

Lackland looked down through the open window of Mags's room, seeing the town he loved so much, hearing laughter and song rising from the common room below. He thought of the massacre in Ludwellyn all those years before, and how everything had come full circle. *I avenged your children, Gronwy. I did it for them and for all the children those monsters murdered. Now they can rest in God's arms.* He stood there, reveling in the sense of peace that thought brought him.

Mags folded the last dress she was taking, packing it into her saddlebag with experienced hands. She looked up, her eyes sparkling. "Alright, lads. Let's go downstairs. I feel like dancing!"

"And so you shall, my dear." Lackland turned, smiling, aware the interlude with Mags would be only a brief respite. "It's good to be home, even though it's only for a while."

"You're right. This town and this place truly is home." Beau closed the book he'd been leafing through, setting it back on the shelf. "And whatever Bess is cooking tonight smells divine. I'm famished, if you want the truth."

"Me too," agreed Lackland.

Holding hands, the three went downstairs to the homey warmth of Billy's Revenge.

PART FOUR
The Last Good Knight

AFTER HENRI'S UNTIMELY DEATH, his eldest son, Harry, ascended the throne. His first move was to retain Lackland as his Lord Commander. Under Lackland's command and with the aid of the Men of Bunder, the Pirates were eradicated. Not surprisingly, the people of Lanqueshire were desperate to become a province of Waldeyn.

Unable to walk past their suffering and starvation, King Harry accepted them, creating the province of Lanqueshire. He immediately sent the Sisters of Anan in to distribute food and seed and help get crops started.

King Harry appointed Lackland as governor and Beau as Port Commander. He also requested that a mercenary company be established there to protect the Lanque merchants as they traveled. As there was no longer a need for mercenaries in the civilized parts of Waldeyn, Billy Ninefingers's son, Brand, bought an inn in Plimpton and moved the Rowdies there. Thus, Mags remained close to the two men she loved.

Lackland and Beau loved the province of Lanqueshire, and their tenure there brought peace to a land that had never known anything but misery. Perhaps it was because, despite its abject poverty, Port Lanque teemed with a vibrancy unmatched by any city. The people were passionate and in love with life. Maybe it was in response to the demise of the pirate kings, or possibly a rebellion against the heavy grey fogs that swathed the city of Port Lanque mornings and sometimes all day. Regardless of why, with the coming of Julian Lackland, the province bloomed.

Lackland and Beau retired after five years. Unfortunately, as they were preparing to end their visit with Mel, King Harry received news that his envoy in Vyennes had been killed in a riding accident.

The two were unhappy at being assigned so far away, but with Jack serving as the ambassador to the Court of Lournes, they understood there was no one else qualified for the task.

In the leisurely way unique to Costa De Sol, their years of exile passed.

Excerpt from *The Life of Julian Lackland De Portiers, Waldeyn's Last Good Knight*, by Huw Owyn, Master Bard of Waldeyn

CHAPTER 22

JULIAN LACKLAND RODE into Limpwater on a dismal afternoon in late spring, hoping to find the place he and Beau had left so long before. As he looked around, he saw many changes that had occurred in the town, some for the better and some worse. He didn't know the place anymore; nothing looked the same.

The town had grown into a city that was far larger than Castleton, and the residents appeared to be quite prosperous. "I knew this place when all that stood here was Billy's Revenge and the smithy," he told his horse. "My old horse, Farroll, hated this place. He was a delicate flower and despised the mud."

Baron snorted his opinion of horses that were delicate.

Even Main Street had changed so much that Julian didn't recognize anything, but still, he kept plodding toward the center of town where Billy's Revenge had always held pride of place, passing several newer taverns of lesser quality on his way.

Nothing was familiar to him. He couldn't find Huw's cottage.

Soon, however, he approached the old inn that had been the scene of so many happy mugs of ale, feeling intense disappointment.

The ramshackle building now leaned somewhat over the cobbled square. The hastily built foundation had finally given way under one corner, just as the masons had warned Billy it would. Peeling grey paint that once had been white was now framed by equally flaking green paint around the doors and windows. The sign hung over the steps, swinging in the ever-present wind.

Once the sign had depicted a bloody knife in lurid colors, but like the rest of the inn known as Billy's Revenge, it was now peeling and nearly colorless.

An immense new building built completely of stone and easily twice as large as the original rose next to it. A sign in front proudly proclaimed the new Billy's Revenge would be open soon, with a grand ballroom and modern plumbing in every room. The masons' scaffold still stood around it, but it looked nearly complete, at least on the outside. The new inn rose in the place where Billy's original barn had stood, the one that had been his father's barn.

Now that he had reached Billy's Revenge, Julian regained his bearings and realized he'd come in on the wrong road—the street where Huw lived on was still there to his left.

He reined up, stopping, and looking at the old inn. The last time he had been in the town of Limpwater for more than a brief stopover, the building had been well kept, and the paint bright. Of course, Billy Ninefingers and plump Bess had been alive too. He smiled, remembering the days long ago when Henri was still King, and he and Beau were the Arms Masters of Waldeyn. They'd always stopped there on their way to and from Castleton.

He thought of the happier times he'd spent there, remembering the summer of the picnic and Golden Beau and beautiful Mags. It had been thirty years or longer.

He didn't really know anymore.

It was the last year he'd spent as a Rowdy, the year that changed his life. "I wouldn't have had all those happy days without the many things that happened that year. I wouldn't have had those years with dear old Beau," he told Baron.

Patiently, Baron stood still while Julian was lost in his memories. The old man smiled at the reminiscence of another golden summer. It was over and gone many years now but still shone bright in his mind's eye.

The summer of the last dragon, Lady Mags, and the field of daisies had been one of the best of Julian Lackland's life. The years with Beau shone as brightly, both memories keeping him warm when the nights were long and cold.

Baron listened as Julian rambled on. "I wish our Mags had come along with Beau and me, but you know how she was. She could face down a dragon, but the ladies of the court terrified her."

He was fortunate to have been given all the summers he had enjoyed. Few people were ever as blessed as he had been. The three of them shared a love story few would have understood, and many would have disparaged.

But other peoples' finer sensibilities meant nothing to Julian. He'd been a part of something wonderful and didn't regret a moment of it. The memories of his grand romance comforted him.

Now Julian was back in Limpwater. He'd come, hoping to find something to remind him of the happiness he'd known as a young Rowdy, wildly in love and with a future full of endless possibilities stretching in front of him.

He'd hoped wrong. The old place was every bit as beat-up and tired as he was, on its last legs, really. "It's a good thing they're building a new inn," Julian told Baron, who flicked his ears in response. "The poor old place is falling down."

He nearly decided to head back down the road to the Powder Keg in Somber Flats, despite the fact it was another five hours' worth of riding a tired horse over ground he'd just covered. But everyone he'd ever known in that sad town was dead, and he'd found the memories too depressing.

He was where he'd planned to be, so he figured he might as well stay even if it hadn't turned out to be the place he remembered. "I'll look up some of the old crowd since I'm here. Huw will be around somewhere if he still lives." Julian felt better, now the decision was made. "He built his college here, and besides, he would never leave his cottage and Lucy's apple tree. Culyn and Belle live here, and so do Annie and Babs. At least they did when Beau was still alive."

Thinking about all the retired Rowdies who might still live in Limpwater comforted him.

Whatever was cooking at Billy's Revenge smelled delicious. His mouth watered just thinking about it.

Lackland tied his horse to the railing and walked through the swinging door. The old place looked pretty good on the inside, immaculately clean and neat as always. He spoke to the innkeeper and paid for a room for himself. "Is there an empty stall for my horse?" The proprietor reminded him of someone. Lackland was sure he knew the man, but though he wracked his brain, he couldn't dredge up the name. He remembered that the Rowdies had all gone down to Lanqueshire long ago but didn't know who had taken over the inn when Billy passed on.

"It's two coppers for the horse and an extra copper if you want a nice bit of grain for him." The innkeeper showed Julian up to his room. It was the corner room that had been the home of Davey Llewellyn and Percy St. John back in the long-ago days. Mags's room had been across the hall. Julian's last room had been one floor up.

"This is fine, thank you," he said, and the landlord went back downstairs.

After stowing his kit under the bed and hanging his armor on the stand in the corner, Julian went out and led his horse around to the stable. The stable yard seemed much smaller than it had been. Indeed, a tall, neatly trimmed hedge now sectioned much of it off, shielding his view of what lay behind it.

Surprised, he noted that the confined area before the "new," larger stable Billy had built out of wattle-and-daub was cobbled, something Billy had always intended to do. But the yard was now only large enough

for one wagon or coach to turn around in at a time.
Long caravans of wagons would have no space to
maneuver in that stable yard, especially with the new
building going up.

Then he realized that probably there was no
longer any need for such accommodation. He hadn't
seen a wagon train in years, but the roads were busy
with traders traveling alone, carting their own wares
with just one or two guards for company.

A neatly painted sign posted beside the stable
door read:

Limpwater Livery Stable and Feed
Full Livery Service, 3 coppers per day, 6 coppers per
week.
Partial Livery Service, 3 coppers per week, you provide
the feed grain

Indeed, the paddock out behind the stable
showed signs of heavy horse traffic just as it always
had, and the stable was as clean and well-kept as it had
ever been. The meadows beyond the stable had horses
grazing, as they always had. Hearing a door open, he
turned, expecting to see Cob John, the Rowdies' old
ostler.

A girl of about fourteen stood there, dressed like
a young Lady Rowdy, but wearing a leather apron like
Cob John had always worn.

Julian spoke to the stable-girl, whose name was
Bessie. "This is Baron. Give him a bit of grain, if you
will," he told her. "He's worth the extra copper, and
he's been foraging much lately."

She nodded, seeing he was a man who took care of his horse first and himself second.

"Is there a farrier here still? He keeps picking up stones since I had him shod down in Galwye," Julian handed her the reins.

"My uncle is the smith here, sir. He'll gladly see to your horse. If you'd like, I can walk him over there for you and have him seen to today," Bessie offered. "Uncle will send the bill here for you."

"I'd like that, thank you. Is there still a bath-house here?" Julian felt every league of the dusty roads he'd traveled, and a hot bath would be a treat.

"Just go through here, sir. It's on the other side." Bessie directed him to a gate in the hedge, which opened onto a neatly kept rose garden. The path wandered past a small fountain where a trysting bench was sheltered beneath a vine-covered arbor, the lush wisteria creating a little privacy for courting lovers. It was the sort of garden fairies favored, and once again, Julian felt disoriented. It was not at all the same place he had known so long ago.

On the other side of the rose garden, Julian passed through another gate in the hedge and at last, came to the familiar bath-house. The old path wound through Bess's privy garden and around to the side door of the common room. Guests still had the same easy access to the bathhouse, which made Julian feel less out of place. Soon he sat neck deep in a gleaming copper tub of hot water. The indoor plumbing and hot water were what had always set Billy's Revenge apart from the other inns on the trade road, and it was still a wonderful luxury to have at the end of a long day's journey.

Later, Julian sat in the common room, waiting for the pretty daughter of the innkeeper to bring him a fine dinner. He'd been offered a menu with several choices for supper. Bemused, he ordered sliced ham and mashed taters with a salad. It was much different fare than Billy and Bess had offered, more like a Sunday dinner at Castleton Keep.

The room was filling up with travelers, merchants, and courtiers. All were strange to the old man who searched for something familiar in this now-alien place. He saw none of the old crowd in the throng.

He listened to a young bard who sat on Huw's old stool, softly playing the harp. The mug of ale he sipped was every bit as good as Billy's had ever been. Resigned to finding nothing he'd hoped for, Julian was unable to avoid thinking about his current problem any longer.

He was worn-out and thinking of retiring. Jules and Mel would both have insisted he go to live with one or the other of them, but he wasn't ready to do that. He would let them know he was alive and back in his right mind, but he wanted his independence.

He had to find some accommodation other than sleeping under hedges and in barns. If Huw was still alive, he would help him figure it out. Julian knew he had more than enough money because he hadn't withdrawn any from his account at the exchequer's office since before Beau had died. It had most likely grown a bit since then. "I'll talk to Huw tomorrow," he decided. "He always gave me good advice."

Soon Julian found himself standing at the bar, talking to the innkeeper, who turned out to be Eddie, the younger son of old Billy Ninefingers. He was the boy he and Beau had saved from drowning that day so many years before.

Other than being a man as large as his father, Eddie resembled Bess, which was why he looked so familiar to Julian. He was married to little Estelle Smith, who had provided him with seven children, one of whom was Bessie, the stable-girl.

"Beau and I were in Vyennes when your parents passed away, and we didn't hear about it for several months. The news arrived the very day Beau died. But never mind." Julian hid the pang of grief beneath a smile. "Your parents were our family and this place was our true home."

"It's amazing how many people say so." When he smiled, Eddie resembled his father. "I've always tried to make my dad proud."

"You can be sure you've done just that. And you can't live in the past—trust me. You need to make your own future." After a moment of silence, Lackland said, "I want to retire, but there's always just one more person who needs my help desperately, and I find myself hunting some creature that's bothering their livestock." It was easy to confide in Eddie just as he'd always done with Billy. "I can't say no, though I should."

Eddie said, "Mercenaries are rare in these parts nowadays because we're too well settled. The boys join King Harry's army, and the girls go down to Lanqueshire because they're welcomed in the mercs there. Brand hung up his sword last year, but he's still captain. His crew stays busy, enforcing King Harry's laws and dealing with those who prey on the unwary."

"I remember when Brand first took the Rowdies down to Plimpton." Julian suddenly felt quite old, realizing just how out of touch he'd become. "Now look at you! You're building a new inn, much finer than this one, and Limpwater is quite cosmopolitan, with a concert hall and the Bardic College. Did I see a cathedral as I came in?"

"You did, indeed." Eddie's pride couldn't be contained. "St Robert's Cathedral, named for our old Fat Friar, Robert De Bolt, who brought the church to Limpwater. We have several smaller chapels too, and a proper teaching infirmary." Eddie's sharp gaze took in the sad, scarred old man who seemed to be so much at loose ends. He felt moved by his despondency, wishing he could help. "I heard about Golden Beau. We sent a letter of condolence to you, but you had left Vyennes already, so they forwarded it on to House Portiers. You and he were together for a long time, and it was hard for you. But I have to tell you—you've been missing for a long while, and folks do worry. Your nephew and the Earl of Bunder in particular."

"I know. I'm not sure what happened to my mind, exactly. It passed, eventually." Julian paused for a long moment, thinking of Jules and Melvin. "I should be dandling Mel and Jules's grandchildren on my knee before a cozy fire instead of dragging my sorry old horse out in the cold and rain to save the world. But I just can't do it. I'd be fine on my own, but my old bones are creaky, and it seems to take longer every day to get the mobility back in my sword-arm."

An idea sparked in Eddie's mind. Lackland had saved his life once. Now he had the chance to return the favor. Smiling innocently, he said, "Why just the other day, Lady Mags De Leon was saying the same thing. Her problem is she's grown somewhat stout as women of that age will. My uncle, Bennie Smith, had to make her armor a bit more expansive, but for all she has silver hair and has plumped-out a bit, Lady Mags is still a looker."

"Bennie's still here?" Julian brightened up. "Let me tell you, Mags was an armful. She was incomparable." His mind's eye saw the mahogany-haired beauty and her dark, flashing eyes, with the swing of her hips that made his mouth go dry and the lush, full lips that were meant for kissing.

"I expect her to stop in anytime tonight or tomorrow." Eddie felt pleased with how well his bait was received. "She had to go and take care of a nest of firesprites at the edge of town, but she should be just about done with it."

Julian thought for a minute. "I'll definitely stay a few nights and wait for Mags. I wonder if she's still as spirited as she was."

"She doesn't tolerate stupidity well, but her disposition tends to improve after a few mugs of ale," Eddie assured him. "She's still like she always was, only more so. A bit tetchy, you might say."

With a spark of his old self, Julian laughed. "She could best me in a fight even in my glory-days. She always said there was no such thing as a fair fight, only winners and losers. She was a woman who mortally hated losing!"

"Lady Mags bought a cottage here in town, down the street from old Huw's place. She's thinking of hanging up her sword." Eddie paused, seeing a customer holding out his mug. He walked down to the other end of the bar, served the customer a mug of ale, and returned. "Babs and Annie retired a long time ago. They have a place not too far away. Of course, their boys went down to Plimpton to work for Brand and Anna."

Julian fell silent, lost for a moment in his memories. "Do you know I once asked Mags to marry me?"

"You don't say," Eddie looked surprised. "She was never the settling down type. I've heard all of Huw's tales of your star-crossed romance, but you and Beau left here together when I was a boy. Besides, she's always been the sort who'll die on the road still swinging her sword in the trade."

Julian said wryly, "I know, and I knew it then. We both loved her, Beau and me. She bound us together in some way in the beginning. Then? If we couldn't all three be together, we had to live the best way we could. Beau begged her to come with us, but she couldn't do it." He stood there, thinking. Then he said, "I'll definitely stay an extra night or two."

Eddie smiled, pleased at how easily his plan had fallen together. "It certainly wouldn't hurt to have an extra hero hanging around town. I think you might be the last good knight we'll be seeing up here for a while."

"Yes, we're a dying breed, Mags and I," Julian agreed.

"There's a nice little cottage for sale just down the street if you're thinking of staying more permanently," Eddie said. "It's right next door to Slippery Jack and Merry Kat's place."

"Are they here then? Maybe I'll look into it," Julian replied. "I could use a place to call home, and my poor old horse would like to settle-down. I'd like to try my hand at growing roses." After a little more smalltalk, Julian went to sit before the fire with his mug, feeling something close to hope for the first time in years. It was the old Fat Friar's favorite corner.

Imagine that, he thought with a small chuckle. *A cathedral and sainthood for good old Friar Robert De Bolt. I wonder how he likes being a saint. Is he up there in heaven wearing a halo? No, probably he's sitting at the ale-barrel like he always did in the old days, wondering what the fuss is all about.*

Soon he was napping, dreaming of a summer long past, a summer of blue skies and endless fields of daisies.

Eddie wiped down the bar and began closing up for the night, shooing his customers out as they finished their mugs. He had to make sure Lackland stayed in town, for everyone's sake. He debated waking the old boy up, or just letting him kip by the fire in peace, and finally decided to leave the poor old man be.

Lady Mags was difficult, but she was a good old thing. The two of them could choose their jobs together, and she wouldn't be so lonely. It was a sad thing when the only people willing to do the dirty jobs were too old to be doing them.

The doors opened, and Lady Mags walked in. "Am I too late for an ale? I'm mortally tired."

"You're never too late. I always have one for you." Eddie's relief at the sight of her emerged in a wide, welcoming smile. He fetched her a foaming mug of ale. "I didn't expect you back tonight."

"I think that was my last job," Mags said, handing him a copper. "I just don't have what it takes anymore. The little buggers almost had me. Firesprites are a pain in the arse to deal with, even when they're only just hatched. The damned sleep amulet just didn't have enough 'oomph,' this time. Of course, there were twenty of them, and it's dark out, which made it tough."

"Huh. Earlier this evening, someone else in your line of work was talking about retiring," he said, watching her reaction. "The old boy says his horse is tired. He's an old friend of yours."

"Really? Most of my old friends are dead now." She wondered who could be stopping over in Limpwater. "Everyone who's still breathing lives here on Rose Street."

"Sir Julian Lackland is here for a day or two," he replied, seeing shock and joy pass through her eyes, followed by hope.

"He's still alive…!" Quickly recovering herself, she said, "He was a gorgeous man, with a smile that could turn a woman's legs to jelly. I was still in Plimpton when Beau died. John De Portiers said Julian had taken the loss badly and was in a terrible state. But if he's still in the business of rescuing people, he's all right, I suppose."

Pleasure at how well everything was unfolding made Eddie's smile brighter. "He's looking to retire, perhaps to Limpwater. He's a little worse for the wear, and his armor hangs a mite loose. But he still has all his teeth."

Mags stood silently for a moment, hundreds of emotions swirling in her heart, and then drained her mug. "Well, as I said, I'm mortally tired. I'm going to head on home. Maybe I'll stop in here for breakfast," she said nonchalantly. "See you tomorrow!"

"You might want to see him now. He's having a kip by the fire as we speak." Eddie gestured toward the alcove before the great hearth. "Go on, I'll just close up. You can let yourself out when you're ready to leave."

Mags walked hesitantly to where Julian sat napping before the fire, remembering a summer day from so long ago. How young and in love they had been, despite the things that were her fault and hers alone.

She saw his golden hair shining in the sun as they lay on his cloak in a field of daisies, watching the clouds after a long afternoon of making love under the wide blue sky which had nothing on the blue of his eyes. She saw his perfect profile and the smile that took her breath away. *Why did I let them go? Why didn't I take the chance when I had it? Why did I let my selfishness get in the way?*

She'd wondered that every night since he and Beau rode out of Limpwater at the end of the last good summer she'd had. She'd lost them when Julian followed Jules to court, and Beau went with him. Then, she'd lost them again when they left Lanqueshire and went to Vyennes.

She could have gone with them, then. She could have married one or the other, and they could all three have stayed together. Then Julian wouldn't have been alone when Beau...died.

That peculiar nagging feeling, the insidious wondering about her poor choices was why Mags finally left the Rowdies. Her sword began to slow, and though no one else noticed, Mags knew, and it scared her. Fearing her sluggish reflexes would be the death of a Rowdy, she officially retired and came back to Limpwater to settle down.

Plenty of the old gang had settled down there, so she hadn't been too lonely. Babs and Annie, Huw, Culyn and Belle and their grandchildren lived near her. So did old George and Johnny Malone, and Merry Kat and Slippery Jack—they all had cottages near hers.

Even though she was among her friends, she was alone. She always had been. Oh, lovers came and went, but none like Beau and never a one to match her own dear Julian. The days she'd spent with them had been the only happy days she could remember.

Her solitary life was her own fault, her own choice.

Now Beau was dead, and it was too late to tell him he was right.

Jules and Melvin were still inseparable and visited her regularly. Just the previous week, they told her how worried they were about Julian being missing for so long. They frequently heard tales of a mysterious knight who went about helping people, but the rumors frequently set him in widely different places, often at the same time.

No one could say for sure who he might be, though they fervently hoped he was Julian.

Huw swore the wandering knight was Lackland. "Who else could it be? As far as I know, he's the only elderly knight who's gone missing."

Jack always agreed with him. "It can only be Lackland. Did you ever know any other knight who would risk his life to save a cow from a bog? Beau is dead, so it has to be Julian."

Mags prayed the two were right but feared she would never find out.

And now, here he was, lost and alone as he should never have been.

Julian was seated on the settee before the fire with his feet up, dozing. She sat beside him and took his hand in hers, watching his face as he slowly opened his eyes. The delight she saw there once he realized who was sitting beside him was heartrending in its intensity. Joy, hope, love, and fear, all his emotions were raw in his still-handsome smile.

"Oh, Mags," he said brokenly, drawing her close and kissing her tenderly. "Mags, I've missed you so. Our Golden Beau is gone, you know. How he would have loved to see you, still so beautiful!" Now that he saw her again, Julian knew what he'd spent all those years looking for—and she'd been here all along. "My beautiful, beautiful Mags. No one could ever compare to you." He tenderly touched her silver hair, not realizing a tear streaked his seamed old cheek,

"Julian, will you marry me?" She blurted it out, terrified he might say no, terrified that he was done with her and had other commitments. "Let me take care of you, let me give you what you should have had all along. Let me try to be as good to you as you deserve!"

"I will! Of course, I will, though I've little to offer you, other than my heart and a tired, worn-out horse who'd like nothing more than to retire from the road," he replied. Happiness roared through his veins, making him feel alive again.

"I've missed you so much, Julian. Don't ever let me go again." Mags clung to him. The pain and tiredness of her last few years fell away. "I feel exactly the way your poor old horse does, and if you'd like to share my cottage, we'll all get along quite well, I think."

Eddie and Estelle stood in the shadows, watching them, smiling so widely their faces hurt. Holding hands, they quietly went to their bed, feeling the tale had ended well.

This time old Huw would be able to write a ballad for Lady Mags and Julian Lackland that ended, "and they lived happily ever after."

Connie J Jasperson, Author

A founding member of Myrddin Publishing group, Connie J. Jasperson lives in Olympia, Washington. She and her husband share five children, an ever growing number of grandchildren, and a love of good food and great music. Music and food dominate her waking moments. When not writing or blogging she can be found reading avidly.

Visit Connie and find her books at:

http://www. conniejjasperson.com

Or follow her on Twitter at: https://twitter.com/cjjasp

Books by Connie J. Jasperson

BILLY'S REVENGE series, set in the world of Waldeyn, and a medieval alternate reality

Huw, the Bard: Fleeing a burning city, everything he ever loved in ashes behind him, penniless and hunted, Huw the Bard is a wanted man. Only the kindness of strangers stands between Huw and the gallows as he embarks on a trek to freedom.

Billy Ninefingers: Billy MacNess has the worst luck. An unwarranted attack by a jealous rival captain seriously wounds him, destroying his ability to swing a sword, and any chance he might have had with Dame Bess. In a world where only the strong survive, Billy must somehow salvage his life and remain Captain of the Rowdies.

Julian Lackland: Despite his knowledge of depths humanity can sink to, Lackland remains naively convinced that good will always triumph over evil. When he is kidnapped and tortured, can Julian survive? Sanity isn't always his best thing, but he just lives as best he can.

TOWER OF BONES, series based in the World of Neveyah

The gods are at war, and Neveyah is the battlefield.

This epic fantasy series opens with *Tower of Bones,* and follows Edwin Farmer as he journeys deep into the lands claimed by the dreaded Bull God, in an attempt to rescue a girl he has only met in his dreams.

Forbidden Road – takes up Edwin's story six years later. When four mages are sent into the shadowed lands claimed by the mad priest of the Bull God, who will return unscathed? Sorrow, peril, and magic await in the Valley of Mal Evol.

Valley of Sorrows – the thrilling conclusion of Edwin Farmer's story. Four men, war-weary and grieving, must face the new Overlord of Mal Evol in a race to close off the Braden Gap and protect the heart of Neveyah. Who will prevail when the Legions of Tauron arrive…? The gods are at war, and Neveyah is the battlefield.

The Wayward Son – takes place concurrently with *Forbidden Road*, but follows John Farmer's story. War looms and John must answer the call to serve, but his terrible secret could destroy everything. A broken mage trying to rebuild his shattered life, he must somehow regain his abilities, or everyone and everything he loves will be lost. John must face the crimes of the past to become the hero he never was.

Mountains of the Moon – Before the Tower of Bones, there was Wynn Farmer, the legendary smith and lightning-mage. Danger, mystery, and dark prophecies lie deep in a gauntlet of jagged peaks and deadly traps. Can Wynn survive the dark secret hidden in Tauron's stolen castle before the Bull God's minotaurs overrun Neveyah?

OTHER BOOKS BY CONNIE J. JASPERSON

Tales From the Dreamtime – a novella consisting of three modern fairy tales told in a traditional style. Available as an ebook, in paper, and as an Audiobook, narrated by the wonderful voice actor, Craig Allen.

**MYRDDIN PUBLISHING's Book List
Can be found at:
WWW.MYRDDINPUBLISHING.COM**